when in december

kendra mase

When in December

WHEN IN DECEMBER
Copyright © 2024 by Kendra Mase
All rights reserved.

kendramase.com
Cover Designer: Wildheart Gaphics
Cover Image: Regina Wamba, reginawamba.com
Editor: Jovana Shirley, Unforeseen Editing, unforseenediting.com

ISBN: 978-1-960254-10-8 (ebook) | ISBN: 978-1-960254-15-3 (paperback)

To those who know their worth and declare it loudly.
And to those who are still getting there.

one

. . .

Poppy

TO BE HONEST, for a while there, I really thought love was dead. Dead in the ground. Torched with flames. Dead. I was never going to find the magical fairy tale—and not for a lack of trying or sparing my own feelings.

I did the dating thing. I went on blind dates that only served to convince me my parents either had no idea who I was at all or they were secretly laughing behind my back at the comically terrible men they'd set me up with. I even tried the more socially acceptable thing where I dressed in something pretty and low-cut so that someone would notice me in a bar, where I sipped a drink that tasted like too much lime, far past my normal bedtime. I even did the relationship thing. And that one? That one nearly ruined me entirely.

Then, everything changed.

Falling in love, I learned, could be situated tightly against the phrase *has potential.*

It was a famous line in an interview from Michelle Maven, my boss and the creator of one of the most recognized home design and entertainment companies in the entire city—and soon, the country.

Home Haven insisted that making a house a home could

easily be the most stunning of mundane magic. It was romanticizing your own life. In this world, we all needed a little of that. That kind of comfort. That kind of love.

It was also what Michelle had said when she took a chance and hired me two years ago.

I had potential.

She'd also told me I had a strong self-starter personality. That was likely why I was still in the office at seven thirty in the evening when I was supposed to go home at five, dropping a bag of takeout on my desk, covered in layout plans detailing my next project and paint swatches that were beginning to look a little too similar to one another.

At the paper bag crinkling, Hannah perked up on the other side of our shared cubicle. She twisted around in her plush, pink-cushioned desk chair, which, though comfortable, squeaked incessantly with every tiny movement. At first, the sound had been annoying. But after Hannah sitting behind me five days a week, at minimum, for the past two years, the high-pitched squeal of metal on metal was almost comforting to my otherwise shot nerves.

Hannah also had a keen sense of hearing whenever food was brought into the office past six p.m.—it was basically her love language.

She leaned back in her chair, a soft blanket hanging over my friend's shoulders. A piece of the black licorice she normally kept in a glass container on her desk dangled between her teeth.

Soft hazel eyes widened behind clear acetate blue-light glasses.

What are you doing here? she mouthed, pointing to her headset, where I could hear the distant hum of someone talking to her over the Home Haven Hotline.

What does it look like I'm doing? I mouthed right back.

With a click, Hannah muted herself. "Clearly, you're not at home, like you should be."

I waved her off.

"You said that you were going to get some sleep for once."

I'd slept. Sure, it might not have been as much as some people within the past week or two, but it was enough. I started to take out the to-go containers. Immediately, Hannah's attention shifted toward the Thai noodles and spring rolls with peanut sauce. Once, I'd made sure to get vegetarian just for her until she turned me on to them.

I could never resist a good peanut sauce.

"I have to go back over the plans for the Hayes-Preston home."

I handed her container over. She took it from my hands and popped open the lid.

"Again?"

"Construction is not to be complete tomorrow, which means I start tomorrow," I reminded her.

Even though, as of now, the construction company we'd hired this past summer to get a head start on the place still hadn't replied to my emails or phone calls for a more updated update.

"And the floor plan is a tad out of the ordinary."

"If you have the place completely done already by the time you get up there to decorate for the holiday, there's going to be nothing left for you to do for the rest of the year. You're taking the fun out of it," said Hannah.

I smirked as I sat down and settled in for my takeout. The place we got the food from was always the best since they were nearby, and somehow, the food was always hot. I could feel the warmth seeping through the plastic container into my palms. "This *is* the fun of it."

"Only you would say that."

I pointed with my fork back to her headset.

She shook her head. "Still talking."

I twirled my noodles. At my pause, Hannah reached up to click back on her headset. Soon enough, whatever story the person on the other end was telling her about their holiday plans would come to an end.

I took it as my chance to murmur, "Michelle also sent out an email, asking if I would be in the office tonight. She's leaving with some of the other senior staff for their retreat tomorrow. She said she had something important to tell me."

"She what?" Hannah gasped before realizing her headset was no longer muted. "No, I apologize. Not you, ma'am. What was your question again? No, of course, I'm not judging your question about vegan options to make this season. We have a whole section on our website categorized by occasion. A coworker of mine came in and—oh, yes, there's tea." Her eyes flicked to me, sparkling. "Verbal, not herbal."

When she said it like that, gossip truly sounded like a disease.

"Do you think it's about the … you know?" Hannah whispered toward me, covering up her microphone this time.

The promotion? I had to think so. It was the only thing that made sense.

I smiled down at my food, feeling the rush of giddiness that hadn't left me since I'd opened the email this morning, asking me to stick around.

Unlike during my first year, when I had constantly felt like I had one foot out the door whenever I accidentally Replied All or tripped over the pointy high heels I couldn't wear to save my life and spilled senior interior designers' coffee, I knew that Michelle wasn't going to call me into her office anymore to show me the door.

Though I didn't want to sound full of myself, once I'd gotten the hang of things, I was good at my job. Enough so that for the past year, Michelle had been teasing me with the fact that my work and seniority over the other entry-level staff meant I was a shoo-in for a promotion to senior interior designer once the budget turned for the year.

And it was almost the end of the year.

The promotion in title, along with what felt like my first-ever big-girl salary at the ripe age of thirty, was another reason I didn't mind putting in the extra hours at work the past few weeks. Months.

Hannah grinned as she talked through her recommendations

to the woman on the phone. She went over the pros and cons of spaghetti squash over butternut and how pomegranate seeds could bring a festive aesthetic into your holiday meal.

In between breaths, she took a bite of a spring roll. As she chewed, she put her hands together as if in prayer to silently thank me.

Hannah might have had the best and worst job at Home Haven, yet she never complained about the hours she spent attached to her computer and headset. I almost envied the way the perky twenty-six-year-old was able to slip on her fluffy slippers under her desk, twirling the cord as if she were a teenage girl talking to her crush about his favorite color instead of the perfect temperature to cook a turkey and how to make your own cranberry sauce.

Almost.

I couldn't handle talking to anyone for eight hours a day, if not more with the amount of voluntary overtime Hannah picked up. I could barely handle more than two meetings in a day with the rest of the Home Haven staff—consisting of interior designers, bloggers, and event planners—whose mission was to make the everyday in your home a little more special.

It was the idea of romanticizing your life that had first drawn me into Home Haven.

Once I, a devout DIY renovation admirer, had found out a woman-owned business of my dreams existed, there was one place I desperately wanted to work, even if it wasn't far from home, like I'd always thought I would end up.

No matter what, I was proud of myself.

I'd done it. I'd made it. Not to mention, I was pretty sure I was in the minority of the world when I said how much I loved my job and meant it.

Pulling off her headset, Hannah dropped it on her desk. She took a huge bite of noodles and didn't bother fully chewing before she spoke. "Look at you. Going to have a big promotion before New Year's. I feel like a proud mother. Seriously, are you going to leave me? You totally are. You're going to be put in one of the fancy side offices now and forget about the sad little administrative assistant turned Home Haven call girl."

"Don't call yourself a call girl."

She barked a laugh. "Now, all we have to do is get you a man, and Poppy Owens's fantasies will have come true."

"I don't need a man."

"No one said you needed one, but take it from me." Hannah looked up toward the ceiling, as if remembering her last online dating rendezvous, which she normally saved to tell me about on Monday mornings. Sometimes, the stories she had were the only things that made me pull myself out of bed and into work with something akin to pep in my step. "It's nice once in a while."

"I don't need someone to be nice to me."

"Why not? It's great. And if anyone needs someone to take them out and treat them like a lady, it's you. Don't let your assbag ex ruin things for you."

Of course, she'd had to bring him back up again. We both remembered the eventful day nearly two years ago. It was one of Hannah's first days at Home Haven. It was also one of the only times I'd cried in the office.

Luckily, it hadn't scared her away.

"Assbag?" I questioned.

"Yes, it sounds right."

"You didn't even know him."

"I don't need to in order to preach the cold, hard truth. I saw him that one time when you asked him to pick you up from work," Hannah insisted with enough force that she had to swat away a piece of copper hair that had flown forward into her freckled nose, which scrunched in indignation. "He made a big deal about it. Plus, what kind of non-assbag without masculinity issues leaves you all of a sudden because—"

A head popped around the corner of our cubicle. "Am I interrupting?"

As if on cue, Hannah's computer monitor lit up behind her. The hotline rang its steady trill.

She grinned brightly up at Michelle as she turned around to affix her headset back into its proper place, where her hair had a permanent indent from her wearing it all day. "Not at all."

Michelle chuckled.

"Home Haven Holiday Hotline, this is Hannah."

Now that Hannah was back to work, Michelle turned toward me.

I started to put away my food, putting the lid back on and sliding it back into the bag. "Sorry about that."

"Don't apologize. Tomorrow is the big day. You start your first large-scale solo project on the ground, correct?" Michelle asked.

I shifted in my seat. Should I get up or sit down? I knew most of the other designers had a comfortable rapport with Michelle, but for some reason, I still could never stop seeing her as the person I'd looked up to for years before I got my job here.

When I compared myself to Michelle, I always fell short. It was kind of hard not to. Michelle Maven was elegant and confident. She was a home design *icon*. She wore crisp, fitted blouses in cool winter shades that didn't wash her out and defined what it meant to style something versus just wearing clothing, like I did.

Every day, I showed up to work in what I knew looked nice enough on me. It usually included one of my multiple pairs of patterned dress pants and loose blouse combinations, which might've been more appropriate for a fifty-year-old librarian than an up-and-coming contemporary home aficionado.

"It's always an exciting thing to sink your design teeth into a whole new palette," said Michelle with a bright smile, stretching her lipstick, but never smudging. "I know the overview of your first big project, but I can't wait to hear more about what you've come up with when we have a chance to talk more. Would you mind coming back to my office with me for a moment?"

"Sure." My flats squeaked on the floor as I followed her

toward the back corner of her office, illuminated by the soft glow of Tiffany lamps.

Surrounding Michelle's wide desk were various mood boards for the larger important projects she was working on with the senior teams. Aside from that, it was just Michelle now who was about to talk to me and … Alison.

Wait a second. Alison was here?

Alison, another junior interior designer who had started a few months after I did, sat in a chair across from Michelle's desk. Her leg crossed over the other, making her pleated maxi skirt flare toward her sleek leather boots.

I might've stood staring at her for a second too long.

"Have a seat." Michelle waved for me to make myself comfortable.

I sat on the edge of the second chair stiffly, turning toward Alison with a short smile. She appeared completely at ease with her long, silky brown hair twisted up into a simple knot.

Michelle sat back in the leather chair behind her desk, cluttered similarly to my own with paint chips and molding corners, yet everything was stacked neatly in its proper place. "I wanted to meet with the two of you before the holidays got into full swing. Let's get right down to it."

I didn't think she was going to fire me. She couldn't. If anything, Home Haven had taken off in the past year and a half to new heights that even Michelle had admitted she never foresaw. I wasn't going to second-guess myself now, but if Home Haven had to let some people go … firing me and Alison made sense. We were both junior interior designers, preparing for news before the budget changes for the next year.

But was it good news? It had to be good news.

"Both of you are up for a promotion at the start of the new year. As you know, we have a biannual evaluation for promotions when they are being considered. However," Michelle prefaced with a deep breath, "our wonderful human resources director, Tabitha, has informed me that since we started the Home Haven publication division, only one promotion from junior to senior interior designer is possible.

"You're both amazing workers. Unfortunately, these things happen. It's logistics. This doesn't mean that you won't be considered for a promotion in the future. For the time being, I thought of a solution to solve our problem." Michelle opened her hands as if in offering to us both. "We have a last-minute spread within our upcoming magazine issue. An article fell through. So, I figured, why not have some friendly competition?"

"I'm not sure I understand." Was I the only one still lost here? "Alison and I are competing against each other for the senior interior designer role?"

"All in good fun, yes."

Fun. *Fun?*

"Both of you are working on some of your first independent design projects here at Home Haven, centered around the winter season. As you complete your projects, one of our photographers will come in. I'll assess from the photographs and progress reports. The best design for our readers wins. You'll get the design byline in *Home Haven Magazine* as well as the promotion."

Was she serious? It was clear she was, but my heart started to beat a little faster in my chest.

After the past two years as a junior interior designer and being told the job was mine more than a few times, I'd thought that, well, it was mine. I'd finally have the job title I always imagined. The job title I'd worked for and deserved.

Earned.

Something was going to work out and fall into place. At last.

"I'm aware this is unusual, but a little friendly competition never hurt anyone. Most of the office will be in and out come December with the holidays, so please feel free to use anyone or each other to help make these two homes places to be proud of. I know you two already will. Do what you do best and make a home a haven." The edges of Michelle's lips quirked up. "That was cheesy, wasn't it? Anyway, you get what I mean."

Alison smiled as if she couldn't have planned for better news. "It was perfect."

"Does this sound all right to both of you then? I don't want to make either of you uncomfortable. Have a good time and use your resources. Poppy?"

Uncomfortable? I wasn't sure what I was feeling, but I was certain that I was past that. I'd just finalized all my plans for the home I was going to see for the first time outside of pictures tomorrow. Now, I suddenly had the desire to throw it all out and start over again. But I couldn't give up. I wouldn't.

I could handle this. I could do difficult things and then some even if it meant pulling another week of all-nighters to make sure that I didn't fail.

I refused to let myself down.

"Yes," I finally replied. "Sounds great."

"Wonderful. Alison?"

Alison shrugged her shoulders like this truly was all in good fun. "Agreed."

"Great. Now, both of you should head home. It's crazy that any of us are still in the office at this time. Get some good sleep and be ready to take on your projects," Michelle advised. "Have a great rest of your night."

"Have a good retreat," said Alison.

Startled by the end of the conversation, I didn't realize that they'd both stood. I jerked myself to my feet. "Thank you."

"Have a great first day on your project tomorrow, Poppy. Give me a call if anything isn't what we've prepared for."

I dipped my head in another nod, heading out of the office behind Alison. Once Michelle's door shut behind us, Alison finally glanced up at me from where she stood, about five inches shorter.

I'd seen Alison's designs before. We'd even worked together on projects within the past year. I liked Alison. She was pleasant enough, though kept mostly to herself. More than that, I was impressed by her truly contemporary style that people oohed and aahed over whenever they caught photographs of the before and after.

Now, I had to go head-to-head against her for a promotion I'd thought … God, how stupid was I to assume it was mine?

"That was a lot, huh?" Alison asked.

"Kind of."

"We're both going to do great," she said. "You'll let me know if you need anything when everyone is out of the office. I have a feeling we're going to be the only two working out on-site once we get closer to Christmas."

"Of course. You do the same."

"Thank you, Poppy."

"Why are you thanking me?"

"I know that you've been here a little longer than me—"

"It's all good. I didn't know you were doing a solo project too," I said.

"Near South Point."

"That's cool."

"Where is yours?" Alison asked.

"Outside of the city actually," I said, suddenly realizing how different our projects were going to be, even compared to a stylistic standpoint. "It's a smaller place up in the mountains."

Her long lashes brushed her cheeks once in what must've been shock. "You're driving there?"

Everyone was saying that to me, including Hannah, who joked about putting out an alert to all the other drivers that I was heading up that way as the weather started to turn. I might not be the best driver. But I could handle a highway.

"Yeah. It should be fine."

"I'm sure it will be," Alison reassured. "I'm headed out tonight. Need to get some sleep before I rethink some things now."

I nodded. "Have a good night."

"You too."

Heading back into my cubicle, I flopped down in my chair.

Hannah started to clean up, looping the cord around her headset. Her eyes studied me.

I covered my face with my hands.

"What happened? Did she tell you that you weren't going to get it?"

I shook my head.

"Wait, you weren't fired, right?"

I shook my head again. I didn't even know what to do now. Slowly, I grabbed the food I'd only partially eaten and started to gather my things into my tote bag that single-handedly held my entire life. Pens and printed directions and more paint chips that I continued to go back and forth on rolled around inside, but none of it was what I needed now.

"Finally ready to head home?" asked Hannah.

"So ready."

two

. . .

Poppy

A HINT of light peeked through my curtain facing the street. The sun was probably pulsing off the hints of snow left behind that had come last night—

Wait.

The sun was up.

My eyes flew open as I bolted upright.

Oh my God. The sun was up.

I swore I'd set the alarm. If I hadn't set it or if I'd rolled over accidentally and hit the snooze, my phone would have gone off with my backup alarm. Wouldn't it have?

It should have.

It was nearly nine. The house was an hour away, and I was supposed to be there by ten a.m. sharp. I'd planned on getting a shower and taking the time to properly wash my hair instead of spraying another layer of dry shampoo, which, like my randomly spaced naps, was taking the place of something much more important.

I tore out of my sheets, not bothering to make them—basically, morning routine sacrilege.

I yanked on a white blouse with a pair of stretch dress pants with red bows printed down each leg. I looped my stiff hair up in a somewhat put-together, yet also very messy, bun.

Seriously, how did Alison get her hair to look so nice when it was pulled up? Michelle would be pursing her lips at me right now if I walked into the office this way during a meeting, constantly reminding us all about first impressions as women who wanted to be taken seriously. Something that still needed to be done in this world, no matter how much talent one had.

However, I believed being on time might be way more important.

All last night, I'd lain awake, going through my plans and trying to convince myself that if I needed to make any changes, the house would let me know when I arrived. Sure, the place still wouldn't be the luxury space Alison was working on with plenty of time to spare. It didn't mean that a small home that the home-owner's family requested be transformed for an ideal family Christmas wasn't going to be just as charming.

Charming.

Based on what had been printed in the first issue of *Home Haven Magazine* so far, I wasn't sure charming would be enough.

Scrambling down the stairs, I glanced down at my watch.

"Where's the fire?"

A chuckle interrupted my internal spiral.

My stepfather, Simon, raised a dark, bushy eyebrow and his holiday-themed mug of coffee. I looked around, and everything was decorated for the holidays—from the cabinets thick red ribbons to an ornament-free plastic tree stuffed in the corner.

I must've missed that yesterday. Mom must've gotten in the spirit immediately post-Thanksgiving this year.

Not even Simon's morning mug, which usually boasted a picture of a cartoon golfer, had been spared. Not that it mattered exactly. Simon golfed as much as he admired the red-cheeked jolly Santa he drank out of. Which was never, as far as I was aware.

"I'm late!" I offered as an explanation.

I yanked my coat off the front hook before shoving my arms through each wool sleeve.

Simon lifted his mug toward the door. "Be careful. It's slick out there."

"I will."

"Your mother wanted to see you off."

"I'm late!" I repeated, shouldering my tote bag over my coat. I was starting to sweat already—and not only from the heat. Adrenaline pulsed down into my knees.

I'd never known it could do that. Or that knees could sweat.

Simon cocked his head, as if considering if this kind of explanation would be perfectly acceptable to my mother. Likely not. When I saw her early yesterday, she'd insisted on wanting to see me off on my first big job as if I were a kindergartener going to school for the first time instead of a very stressed DIY lover turned interior designer about to be scolded for not showing up on time, let alone having any clue of where I was going beyond what I punched into my phone's navigation system.

Jogging back up the stairs, I tried not to sound out of breath by the time I made my way through my parents' room and knocked on the bathroom door. Steam snaked under the crack of the door from the shower.

"What is it, Simon?" my mom called.

"It's me, Mom. I'm headed out."

"Open the door!"

Humid air from the steaming water rushed out as my mom stuck her head out of the shower's sliding glass door. A clump of bubbles from her shampoo was still clustered on top of her head in a soapy crown.

"Oh, don't you look nice? I didn't like those pants at first. They're quirky, but very *you*."

"Thanks, Mom." It was best not to read into her unfortunately detailed compliments. "I need to go, but I'll hopefully be back before you guys go to bed."

"You were out late last night. Were you on a date?"

"No, Mom. I was working."

She huffed. "Excuse me for asking."

"I'm running kind of late," I said, looking over my shoulder.

"We'll talk later—no, wait. We'll be out with the Carmichaels tonight. Don't wait up. We're trying that new Mexican restaurant even though Simon has been going on about how he hopes there isn't any cilantro anywhere." She rolled her eyes. "Let me know if we can bring you back anything."

"Okay." I reached to shut the door.

She waved a hand out into the bathroom, stopping me. "Have a wonderful day. You're going to do great things. I can't wait to see what you do with the place. It's like a cabin, right?"

"Kind of."

"Oh, then I'm sure it will be so cozy. Remember what you did to Aunt Shannon's place after she broke up with that awful man she was with? You know, she went back on one of those dating apps and found her new partner. You would probably be a catch on one of those—"

"I'm running *really* late."

"Well, excuse me for trying to build your confidence."

"Consider it overflowing," I said. "I have to go. Thank you. See you."

"Make good *design* choices!" she yelled after me.

In these moments, I saw how my mother and Simon worked so well together. Though my mother was loud and often over-bearing, somehow, Simon, who was a little too book smart for his own good, mellowed her out. Yet even he couldn't explain how they both had the same dorky sense of humor.

They just fit.

I shut the door to their bedroom, and my feet nearly stumbled over themselves down the steps until I was against the front door again.

Simon called out after me, "Have a good day. Be careful with the car!"

I jogged around the corner. Simon used the car more than I

did, though he'd gifted me his old blue hatchback shortly after I graduated from high school, thinking I'd need it when I planned on moving for college or work.

It ran well enough.

Unless—

"You've got to be kidding me." My shoulders slumped as I stopped in the middle of the sidewalk.

A few cars flew by, honking while their tires shoved more slush in my general direction.

At some point, the city had thought it was trying to help, and the roads had gotten significantly more snow-filled in the past ten hours. My car was another snowplow casualty, covered in the white mounds of heavy frost.

Now, it was a car snowman.

I shut my eyes and took a deep breath. It was fine. Everything was perfectly one hundred percent fine. It was going to be a good day—

No, a *great* day.

I was starting my solo project on a cute home along the edge of the woods from what I'd seen in the picture. If that didn't scream traditional holiday magic all by itself already, I didn't know what did.

I balanced my stuff in my arms as I yanked one of the handles until the passenger door flew open enough so I could reach for the snow brush stashed under the seat.

I dug my way through the snow mounds blocking my tires. Water seeped through my shoes.

Once I was behind the wheel, I let the heat run on full blast, though it only started to get warm by the time I hit the highway, clenching the wheel and trying not to wiggle my toes.

When I did, I swore I heard them squelch.

Today is going to be a great day.

Even if my radio was also going in and out and—

Why wouldn't there be traffic?

I slammed on the brakes. Blinking, I watched as a car swerved in front of me before the next exit.

Deep breaths. Deep breaths.

Great day.

By the time I pulled in front of the address my phone assured me for the second time was on the left, my hands were shaking. The drive would get better as I drove it more. I just wasn't used to being behind the wheel for so long.

I nudged the car into park and twisted the key until the engine stuttered to a stop. My body slumped over the wheel, and I sighed in relief.

Made it.

Turning my head to look at the window, I held back a gasp. The pictures had not done the place justice.

The home I expected definitely wasn't a warehouse, like my mother had insinuated. It wasn't even a shack on the outside, considering I'd only seen interior pictures. What I was working on could only be described as the world's coziest-looking cabin I'd ever seen.

Damp snow traveled up the exterior, sticking between the sharp edges of stone like icy vines. The porch was refinished, along with a metal roof, layered with dark brown gutters that dripped down into rain pots already coated in a shiny patina, which must've made it sound like wind chimes in the summer.

Everything was almost idyllic. Every thought I could've ever had to make the house stand out, as well as look at home among the thick shade of pine trees had to be considered.

This cabin was the perfect, cozy retreat in a storm.

I bet *Home Haven Magazine* could even quote me on that.

I gathered up my things, and my phone beeped from where I had it in the cupholder. When I looked at the screen, a notification popped up from my affirmation app.

I can do difficult things.

I smiled. I could do difficult things. Starting with my first big solo project today.

I fought a whistle as I made my way toward the side door that should lead to the mudroom. This way, I didn't track snow through the house.

Those cheesy holiday film producers who dragged me into watching at least half a dozen movies about a girl finding love in a small town would be so jealous right now.

Here we go.

Today was day one of thirty—give or take. The client hadn't specified when exactly they'd be traveling to fully occupy the house for the holidays quite yet. She was a high-earning lawyer with a family who was very busy. That was why it was my job to make sure the final renovations and everything for the holidays—from decor to planning the meal day—went according to plan so they could simply enjoy.

Home design wasn't only something you lived in every day after all, and Home Haven saw to that as well. In some cases, it was all about the experience. You needed to properly set the stage for all the memories to happen.

It was what I was going to make happen.

Everything would be better from this moment on. The moment I walked through this door mattered. Not only for me and my promotion, but for them too. I made sure I remembered that, no matter what project I was working on.

Lifting my hand, I knocked.

No one came to answer. Eyebrows pinched, I knocked again.

The client was supposed to be here to meet me to confirm the design plans in person. Maybe I wasn't as late as I'd thought I was.

Maybe she was just someone who ran even later than I was today. Wouldn't that be amazing?

I reread the last email on my phone that had been forwarded to me from Michelle and another designer who was first going to take over the assignment; the homeowner said that she should be there, but could be running late. If she was, I could use the key left for Home Haven.

Fishing through my bag for the key, I unlocked the side door before I pushed my way inside. "Hello?"

There was no reply, but I didn't want to startle her if she was here somewhere and didn't hear me.

"It's Poppy from Home Haven. I'm here for our initial home consultation."

I pressed the phone to my ear, letting it ring until it went to voice mail.

"Hi, Ms. …" Oh God, I was suddenly blanking on this client's name. Was it Robinson? Reynolds? "Sarah …"

I remembered that much.

"This is Poppy Owens. I'm currently at the property. I let myself in, using the key you sent for Home Haven. I know you were unsure if you would make it today, but I thought I would check in to see if you are on your way to configure plans for the space going forward. If you could give me a call back, that would be great. I'm looking forward to working on this project with you. Yes. Thanks—thank you! Bye."

I sounded way too chipper. I needed to get better on the phone.

Unprofessional, I chastised myself.

This was good though. I could take this time to get a picture of the place on my own. Let the house—cottage? Cabin? Definitely cabin. Let the cabin speak to me.

Shrugging my bag off my shoulder, I toed off my boots in the small mudroom, leaving me in my knit socks. The floor was cold. The heat must not have been on or maybe not working as I walked inside the cleared-out kitchen, already installed with new cabinets. They looked amazing, though the handles weren't attached, and the appliances hadn't been put in yet.

I made a note.

Exposed beams lined the living room and extended into the kitchen, creating a large yet intimate space. Michelle, or whoever had started the renovations this summer—taking down a wall and adding French doors that led to the outside patio, complete with a fireplace—had done an amazing job already, creating the bones of this place for me.

I could see the *potential*.

I could see the greenery to decorate around the old-fashioned brick fireplace that still had its original chips along the edges. Tapered candles and a tree in the corner for presents to be under.

Traditional yet elegant. Comfortable, yet with a creamy contemporary edge that Home Haven readers could replicate.

I bit my lip to contain my smile as it all started to come together. Kids would be running around the cozy space with the wide windows overlooking the acreage out back.

The walls needed to be painted … green. Definitely the darker forest green.

My previous ideas were added to and thrown out the window. They wanted a classic, elegant, yet family-friendly Christmas aesthetic while also creating a sustainable living home for year-round use.

They were going to get it and more.

The cracked flooring creaked in front of me as I finished jotting down the last of my thoughts, not making it to punctuation.

A deep voice snarled from across the room, "Who the hell are you?"

I might've screamed.

three

. . .

Aaron

THE WORST INTRUDER I'd ever laid my eyes on was screaming.

I raised my eyebrows at the strange woman with strawberry-blonde curls twisting at her temples. She covered her parted lips with the palms of her hands. She dropped a pink plastic stylus on the floor.

"Oh my God," she breathed.

"Who are you?" I was pretty sure I already asked. It didn't matter.

A guy couldn't even shower in his own house without someone walking in?

I'd locked the door. *I did lock it, didn't I?*

I was sure I'd locked it. I double-checked. No. I'd triple-checked before climbing in the tub like some girl taking a bubble bath to calm her nerves. My nerves were not going to be calmed. Not when I no longer had a working shower head since I'd moved in five days ago, let alone peace of mind that someone wasn't going to come barging in.

I had locked the door—all of the doors.

The real question was, how in the hell had this chick gotten into my house?

Putting a hand to her heart, the intruder shook her head once, as if to compose herself. Strands of hair caught on her chin before she brushed them away. "I'm sorry. I'm Poppy Owens. I'm from Home Haven. Our client ..."

Not only was she a terrible intruder, but she also wasn't the brightest bulb in the shed.

Great.

I guessed that explained why she wasn't wearing shoes. The only thing she had on her feet were bright red socks that looked like something my grandmother would've knitted.

I blinked at them, remembering how my grandmother would wander the house in thick socks and slippers, refusing to turn up the heat, even when the snow got as high as the windows. I'd complain about it all the time when I was here through my last years of high school. She'd tell me to add another layer.

That was one thing I'd noticed was different since I'd gotten back here a week prior. Central air and heat had been installed at some point.

"Sarah."

The name startled me out of my thoughts.

"Sarah?"

"The person who reached out to Home Haven. That's her name. *Sarah.* I'm Poppy Owens, your home designer—or planner. Whichever you prefer. I'm here to make this house a home. Sarah sent me to help oversee final renovations and decorate the house for a picture-perfect holiday." She waved her hand around the empty room as she delivered her informercial, her expression slowly falling as she took another step.

I took a step back. She stopped in her tracks.

Honestly, I'd barely noticed that the place wasn't completely together when I got back to the house last night. I hadn't realized until I tried to shower this morning that both bathrooms looked like someone had taken a sledgehammer to them. There was also no furniture anywhere, except for the mattress currently lying in the middle of the main bedroom.

"I thought the renovations on this place were supposed to be done this past week," the woman asserted, voice soft, uncertain. "And Sarah didn't say anyone would be here other than her. I swear I had no idea. I'm at the right address."

This chick did not stop talking, did she?

"You said Sarah told you to be here," I asked her once more.

"That's correct."

I was already reaching toward my back pocket. You know, where my phone would be had I not paraded into the hallway, wearing nothing but a towel. For a minute there, I was lucky I'd grabbed that.

I would've loved to see just how red her face would've turned. Already, a blush stained her cheeks up toward her forehead.

I pointed at where she stood, unmoving, hands clenched around her tablet like it was her firstborn. "Stay right there."

The blonde bit down on her bottom lip but nodded.

Rolling my eyes, I headed down the hall and swiped my phone off the charger. In the process, I sent a few tissues and other misplaced pieces off the bedside table and to the floor.

What the hell was my sister thinking?

The phone rang twice.

Sarah answered, out of breath. "Hello—"

"What do you think you're doing, sending random strangers to my place?" I snapped.

"You're …" Sarah paused before she scoffed, excusing someone around her. "What are you doing at home? You were supposed to be out of town until at least the fifteenth."

"If you thought I was going to stay in some stupid rehab—"

"Rejuvenation retreat. It's basically a free vacation."

"Vacation." Now, I was the one about to scoff. I paced back and forth, ignoring the sharp pain that spread from my hip down to my knee.

"Phantom pains mostly," the doctor had told me, though they felt real enough.

I tripped over my pulled-apart duffel bag and dirty clothes that hadn't made it to the hamper and swore.

"Yes, a vacation gladly paid for you by your caring sister. Only you would turn down massages and meditation, Aaron." Sarah sighed. "I pulled strings to get you in."

I thought enough on my own. I didn't need meditation time to contemplate my life.

"You're supposed to be easing back into daily life."

I wasn't talking about this right now. Like I was some traumatized civilian.

"Why is there someone in my house?" I repeated slowly.

"I was about to call her back. Please tell me you didn't scare the girl off. She sounded squirrelly on the phone."

I was getting the same impression.

"She's not a stranger. The place I hired came highly recommended. Her name is Poppy, I think? She'll be overseeing the final touches of the place you're apparently living in," Sarah informed me.

Too little, too late.

"Final touches? This place needs a freaking overhaul with how it was left," I told her.

Her highly recommended place was trying to pull a hack job here without anyone to look over the place.

"You're kidding." My sister dared to sound shocked.

"There are no showers. I had to give myself a sponge bath in the sink."

"I'll look into it." Of course she would. "We need to get it ready for the holiday."

I rubbed the space between my eyebrows. "The holiday?"

"Yes, Aaron, the time of year with lights and presents and Christmas cheer. *That holiday.*"

Every minute my sister remained on the phone, the more exasperated she sounded. I could always tell by the way she started to mutter to herself, thinking that the person she was frustrated with couldn't hear her.

Luckily, I was skilled in ignoring it.

"You won't come to our place—"

"I'm not coming into the goddamn city."

"So, we are coming to you to have a good ol'-fashioned Christmas in the mountains," said Sarah. "That includes not getting lead poisoning from whatever is in the paint there from when it was built in the 1800s or whenever it was."

"You plan on licking the walls, sis?" I asked. "The place is fine."

"No, it's not. It's falling apart. It's been falling apart for years. If my kids are coming, they're going to have a nice Christmas there. It could be nice, and so, yes, I hired someone so that I wouldn't have to deal with all the logistics. I have enough to deal with on my own. You weren't supposed to be there to notice."

My sister went on about how she couldn't possibly plan the entire holiday now that she was back at work yada yada. I couldn't fully understand, according to her. I never held down an eight to five job in a professional office or become a parent or even had a family other than her who called occasionally to bicker at me. So how could I? But, you know what? I didn't want to. Mostly, because I was still hung up on what she said a minute ago. I wasn't supposed to be here?

I agreed. However, that wasn't the point.

Where else did anyone ever expect me to be?

After I'd spent more than a couple of tours overseas, you'd think they'd be glad that I was still answering the phone at all, let alone not completely biting my sister's head off for hiring some fancy home firm to make the one place I had left to look like something out of a magazine you saw on the shelves at the grocery store. I was sure, knowing her taste, it'd probably be stark clinical whites and pops of gold.

"How often will she be here?"

"As often as she needs to be until Christmas. Do I need to repeat that no one was supposed to be in the house until the thirteenth of December, if not after?" reminded Sarah.

"And on the twelfth day of Christmas, your true love gave to thee, your fucked-up brother returning from overseas?"

"If you'd like, but I think he already did that part," said Sarah. "Now, we're just waiting for you to actually come home to us and stop being an asshole."

Well, she'd certainly gotten Mom's guilt-trip abilities down. It was going to be red-and-green plaid everywhere, too, if she got her way.

Fuck.

I grunted.

"Thank you," she said.

"If I don't like what happens, if she gets in my business—"

"Aaron—"

"Then it's over."

"Give it a chance. Like I said, you weren't even supposed to be there to notice. Don't be difficult."

I wasn't the one making things difficult.

"I have to go. Let the designer they sent know that she has free rein and to message me if she has any other questions since I'm not going to make it to the consultation there today. She can also message me if you give her problems," my sister added.

"Would've been nice to know someone had a key to my house."

"You weren't supposed to be there!" Sarah cried. "I'll talk to you later. Next time, it might be nice to call when you *want to* talk to me."

I hung up the phone and made my way back toward the door before pausing. I still only wore a towel.

This day couldn't get any better, could it?

The girl was still standing exactly where I left her. Her attention locked on where I gripped the towel in my hand before her eyes swung up to meet mine. Her eyes were wide and the oddest gray-blue, as if the color began to fade out of them.

How old was she? She looked like she could still be in school.

At the very least, she looked the epitome of a preschool

teacher, if a preschool teacher wore pants with little pink bows all over them.

Along the back wall, double French doors had been installed. There used to be a single window there that leaked when it rained. The fancy glass doors led onto the brand-new patio I hadn't taken notice of until now either, mostly covered in waves of white.

My sister must've been busy on this place since they'd found out I was coming back.

So was the weather. It'd snowed.

Huh.

Carefully, the girl—what had Sarah said her name was again? I couldn't remember and wanted to curse myself for forgetting things so easily—cleared her throat. "I'm sorry if I startled you. Before."

I cut her off with a hand, her eyes flying this way and that, as if I were a flight attendant directing her attention on where to land. "Do what you need to do."

She didn't move. In fact, the moment I started speaking, her eyes drew back to my other hand, still clutching the knot on my towel.

What? Did she want a show?

"Then you can get out," I said. "As you can see, I'm not prepared to receive visitors."

"Oh." She shifted on her feet. "Okay. Of course. I just need to look at a few more spots around the home. It's a nice house. I have lots of plans. It's going to be great. We want to enhance ..." Drifting off, she still seemed unsure.

Then, she walked toward me.

What is she doing? I flinched back.

She pointed behind me. "I, uh, planned on peeking in the bedrooms, if that's okay? I want to make sure that things are on track and the photographs received were accurate."

I waved a hand for her to go on. "Fine."

Her eyes glanced back down at the towel still around my waist once more.

Was she shitting me?

"The faster you move, the faster I can get dressed, homemaker."

"I'm not a homemaker," she immediately corrected. "I'm a designer."

"You said you made houses homes, didn't you?" I raised an eyebrow.

A hint of glare at me crossed over her face. Before it went too far, she dipped her head as she walked down the hall, writing something down as she went.

"What are you writing?"

"Notes," she explained meekly. "The living room was supposed to be finished. Both bathrooms were supposed to be completely done by now too."

I grunted. "Neither of them are."

"Can I see the second one?"

Huffing, I extended a hand toward my room across from the guest bedroom that used to be mine when I'd grown up here—or at least finished growing up in high school.

The homemaker clenched her jaw when she looked at the new tiles that were half finished in the new walk-in shower off the main bedroom. I had noticed, but hadn't cared to look into it much. The sink, too, was a mess aside from the faucet which looked somewhat more ornate compared to what I would've expected from Sarah. She was all about bland beige minimalism and whatever was in style.

The homemaker moved back through my room, careful to step over the strewn blankets and clothes still half unpacked from my issued duffel and backpack without a word. I didn't apologize for it. Wouldn't. This was my space, and at this point, those two pieces of luggage were all that belonged to me.

Other than the mostly empty house we stood in.

A box of old books was all that was left stuffed into the corner of the closet. The old classics I'd had to read for school were stacked inside with my grandmother's historical romance with bent edges and spines so creased that you could barely read the titles.

"Well-loved books," my grandmother liked to call the used copies she picked up at library sales.

She had at least three or four dozen small books stacked inside the box. Some of them I remembered reading when I ran out of other material. The two of us had been in a constant loop of fifty-cent thrift paperbacks and library books until I'd enlisted. Nights had been for warm dinners and reading by the fireplace.

What else was there to do in the middle of nowhere with no cable television?

"Okay, well, um, I think I mainly have what I was looking for today. I mean, I wanted to start on ..." She clicked her tablet off and tucked her stylus into the palm of her hand. "But I guess that all can wait. I'll make some calls about the bathrooms. And the living room. And everything else. I already have a lot of ideas I think will turn out great so long as the crew keeps on schedule."

"Crew?" I cut in.

I didn't just have to deal with her, but other people now?

Long eyelashes peppered her cheeks. "Yes. They were supposed to be done last week, but it doesn't seem like that's the case. I'll need to call them to come back to finish the bathrooms and the kitchen, among other things. They were supposed to be farther along by now. I'll be putting in the order for the rest of the house now that I've seen it too."

"Order for the rest of the house?"

Why did I feel like this chick was speaking a different language?

"Furniture," she clarified. "Is there anything specific you think you'll need? If there's anything, let me know. Then, I'll be working through the holiday decorating and—"

"Decorating. That's what you do?"

Up until now, the homemaker had been looking around the space—anywhere but at me. Now, she lifted her eyes and nodded. "Part of what I do."

"They pay you to do that?"

Her face screwed up as she looked away from me again.

For some reason when she did, I wanted to reach out and turn her chin back toward me. I wanted her to look me in the eye instead of away.

Did I frighten her? Maybe it would be a good thing if I did. It would better if she knew to leave me the hell alone and out of whatever scheme my sister had tried to come up with to make this some big holiday celebration that I wanted no part of.

I was the big bad wolf. She was Little Red Knit Socks, walking straight into my den.

"And events. Sometimes. Not lately."

I snorted a short, unamused laugh. "Impressive."

The homemaker bit the inside of her cheek, though her face revealed nothing of the frustration I'd expected to be there at my comment. "I'll send along the tentative schedule to you. That way, you're not surprised by anything. I'm confident that this project will come together perfectly. Thanks for not calling the police or anything on me."

"Then, even more people would show up?" I chuckled. "Yeah. No, thanks."

"Right. All right then."

Now, get out.

Light brows furrowed. Without any further ceremony or rambling, the flighty blonde headed back the way she had come through the kitchen. I followed her out, making sure she made it as she slipped her shoes back on and donned her oversize puffer coat.

"Have a good rest of your day, Aaron—Mr. Hayes."

The heavy door shut behind her.

Finally, I was left alone. Again.

I stood frozen in the cold and empty living room, listening to the echo of her lapsed presence.

"Aaron," she had said. Hadn't she?

When I had started in the military from the beginning, my name had changed. I was no longer Aaron. Nearly everyone was called by their last name, unless given a call sign or they were special.

And I quickly learned from training and becoming the best soldier I could be in the Army—from basic to infantry to special forces—I wasn't special. None of us were.

I learned that on day one—from the time I got off the plane to where I was supposed to report alongside my friend, Barrett. The tall, lanky blond kid had shown me around my first day of school after I moved to the cabin with my grandmother outside the city. Eventually, he enlisted right alongside me. He said that he always planned on doing it. It wasn't just because I had brought it up or because we joked that he had to if I beat him at the push-up competition, which I did, even if my arms felt sore for days after.

Barrett's father was in the military. Barrett had lost his father, too, by then. His mother had still tried to convince him to stay home by the time basic training came around.

"Hayes!"

The deep voice of the sergeant still shocked my system whenever I remembered it. Raspy and guttural. The way his boots were always polished and most of all how his gravelly voice never had a volume lower than loud from day one.

"Looks like you didn't get out of sharing your bunk yet. This private decided he didn't need to follow direct orders and show up on time." The sergeant, who all of us had already met—at the time, we were still slightly quaking in our newly issued boots at being called little girls or much worse—addressed me.

Standing behind him with what could only be considered a smirk under his high-and-tight haircut, which looked like a puff of black curls, was another recruit. He at least had the sense to wait until the sergeant was out of earshot to smile and look between me and Barrett—we had somehow lucked out and gotten bunks across from each other.

"Hey." The new guy smiled, stretching his thick coating of freckles across his tanned cheeks. Soon, I'd learn that he rarely wasn't smiling. "Warren Vassar. Nice to meet ya." He met my eyes. "We bunking? Cool stuff. Haven't bunked since I went to camp in seventh grade. Guess I get top."

Immediately, Barrett smiled back at this new character with a wave across the aisle. His bunkmate was somewhere else, probably getting teeth pulled or making sure he could see out of both eyes in medical. "Joseph Barrett."

I rolled my eyes. "His name's Barrett. I'm Aaron. Aaron Hayes."

Vassar dipped his chin as he threw his duffel onto the top bunk. "Got it. Nice to meet you, boys."

For some reason—maybe it was the fact that basic training managed to bond us more than break us somehow—it wasn't just me and Barrett anymore. The three of us made it through basic training together during the rain, shine, and the sergeant screaming at us like we didn't have eardrums and he didn't have vocal cords he was afraid of ruining.

Case in point, the day we were all doing one of the famous runs. Someone always ended up either puking or passing out from sleep deprivation or how hot it was. Either way, you ended up covered in a layer of sweat you hadn't known was possible.

With Barrett leading the three of us and Vassar keeping pace at my side, he stopped.

Leaning over his knees, Vassar picked up a stick on the side of the path, turning it around like it was some kind of treasure.

For a second, I considered that he might have heatstroke.

"What the hell are you doing?" I sneered at him, reaching to drag him with me if I had to.

Barrett was turning around as he ran to keep up with the rest of the pack, peeking over his shoulder to see what the holdup was.

Unfortunately not before the sergeant did.

"Are you holding a stick, Private?" Sergeant screamed.

Vassar looked down at his hand, still holding the stick like a toy wand, and then back up to the sergeant. After a moment, he nodded. "Sir, yes, Sir!"

"Good," said Sergeant, catching me still watching the two of them. "What are you looking at, Hayes? Get running! Now, you, Private, what the fuck is that? Vassar? You, Private, get to hold that stick for the rest of your time here in the Army. That way, it can replace the oxygen that you're wasting!"

I didn't know what the sergeant thought was going to happen when he gave that order. I'd already started to keep running to catch up with Barrett, but Vassar nodded harder.

"Sir! Yes, Sir!"

And Vassar laughed.

His laugh had been loud enough that when he was inside, I swore it nearly shook the entire building. It was deep and brash and never held back. It made the sergeant and anyone else all through our years of training up to special operations make him run double, train double, be as good as his humor was.

But for the rest of basic training, Vassar had run, eaten, and slept with that puny stick until graduation day.

Eventually, years later after basic and special training, all three of us ran back into the sergeant between deployments. He looked at the three of us in recognition before his eyes caught on Vassar—because everyone remembered Vassar. Only now, it wasn't just Vassar to look at. Vassar stood with one of the best work dogs I'd ever seen in the Army at his side.

"If that ain't the best shit I've ever seen," the old drill sergeant muttered, looking at Vassar. "Congratulations. You might be the only soldier I taught with follow through. Hayes! You'd better be keeping this soldier in check."

When we walked away, I turned to Vassar. "What did he mean about follow through?"

Vassar shrugged. "Always figured he mean to make sure every breath you take here counts."

I stared at my friend, shocked at his thoughtful answer.

"Now, come on, you're supposed to keep me in check," He shouldered me, and it was back to the same old Vass.

I was supposed to keep him in check.

I'd sure as hell tried.

The final time I had heard my last name outside of a hospital room, I could nearly still hear Vassar and Barrett—I swore it was the two of them—screaming my name still, like a piercing, high-pitched ring looping through my head over and over.

"Hayes! Hayes! It's gonna be all right, Hayes. We got help. You gotta let go."

Or at least at the time, I'd thought it was Vassar. I'd hoped it was.

I shook myself out of it. No one had called me by my first name, other than my sister, in years. Not since high school.

Had my sister given cheery homemaker my name? Had I at some point since I'd caught her sneaking through the place?

Did I not remember?

I ran my hand through my hair, feeling how long it'd been since I'd last cut it. I shuffled back to my room. Without bothering to change, I dropped onto my mattress. It did the job well enough. Certainly weren't the worst conditions I'd ever slept in.

I shut my eyes, squeezing them for a second as I pretended the world didn't exist. I wished it didn't.

Aaron. Aaron Hayes.

Funny. It hadn't sounded so terrible when she said it.

four

. . .

Poppy

I WASN'T a prodigy when it came to home design. We all made mistakes; it was how we learned. This was especially the case when the thing you needed to learn and evolve aligned with fashion.

My first project, for instance, like most interior wannabes, had been my own bedroom. I thought I was the coolest, wanting to slather my walls in a rich golden yellow with a classic white border that made the entire room look somewhere between a sunset and a Victorian tearoom. My bedspread was offset by having the comforter in a now-cringe-worthy chevron pattern—because at that point, everything had been chevron.

I knew better than a lot of people how easy it was to get caught up in trends and what was hot right now rather than what would always be classic and homey for years to come while still making guests speechless and wondering how exactly they could live just as stylishly.

Of course now, all the things I learned and all the ways I knew I was more than sufficient to complete a job like the Hayes-Preston holiday home were thrown out the window. I felt like I reverted back to being that same girl—when I had been fifteen in high school, awkward and clunky and desperately trying to pretend that she wasn't—the moment I stood stock-still in front of Aaron Hayes.

Aaron Hayes, who had once stood in front of me similarly. Only then, we weren't in a small cabin. We were at school, in a locker room, and I was hidden behind a wall that he didn't see me or my so-called friends who I soon enough realized only kept me around for comic relief. Or it was more likely that they'd kept me around so that I could tell them about the parties on the college campus nearby, courtesy of Simon, and divulge to them at least one secret to trauma-bond us all together.

"What do you mean, you don't like anyone?" Cassie, an almost-dreadfully-stereotypical cheerleader—whose mom took her to get her blonde highlights redone every month until she was no longer the brunette—gaped at me. "Come on now. You must like someone. Tell us."

All the girls pushed in on me closer that day during school.

I bit my lip, and they all squealed, cheering me on to let the name loose.

"Well," I finally broke, my voice nervous as I picked at my perpetually short fingernails, "Aaron Hayes."

The next day, they pushed me into the boy's team locker room to hear Aaron tell all his friends that I would be the last person in the entire school he would ever consider kissing on a bet, let alone asking on a date.

I was *that* repulsive to him.

And that was how he had looked at me today when I stepped into his house. Onto his property.

Even though he shouldn't have. Not when that day on the edge of the locker room, where he and his friends were changing after practice, hadn't been the final time I came into contact with Aaron Hayes.

No, that wasn't until a few months later.

After the start of a new school year, when everyone turned a little boyfriend crazy, and after the holidays, when everyone heard about the reason the popular quarterback for the team hadn't been in school for over a week was due to a tragic car accident involving his parents— One of his football teammate's, Isaac, had parents that were out of town and decided to throw a party.

I snuck out to attend at the behest of Cassie. She'd insisted if I didn't come, I would be a major loser—even though she barely talked to me when I got there.

Aaron Hayes had been nearly buried alive by a pile of puffer coats in the guest room. He was also very drunk. I asked what he had to drink that night.

"Uh," he sputtered, squinting at me as if he couldn't quite place who I was. "I dunno. There was a beer and then some stuff out of a bottle ..."

I chuckled.

"You're laughing at me," he said, as if he wasn't sure.

I shook my head. "No. I'm not. Are you okay?"

"Course I am." Aaron snorted. "Why wouldn't I be okay? I'm fantastic."

I looked him over. "I'm sorry. That was kind of a stupid question."

"Yeah? Why's that?" he asked, waiting for my answer.

Because I heard your parents died, I wanted to say.

Instead, I sat down next to him. "You're kind of lying in a mountain of coats."

He laughed as if I had said one of the funniest things in the world. "Freaking comfy pile of coats."

I pressed my lips together, trying not to laugh with him. I shouldn't. I knew laughing with him would be wrong considering the state he was in.

"You can laugh at me."

"I'm not laughing at you," I said.

"You are," he insisted. "I'm certain."

"Are you?"

He shrugged, less confident in his answer. "Stupid party."

It was, but I didn't answer. If I contradicted him, I'd be lying. If I answered honestly, I would be a big loser, like Cassie always said I was.

" What?" Aaron tried again. "Don't you think so?"

I shrugged.

"You wouldn't have any fun."

He was right; I wasn't.

"Why did you even come here?" he asked.

"I was invited."

"So?"

"So, I … my friends …" I tried to come up with a better answer, feeling my heart race as I thought of one that would make me sound better than simply coming up with the answer I'd had all night before I escaped down the hallway, away from the music and people who hadn't given me a single ounce of care whether or not I'd shown up in the end.

I didn't know why I was there.

"And where are they?" Aaron asked me. He raised his eyebrows, which had a tint of red to them, especially in the dim lighting of the room.

The lamp on the nightstand was on, leaving the smallest amount of yellow light to bounce onto the bedspread and across his face—warm brown eyes, half closed yet rimmed in a red, which I couldn't tell if it was from the alcohol or tears. Though this was Aaron Hayes, so it had to just be from the alcohol, right?

His chapped pink lips parted as he took heavy, uneven breaths.

"I don't know," I answered him. "Probably out there with their other friends. Dancing, maybe with their boyfriends or getting boyfriends … I don't know."

"Don't you have a boyfriend?"

I barked a laugh.

"You think that's funny," Aaron said.

"Yes, I do."

"Why?"

"Because." I shook my head, looking down at myself. I wore my tightest jeans and a turquoise-blue sweater that I thought made my eyes pop, even with the minimal makeup my mom let me use, still telling me I was too young for such things. "I don't have a boyfriend."

"You're pretty."

I shook my head immediately. "No, I'm not. You probably don't even know who I am."

He certainly wouldn't be talking to me if he did, I figured, would he?

"Yeah, I do. You're nice at least. And smart."

I felt myself blush so hard that I put a hand on my cheek when he complimented me. He reached up to pull my hand away, and I was forced to look straight at him again.

"That's a whole lot more than anyone can say for themselves. Your friends. Me."

"I don't think so."

He rolled his eyes.

"I mean it," I told him, cocking my head to check that he was listening to me. "I think most of the time, you're a pretty great person, Aaron. You're a good athlete."

"A whole lot that does me now. Never even liked it."

"You didn't? You're so great."

He shrugged. "I mean, I like it. I do, but ... my dad was the one who said that it was worth anything. 'Always keep busy,' he said. He did. So much so that he was always too busy that he didn't even show up to the games. Didn't anyway."

"Well, you're a good student too," I said. "You always have an answer and try to start conversations in English with Ms. Markle. Your interpretation on Romeo and Juliet when we read it last semester as a comedic tragedy and not a romance was really thoughtful."

"You remember that?"

Embarrassingly, yeah, I did. "I'm sorry about your parents too, you know."

He didn't say anything for a long time.

"I guess I've just been sitting here, thinking that I have no idea what's going to happen next," he said. "I mean, I knew that I was never going to make anything of myself worthwhile to them, not like my sister did, going to school to be a lawyer or that kind of shit. It's just not me. And now … I'm really not going to."

He sucked on the inside of his cheek, holding back the water that I watched well in his eyes and sit on the edge of his lashes, never falling.

"You can be whoever you want to be, you know. Make it worthwhile, I mean."

I tried not to blush again, embarrassment swelling in the pit of my stomach the more I talked. Swirling around with the words I tried to make sound right and sophisticated rather than desperate, like I was sure he must've thought I was. He'd basically said so before.

Though as he sat in front of me, red-eyed in a way I could tell then was more sad and tired than tipsy, I didn't see how we were all that different.

I swallowed. "I think you're pretty great."

"Worthwhile," he whispered.

"Yeah, worthwhile like—"

I almost missed it when he reached out to hold on to my cheek, bringing my face down to his—and he kissed me. Aaron Hayes kissed me in a pile of random teenagers' coats that crinkled under our hands as we sought balance.

His lips were soft, and he kissed the same way he talked when he was a little drunk. Or a lot drunk. Smooth and easy.

And kind to me.

He tasted like sharp liquor that burned, sticking around long after I left, making sure he fell asleep on his side before I did.

After that night, I'd never seen Aaron Hayes again. From what I'd heard, after his parents died, he'd moved in with another relative somewhere outside of the city. But still, in the back of my mind, I never forgot him. I never forgot my first kiss. Our kiss.

Or the fact that somehow, it still managed to be the best in my entire life and made the lecture of a lifetime that I'd received from my mother when she realized I'd snuck out—due to the fact I'd never snuck out of the house before and I'd forgotten my key to let myself back in—all worthwhile.

five

. . .

Poppy

"GAH!" I dropped everything in my arms, sending the old, beaten Home Haven office chair rolling away on its wheels. I pulled it back toward me before falling into it with an unattractive grunt.

Today was supposed to be great. Nothing had stood in my way.

I could do difficult things.

Until, of course, something had stood in my way, and it was far past difficult.

Right in front of me and in nothing but a towel, no less.

It was supposed to be the start of winning this promotion and becoming Poppy, senior interior designer at Home Haven. None of this was how it was supposed to go. Could it get any worse?

"Did you seriously just say *gah*?" Hannah tapped her headset as she turned around toward me. She took a sip from her oversize hot-pink water jug before glancing back toward her screen again, checking the time. "Wait a second, aren't you supposed to be still at the house right now? I thought today was your first big day."

Not answering, I took a deep breath as I took my things out of my bag to set up on my desk in my tiny cubicle.

I needed to take a deep breath. I might've needed two because I had driven over three hours in less than that. I was supposed to be measuring and taking my time right now as I put together a plan to create the best project out of this assignment I possibly could.

But then I'd met the real owner of the cabin. Or rather re-met him.

Only clearly, he'd had no idea that he was re-meeting me.

The real owner of the cabin was so much worse than the possibly uptight corporate lawyer I'd thought I was going to be dealing with. The kind of person I was used to dealing with.

I put a hand to my head.

Aaron Hayes.

We were adults now anyway. I could move on from what had happened. Even if he already was looking at me like he had in high school, like I was the most repulsive human being he'd ever seen.

You know, after he got over the fact that I wasn't a home intruder.

I wished I could say that he had gotten worse-looking in the past decade or so. But no. If anything, Aaron Hayes had gotten even handsomer than I remembered. He was tall, and his shoulders had somehow turned even broader than they had been when he was playing football, though those eyes piercing into me had felt just as heart-stopping.

Maybe it was a good thing. I didn't look at all like the girl who had bulky braces and didn't know how to apply even the basics of makeup anymore because, Aaron Hayes did not remember me.

How was that even possible? It didn't even seem fair in the whole balance of the universe. Instead of the sweet boy next door, Aaron looked like a ruggedly handsome model as he'd stood in a towel and only a towel, which I couldn't tear my eyes away from, along with his side, puckered with scars.

Hannah watched me as I chaotically confessed my traitorous eyes and even worse past—about a client.

What happened in the cubicle stayed in the cubicle.

By the time I finished, I put a hand on my warm cheek. My face had turned a bright red in frustration and embarrassment.

I probably looked like a tomato.

Or like I had two heads by the way Hannah was staring. Had I ever seen her speechless?

"Wow."

"I know," I whined.

"Poppy Owens is honestly admitting that she has a crush. This is a moment for the record books. Poppy Owens is having a meltdown before our usual afternoon teatime and she liked a boy."

"What?"

"Likes? Present tense?" Hannah corrected.

I scoffed. Hannah had missed the point. That wasn't what I had said at all.

The house was a mess! Aaron Hayes was there, looking at me like I'd committed high treason for ogling his abs!

"He was a little high school crush. Don't look at me like that. Yes, I'll admit it. But that was then. Nothing more."

"Nothing?"

"Well ..." I paused.

"What more, Poppy?"

"We kissed in high school. Once," I admitted. "But he didn't know that it was me then either."

Or at least, I didn't think he had.

Hannah stared at me, wide-eyed. "I think I need popcorn for this."

I didn't know what I'd expected, but the lack of an appropriate response was even more concerning.

"I'm just wondering how hot this guy is, quite frankly." Hannah leaned her head against her fist, studying me. "More than a seven on a scale of one to ten, right?"

"Did you not hear anything I said?"

"Tell me. Is he hotter than Henry Cavill?" Hannah gasped as if the thought was incomprehensible, reaching up to take off her bulky blue-light glasses. "Oh my God, he is."

I fell back into my seat. I could see this was going nowhere.

I stared up toward the ceiling. "Different kind of hot."

His body was … and his arms … God, his arms.

Stop. This was a client I was thinking about!

I was being terribly unprofessional.

He might have been Aaron Hayes who had made me feel awful and caused a minor break in my extremely fragile sixteen-year-old heart, seeking validation, but he was my client now.

"Today really couldn't have gone worse, could it?" I asked.

"To be honest, Pops, I'm just impressed you made the drive alone. Give yourself some credit," suggested Hannah. "Your first day didn't go so great. You still have your notes of what you need to do on the admin side for the rest of the day, right? It doesn't sound so bad. He's probably embarrassed. I'm sure you think it's a hundred times worse since you've been spiraling the entire way back."

"You're probably right."

"I usually am."

"But …"

If all went well, it would be a few weeks, and then I would never have to look at the man I'd made a complete fool of myself in front of again. And hopefully, he wouldn't tell Sarah Hayes-Preston that I had made a fool of myself either and fire me.

"You just—you wouldn't believe this guy, Hannah. Beyond the whole …"

"Crush you have on him?"

"*Decorating? They pay you to do that?*" I openly mocked, quoting his words that had sent a flash of red-hot anger through me. "Now, I'm also going to have to deal with him for the next month."

"Gah," Hannah said, dragging out the word in understanding. "Never mind. Keep ranting if you need to. I have a call coming in. Hold on a second.

"Home Haven Holiday Hotline, this is Hannah. No, no, no. Ma'am, when I said take out your turkey to defrost, I didn't mean to defrost it in the oven. There's a setting to defrost in the oven? The microwave. Ah, I see. No, don't panic. Let's remain calm. It's all right. I mean, most people like the leftovers better anyway. Our goal now is to make sure it gets in the oven to cook."

Another ring startled me as I turned toward my monitor. I looked back at Hannah. She looked at me with wide eyes, shaking her head. It wasn't her phone.

I shifted through my bag until I found my own. I stared at the lit-up screen filled with numbers before I finally had enough sense to answer. "Hello?"

Hannah was still staring at me while her call went on in the background. She cocked her head to the side, as if waiting for me to continue. Apparently, I needed to work on my phone-answering skills.

Home Haven, this is Poppy. I wasn't sure I could pull it off.

Carefully, I got up and headed outside the cubicle. A few others were in the office today. The sound of the copier whirred, and a hum of voices remained minimal enough that I tried to keep my voice down.

"Hi there. Is this Poppy Owens?"

I cleared my throat, trying to sound professional. "This is she."

"This is Sarah, about the house."

"Yes!" I nodded into the phone immediately. Of course it was. I needed to put her number into my phone permanently. I added it to my mental to-do list once I got off the phone, switching from my minor meltdown back into business. "It's good to hear from you. How are you?"

"I'm fine. Thanks for asking," she said before pausing. "How are you?"

"Me?" I asked before I could stop myself. Quickly, I cleared my throat. "I'm perfectly well, thanks. It was a pleasure to finally see the house and meet the homeowner on-site today."

"Uh-huh," Sarah intoned as if she didn't believe me.

My forehead creased as she murmured to someone in the background. A few eyes in the office glanced toward me, but only for a second before returning to whatever else they were working on.

"I'm sorry I couldn't make it out to the house for your start date today. I made all the preparations and plans to be there, but unfortunately, things got a bit out of hand at work," said Sarah.

"Completely okay. I understand. That's why I am here. It's expected that these things happen, especially around the holiday."

"And the house?"

"The cabin is really lovely." I mentioned, "I'll admit that I expected some of the larger renovations to be further along. A few of the rooms have not been finished yet by our renovation team."

Another thing to add to my to-do list.

"Will this push back our finish date?"

No. It wouldn't. Couldn't. "It will all be taken care of."

"I love to hear that."

I could hear her smile over the phone. It should've relieved me. Instead, it made my heart race.

"I'm sure seeing my brother there, however, was more than just another surprise."

"Oh, well, it's all right. I mean, I did walk in, unannounced to him," I told her, explaining the situation in case he exaggerated the situation. I wanted to be calm and professional. I did nothing wrong. "Though I did knock first."

"Don't apologize. I apologize for him. I didn't believe it when he said he was already living there, especially considering how the house isn't …"

"Completely livable?"

"Exactly."

I wanted to laugh at the huff in her voice. Oddly enough, along with my frustration towards Aaron, I was also disappointed in how today panned out. With the house, sure. But also with our interaction. Despite knowing how he'd acted when we were kids and how he'd acted today. I'd forgotten that Aaron had such kind eyes, even when they were staring you down.

They were wasted on him.

I kept my voice bright and upbeat so the conversation didn't sour. "I don't want you to worry. That's my job. Everything's going to come together. I'm sure that if Mr. Hayes is living there now, perhaps he would like some input on the direction we are going."

"Don't worry about any of that. I'm calling for one other reason. Or two, technically." Sarah stopped me before I could ramble on.

"Yes?" I was pretty sure I'd squeaked.

"You have one hundred percent creative freedom on this project," Sarah informed me.

"Wait … what?"

"The plans you've sent and already written up look amazing. Honestly, they're above and beyond what I expected of the place, knowing what condition it was in. Feel free to do whatever else you need to make the home a cozy, holiday space. I need it to be."

Free rein. My heart might've stuttered in my chest.

"I understand."

"I hope so. We need it to be the best Christmas possible. Extend the budget another ten if you need to. If you need more for the day-of planning, let me know, but as of now, my family and I will be there promptly on Christmas Eve."

"I understand," I repeated.

"Good. Because I'm sure you're already getting the feeling that this job, so long as my brother is around, is going to come with a few obstacles. I have entire faith in you from our correspondence."

"Thank you."

"I want to warn you again. Right now, Aaron is … he recently returned from deployment in the military. He's still finding himself back home. I hate to tell you to be patient with him. Maybe it's the sister coming out in me as I say this."

She continued, "I understand it's a big job, especially since I want to make sure you don't take whatever that lunk living there makes you deal with to heart. Aaron can be an ass on a good day, let alone when he's been grieving."

Grieving?

It didn't seem like it was right to offer Sarah my condolences.

Luckily, I didn't have to as she rattled off some more information, along with, "You have my permission to be just as stubborn and frustrating to him if you need to."

"I—"

"You understand?"

"Yes," I said after a minute. "I understand. But I'm sure that won't be necessary. You want this holiday to be perfect. That's why I'm here. Everything will come together as you envision, Ms. Hayes-Preston."

"Thank you. Have a great day, Poppy."

"You too."

I wasn't sure I was able to move. I let my phone hand at my side.

One of the online magazine writers at their desk paused their typing. He raised an eyebrow. "You okay over there, Poppy?"

Hastily, I nodded. "Yes. Thanks. Need a minute."

He looked bored and unconvinced. However, he turned back to his screen, letting his fingers jump over the keyboard.

Hannah watched me as she finished her conversation on her headset, though it didn't sound like it was still the woman with her rubbery microwave turkey.

My phone pinged with a text.

Michelle: I got a message from the Hayes-Preston home.

Three dots came across my screen as she typed.

Michelle: She's very impressed with your designs and with you for taking on the extra work she is asking in stride. Please let me know if you need any help at all or if there are any obstacles. We're here to help however you may need.

Me: Thank you. I'm excited about the project already. I will let you know if anything comes up, but enjoy your holiday. I have everything in hand.

Michelle: I'm so excited to hear this for you, Poppy. I know you won't let us down.

I reread the message. I wasn't going to let Michelle or Sarah down. I wasn't going to let myself down.

I was ready for this.

I took a deep breath before I realized Hannah was staring at me.

"What was that?" I asked.

Hannah cupped her hand over her microphone and turned back to me. "I'm just surprised you're holding it together this well."

Honestly, so was I.

six

. . .

Poppy

DAY TWO. Day two was always better than day one.

Right? I was going to pretend that was a thing.

My phone chimed with my affirmation app. I peeked down to see it announce across the screen, *I am exactly where I need to be.*

I was. Even if that included my knuckles gripping the steering wheel just as hard as I had the last time I traveled up the highway. I focused on the road, trying not to zone out within the mental checklist I already had formed for the day.

The new renovation crew was set to be there by noon—with me present. The appliances would be coming in by the end of the week. Then, once I managed all of that, it would be my time to shine.

I balanced my phone between my shoulder and ear, listening to the static-filled ring.

A gruff voice answered. *"What, Sarah?"*

"Oh." I was startled at his greeting. He certainly didn't answer the phone with the usual *hello* I had expected. "It's not Sarah. I'm coming on-site and—"

"Yes?"

I took a deep breath.

This was my job. *My joy.*

"Good morning, Mr. Hayes," I restarted. "This is Poppy Owens from Home Haven. I wanted to let you know that I will be working at the house today soon and assure you that despite the lack of renovation in certain spaces of the house, everything is very much under control—"

The line went dead, along with my hopes and dreams.

Okay, maybe I had been spending too much time with Hannah in a six-by-six space. My reactions were starting to take on a flair for the dramatic.

I dropped my phone in the cupholder. When I finally arrived up the long, hidden driveway, I let out a sigh of relief.

I wasn't sure if there would ever be a time when I wasn't secretly shocked that I'd made it.

Today was going to be better.

When I knocked on the door, it swung open.

Aaron Hayes stood in the middle of the doorway. He stared at me as if I were number one on his Most Hated list. Or maybe he hadn't gotten enough sleep. A lavender haze circled his warm honey-brown eyes. Not only that, but he had to be cold. From rolling out of bed with his dark blond hair sticking up in all directions, he hadn't even cared enough to put on a shirt. Gray sweatpants hung over his hips.

I forced my traitorous eyes not to dip toward his toned stomach again, locking my stare on his so that I wouldn't be tempted—since it appeared around Aaron Hayes, I was worse than a man.

His eyes narrowed further, as if he wasn't quite sure where he could place me as I stood on his front doorstep.

Do you remember me?

No. He didn't.

That was fine. Aaron not recognizing me from all those years ago could be a great thing. This way, I could focus. I could start fresh and be completely professional.

"Oh." I tried not to appear as startled as I felt. "Good morning, Mr. Hayes—"

"Your so-called workers are already here," he interrupted.

"Excuse me?"

"Been here for hours, homemaker," Aaron stated, his voice gruff with displeasure. "Maybe you don't have this whole place under control as much as you thought."

Stepping inside, I could hear the few voices echoing through the cabin. The workers weren't supposed to be here for another hour, I'd thought, but when it came to this house, I should've known to expect the unexpected.

The fact that there were no showerheads in the showers yesterday was case in point, and it appeared that no one knew where those fixtures had gone in the hustle of them clearing out last week, which meant another order. Another change.

The door shut from somewhere behind me. I didn't bother to take off my coat as I made my way to the group of men standing in a circle in the middle of the empty living room.

One of them turned around, moving toward the hall.

I stood a step back, trying to move out of the way. "Um, hold on a second. Excuse me."

The man wearing a threadbare T-shirt laughed, hopefully at something his coworkers had said and not about the fact he'd almost run into me. His eyes were half lidded as he waved his hand somewhere over my shoulder. "Care to move aside so we can get finished already?"

"I apologize," I said kindly enough, though my hands went to my hips. I didn't move from where I stood in front of him. Hannah would be proud of me right now. I was standing my ground like the badass interior designer who would own that senior designer title. "I didn't introduce myself. My name is Poppy Owens. I'm the contact person for the home design."

The one guy raised his dark eyebrows. Dear Lord, was this area filled with men who wanted to look at me like I was some sort of confused animal wandering in here? If this was the foreman who had started on this project in the summer, he certainly didn't have the same gruff yet kind consideration in person.

"You?" he asked. "You're the person who brought everyone out here when we were already on a tight schedule before the holiday?"

It wasn't right before the holiday. Near the holiday perhaps. Sort of.

The man I'd talked to on the phone didn't sound slightly as put out.

I cleared my throat. "Yes. Me. Thank you so much for coming out after it appeared some of the work here was incomplete by the precious crew that we employed."

"Are you lot giving this woman a hard time?" a voice called out behind me.

All attention went to an older man shaking his head until his eyes found mine. One hand reached up to scratch his thick beard. The other waved off his workers.

"Give us a second, will y'all?" he asked, though it wasn't much of a request.

The other guys mumbled around something but found other places in the small home to be as the man, whose voice more so resembled the man I had talked to and who was recommended through Home Haven's directory, made his way until he stood in front of me.

"You must be Ms. Owens."

"Poppy is fine," I said. "Thanks for coming in and looking over the place. I'm sorry I wasn't here earlier."

"We had an early start. Don't you worry 'bout a thing. My name is Frank. I don't care for no titles much either, so I have a feeling we'll be gettin' along just fine, working together."

The corner of my mouth curled up for the first time since I'd walked in the door. "Nice to meet you, Frank."

"We don't have much time to waste, so let's talk house. I don't understand how such a project was brushed to the side like this," he muttered, though not with me. According to Michelle, whenever she hired this man, he was thorough with his work. This place right now must've looked like a disaster. "Whoever was in here before us got lazy."

That was putting it lightly.

"It looks like whoever did the exterior on this place during the summer months did a fantastic job. The inside looks like it was done by an entirely different team."

I inhaled sharply, causing him to pause. I had known it didn't look right the moment I saw that part on the project listing the other night when I was double-checking everything. Sure, it wasn't completely out of character for Home Haven to assign two different crews to a house that needed a large overhaul. In some cases, it was too much work for just one, and Home Haven dealt in design and design only. The rest was hired out.

But in this case, it was a mistake.

And in the end, it was going to be my *mistake*.

"It was."

"Whoever they are, you should make sure they're off the list to work for you ladies at Home Haven."

"Already done. After Michelle reached out, I let her know of the situation and that I was contacting a different crew to see if they could spare any time for us on such short notice."

The foreman dipped his head. "I appreciate you thinking of the small business I have going here. We're happy to be in contract, working with you all, and I'll be damned if someone took advantage of you not being on-site for the start of reno. This place is basically a historical landmark. It fires me up to see such a project treated this way. Would you like me to walk you through what I see has already been done to make sure we're running at the same speed?"

"Yes." I breathed a sigh of relief. "Thank you. I read through the report, and I have been following the schedule of what should've been done."

"And it's just you on this project?"

"Just me," I confirmed, hoping there was more determination than nerves in my voice.

"I got a good overview of the house before you walked in."

I tried to stand strong. He wasn't judging; in fact, he looked a little nervous.

And nervous could only mean …

"Oh no."

"It's nothing to worry about," he assured. "But we did find a problem in the bathroom."

"The one we just finished?" For some reason, I could tell he wasn't talking about the vanishing showerheads or the fact that not everything was properly grouted in the tile work.

"The problem is the original shared bathroom off the hallway. There's mold."

"Mold," I repeated.

"It was likely left when they attempted to redo the panel. They weren't paying attention, is my guess. It's not too far gone, but it does put us another few days behind. There's no way around it. We need to redo it to make sure the space is as it should be and won't be getting anyone sick in the long run."

"Right." Mentally, I started to push things back in my schedule.

"But we also have other jobs coming up that we need to leave the site for. We have a week we can offer. Maybe a few days after."

"A week," I repeated. There was so much left to do. "Only a week?"

I had the list written up, and suddenly, I wished I had it on my tablet, which had become the singular thing keeping me together and everything straight. There were the bathrooms, of course. The mold needed to be dealt with. I was happy it had been caught. But there was also putting the final touches on the kitchen once the appliances made their way in. There were the floors that were never refinished, as was part of the prior contract. The bookshelves weren't built in the living room. None of the walls in any of the rooms, besides the kitchen, were painted and couldn't be by the team I hired until the rest was complete!

Uncertainty brewed high in my chest. No team was ever going to be able to do all of that before they left. They wouldn't be able to.

"We can finish up the bathroom and floors if you already have the stain picked out, but that's the final part of our job here on this project," said Frank. "The rest is up to you. I'll let your boss know what's going on."

I shook my head. "It's all right. I'll make sure it's covered."

A huff sounded behind me. As I turned around, I noticed Aaron moving away from us toward his bedroom. The door shut quickly afterward.

At least I wouldn't have to worry about him. Maybe, if I was lucky, he'd stay out of the way entirely.

Frank seemed to understand immediately. "We'll get started right away."

When it came to renovation, things often got worse before they got better. It was just how things went.

I'd watched the up-and-down process secondhand when shadowing other designers. It wasn't out of the ordinary that when they were in deep with a project, they got a little more than they'd bargained for. Creaky floorboards, lost shipments of throw pillows, cracked paver patios no one noticed until the day before everything was set to be complete for a final walk-through. It was rare that when it came to a home project, everything went right.

A good interior designer was calm, cool, and collected. I took a deep breath with each new heartbreak and news.

That didn't mean I didn't want to cry about it.

Just a little.

I was starting to doubt anyone in the history of Home Haven had ever had to deal with a renovation monster like this project.

For so many reasons.

"What do you mean?" My voice shook in a way that warned everyone around me that I was about to be reduced to a full-on mental breakdown.

I didn't think anyone would blame me at this point.

Not even Frank could hide his disbelief at the chaotic mess this project had become in record time.

He and his men had been working nonstop on my to-do list. Bathrooms were being completed, light fixtures were being wired correctly this time before being hung, and the floor was re-stained the correct color after I'd realized it was incorrect on my second day—and not just because Aaron Hayes wandered by to second-guess if I was *sure* about that color. Luckily, I was able to reorder it by the third day in the correct shade. But then the painters had to wait to come in since they couldn't paint the walls when there was a tacky floor. There were still no appliances in the kitchen for some unknown reason. Not even the distributor could give me a decent answer for that one when I forwarded my email that matched my calendar, saying that they were supposed to have arrived on Tuesday.

Now, Frank took off his hat and rubbed his nearly bald head. How could men be bald on top but have a monster of a beard growing a few inches down? Was that a genetic thing that just affected the scalp or due to a hormonal problem? Either way, it was never a good sign.

"We need to tear down the tile along the one wall in the bathroom to fully remove the mold. It went further than we thought."

My eyes flicked back and forth between his naked scalp and sincere expression.

"The main bed and bath are complete now, which is a positive from where we started. The walk-in shower is set. Fixtures are in, spick and span. The tile is immaculate. My workers didn't cut corners, like the last crew."

I hadn't gotten to see it. Every time I snuck in, our not-so-gracious homeowner huffed about an invasion of privacy before I could get a good enough look.

But the foreman had taken a few shaky photos of the bathroom for me on his phone that proved they had gone above and beyond what I had pictured. It was clean and airy while managing to pull off dark graphite colors to give a cozy, masculine look.

It was so much better than the hack job before.

"Okay. I understand. You can do it?"

"Already started. There was no time to waste and figured you wouldn't want to," said Frank.

He was right.

"We're already halfway through."

At least that was one thing going my way.

"I'm afraid though, with this and the living room bookcases and detailing …" he drifted off, but I knew what he was talking about.

My built-ins, which were supposed to have already been built in, were no longer part of the deal.

Deep breath.

"It's okay. Don't worry about it," I reassured him.

He shouldn't be looking at me that way with such concern.

There was nothing to be concerned about.

"I can spare another day starting next week and send my guys to the next project we have," offered Frank.

I shook my head. "No. I'll work it out. You're already doing so much more than I could've ever expected on a time crunch. Let me—I'm sorry. I just answered the door and need to go back to make sure that the lights people outside know the plan."

Frank nodded his head in agreement. "You know where to find me."

In *the bathroom from hell*, as it had been dubbed.

For the past week, the rest of the house had been full of noise. Unfortunately, it wasn't only coming from the power tools and construction crew that had managed not to throw any more snide comments my way.

Aaron Hayes, however?

If I'd thought that I could make it through this project without having to see him more than necessary, I could consider myself vastly disappointed.

I tried to ignore his constant comments from when I showed up at the house to work to the moment before I left. It was a constant feeling of being torn back, only to have to build myself all the way back up again by the end of the day. And then …

The backlash was never-ending.

The workers are too loud. The reno is taking too long. Why are you still here?

When are you going to be done?

December? When in December?

Whenever I'm finished and this place looks nothing like the run-down shack it once did. That's when, I wanted to snap.

But I didn't.

I gave him the tentative date instead of saying what I wanted to, along with a very nice and detailed list of when he could expect people coming in and out for deliveries. I was hoping it would put his mind at ease—not that he appreciated the heads-up and extra work I had to do to make sure that he was comfortable while sleeping in the middle of what had turned back into a renovation site no better than the house had been a few weeks ago.

So far today at least, it seemed I'd gotten through half the day without a battle.

I paused once I got to the living room hall leading to where I'd left the outdoor light workers.

They weren't there.

Did they already head back outside and start?

Leaning out the front door, I looked around the front yard. A gust of air hit me in the face. I crossed my arms. Most of the snow had melted over the past few days, aside from the big clumps that had formed into ice, glittering under the sun.

There was no one there.

Absolutely no one.

That couldn't be. The Christmas light people had been right here. Just a second ago. I didn't imagine them. Now, nothing. Not even the van of the few people, who, moments ago, were standing on the crinkling renovation paper in the entryway, remained outside. It was as if they'd disappeared.

Or ran.

No. This wasn't happening again.

This cabin might be a shit show, but there were going to be Christmas lights.

I reached for my phone and dialed the number I'd confirmed earlier this morning.

"Hello. I'm inquiring about the outdoor light service that I had. They showed up, but didn't do anything before they left."

"Oh dear. Let me look into that." There was a pause. "There's a note on the file that says they were sent away about ten minutes ago."

"What are you talking about? I just saw someone. They were right here on the doorstep," I stammered.

"The holidays are a very busy time, Ms. Owens. Unfortunately, this is the second time we've had to reschedule. We will be moving forward elsewhere, and you will have to make your arrangements with another company."

"But there is no other company," I let slip.

It was the truth. No one around this area was able to put up the lights at this point. Everyone was booked solid for the next month. It didn't matter if it was a small cabin or a million-dollar home by the coast; everyone wanted to make sure they were in the Christmas spirit, and I needed to make sure that it happened now.

"I'm sorry to hear that. I'll be sending an email to the addresses we have on file to confirm this change of plans as well as the cancellation charge. Have a good day."

"Yes, thank you. Oh! Wait!" I tried to catch the woman before it was too late.

The light company was going to send the update to the Home Haven email. But I knew what email that was, and it wasn't only mine. The email they had on file was *powens@homehaven.com*, but it was also going to be cc'ed to my supervisor footing the receipt. And on this project, it was the one and only Michelle Maven.

I covered my face with my hands, my phone hot against my cheek.

Don't scream. Don't scream. Don't scream.

What was going to happen now? What was Michelle going to think when she saw that I couldn't even handle getting lights up in this place?

All the little mistakes were adding up.

There were only so many I could keep under wraps.

Swallowing, I took a deep breath, feeling the air get caught somewhere midway down. A balloon couldn't stop expanding between my throat and chest.

Stop it.

This wasn't going to happen.

I would not scream, but most of all, I was not going to cry. Not over lights. Not over mold—

"Falling apart on the job so soon?"

I whipped my hands away from my face. My phone slipped out of my palm and onto the floor. Great. Just great. I leaned down to swipe it back up, checking the corners for cracks.

My arms sagged, though I still didn't look up at the presence sneaking up alongside me. He'd likely watched the entire thing.

"Can I help you with something, Mr. Hayes?"

"Just one thing after another. It's almost like someone doesn't want you to be here," Aaron mused.

I bit the inside of my cheek, letting him speak. I was going to be kind. I was going to be professional.

"Just stating facts, of course," said Aaron as he turned on his heel and walked away. "Feel free to call my sister and call this whole mess off whenever you'd like. There is still time after all."

"It'll come together."

"You sure about that?" Aaron asked the same question I had asked myself every day when the renovation didn't seem like it was coming together or getting easier, only getting more difficult.

I lifted my gaze to Aaron. He shoved his hands into his grimy sweatpants pockets. He'd been wearing the same thing, I was pretty sure, since I'd arrived the other day.

"Call it quits. It sure looks like you need to cut your losses at this point."

Air stuck to my ribs. "Don't worry about a thing, Mr. Hayes. It will all come together in time for your family to enjoy the holiday with you."

"Huh." He nodded, looking around the living room. The space between his eyebrows crinkled.

"Yes?" I asked.

"Wasn't there supposed to be built-in shelves or something over there in that big bare spot?" He jerked his thumb toward the one still-very-empty, unpainted wall.

I couldn't stop the glare. I managed to direct it down to the floor as he sauntered away.

Frank hesitated in the doorway where Aaron left the room. He dipped his chin toward Aaron before walking toward me, checking over his shoulder once. "This house is challenging us all, Ms. Owens. First, there was the delay in the kitchen appliances."

Kitchen appliances where the delivery to this address was mysteriously canceled.

"And then the paint order coming in incorrectly."

Another strange occurrence that didn't feel so strange at all as I looked where Aaron Hayes had wandered off to, alongside the painters having no clue what I was talking about when I called to reschedule after they were supposed to come and didn't show up, floor stain or no floor stain.

"Almost like someone doesn't want you to be here."

"And of course, the electricity going out a few days back with the last storm. Remember to take a deep breath."

My throat felt like it was closing in on itself. My right hand drifted up to it, as if I could somehow clear it with a touch. If anything, it made me feel like I was being strangled. "Uh-huh. Thank you. Everything is going perfectly fine. We'll make it work."

He raised his salt-and-pepper eyebrows, but didn't dare to contradict me. "It has been nice working with you, Poppy. I can see what you're trying to do here, and if you can pull it off—which I have no doubt you can—I can't wait to see the photos. It's a great place. Lots of potential."

It did have potential. I knew it from the start.

Yet the reminder was still nice.

"Thank you, Frank."

I started to get my new game plan together when I was cut off by the ring of my phone. I stared at the name lighting up the screen before I could no longer put it off. Pressing the phone to my ear, I braced myself.

"Poppy?" A hint of question tainted Michelle's voice as I shuffled away from everyone into the mudroom. Though the house was heated, I crossed my one arm over my center to fend off the chill creeping in.

"Yes. Hello, Michelle."

"Hi there. How are you doing?" she asked.

"I'm great. Thanks for asking."

"Are you sure?"

There was no doubt that she already knew how badly I was screwing up.

I tried to correct it. "I knew from day one that this project would be a little more intensive than previously thought with the amount of renovations planned before I came in. There have been some product delays and, um, mis-scheduling as well."

"I got an email from Ms. Hayes-Preston about the extra challenges this project is presenting. I have had nothing but confidence in you," said Michelle.

"Thank you."

"But I need to ask you right now." There was a stagnant pause. "Are you capable of completing this job?"

My heart slammed into a brick wall. "What? Yes, of course."

"I need you to be honest. This job has had a lot more issues come up. You're right. Some of them were unavoidable from what I can tell and not your fault in the slightest, but as the holidays begin, I need to know before I go on my leave if I need to put someone else on this job to make sure it's up to our standard. Any other time, Poppy, I'm sure that this would've turned into a two person job."

"No," I assured her. "I've got this."

"Are you sure?" Michelle asked once more. "I want you to be one hundred percent positive. You've been honest and kept me up-to-date with everything going on. I appreciate that and how you're making sure that things are transparent, but—"

"I've got this," I repeated.

Did I though? I looked around the place. What was the likelihood that I could make sure the furniture got here after the floor was finally refinished and not before, let alone decorate and plan the best Christmas the Hayes-Preston family had ever had, like I'd promised Sarah?

"One hundred percent," I confirmed.

"Okay." Michelle took an audible breath. "You're one of the best interior designers I've ever had on my team, Poppy. You have an eye. Not just for what is in style right now, but for what truly reflects the client. I need you to be on your toes and complete this job, no matter what it takes both for the client as well as to be in the running right now for the promotion we talked about."

"I understand."

"Please reach out if you need anything."

"I will make sure this place is everything envisioned and more. No matter what it takes."

"Make sure you're also taking care of yourself, Poppy. Check in with Alison or anyone in the firm available to see if they have any ideas to assist you. It's not a crime to ask for help. Sometimes, it's the best thing anyone can do. Designing might be a solitary practice when deep into a project, but it can get lonely if you don't have a team. It's part of what made Home Haven what it is today for everyone in the office and those in their own homes looking to us to be their team," said Michelle. "I have to go. Have a wonderful rest of your week."

"Thank you, Michelle. You too."

Ending the call, I shut my eyes and cradled my head. My head hurt. But no. I could do this. I didn't need anyone's help.

I was going to make it to the end of this project and get this promotion.

I was going to surprise them all. Including myself.

I eyed the plywood and other materials I'd already been gathering since the afternoon they had been left in the garage, alongside the few containers of paint that were correct for the living room.

Fine. If the crews weren't going to do it and no one was going to show up to complete this home …

I was.

As an interior designer, working with my hands was one of the things I wasn't exactly supposed to do. I developed a vision. The comfort. Aesthetic. I wasn't actually supposed to create. Making things physically happen in the main scheme of the house was for the heavy lifters.

The renovators.

But those pieces in the end were something that made me feel even more at peace with each step I took and were part of the first reasons I had gotten into home design in the first place years ago. But this felt different now. It was different.

In fact, with each board I laid out, the more satisfied I became. Stress leached out of my shoulders, and my brain, previously full of schedules and worries, quieted.

There. This was working.

There. That was working too.

I was doing something. It was all in my control.

By the time I laid down a sheet and started measuring, the day was already starting to look up.

seven

. . .

Aaron

POPPY OWENS WAS INSANE. Frustratingly, certifiably insane.

Poppy Owens stood outside in below-freezing temperatures, painting. A cloud of her breath swirled as she mixed the dark green paint before brushing it in long strokes onto a stretch of wood.

No wonder it didn't take her long to all but bite my head off since starting her maddening twenty-four-seven work on the cabin. To be honest, I'd expected it to be sooner. It didn't mean it didn't feel just as sweet. Just as awful. Maybe that was why I'd kept trying to make it happen for the past week.

The first time, I admitted, had been an accident. When someone called her phone, which was sitting on the counter while she was talking to the construction crew, the ring felt like someone was stabbing an ice pick straight through my skull. So, I answered it. Turned out, it was the painters, confirming that they were rescheduled to paint the walls inside the house on Wednesday.

Irritated, I snapped at them that the walls were fine.

For a moment, especially when I saw the homemaker rushing around like a chicken with her head cut off, I felt bad. But then, more than that, I felt sweet, sweet satisfaction. Maybe that made me a bad person. It certainly made me a bad person. But for the past few days, since I'd started the charade to see how long it would take the homemaker to realize that her house she was determined to make a home wasn't a lemon. The homeowner on the other hand?

It had become my favorite form of entertainment.

There wasn't much else to do other than read the books I'd left behind, along with my grandmother's tattered romances. There was no television or anywhere to sit since the furniture had been delayed as well.

"What?" Poppy snapped as I interrupted her work for what had to be the fourth or fifth time. "What else can I do for you today, Mr. Hayes?"

And Mr. Hayes? What the hell was up with that?

I didn't think I had ever been called *Mr. Hayes* in my life, except for when I returned home and had to make a very painful trip to the bank to assess my finances, or lack thereof. I'd probably looked similar that day to the sad, pitiful face the homemaker had had when she watched the rest of the construction workers pack everything up and head out two days ago.

She now wore paint-splattered pants. The faded jeans hugged her hips a whole lot more than the fancy dress pants she wore every other day. But those pressed pants hadn't given her enough stretch it seemed since she pressed down bright painter's tape that wasn't just to give the professionals she'd hired before I canceled the appointment a head start. Nope. Within twenty-four hours, the entire living room was coated in a warm forest green.

Power tools were also becoming involved in the setup in the once clean, albeit empty, living room, now crowded with crap.

Obnoxious Christmas music played through the old, dusty radio, once properly hidden in the cellar. Gone was the put-together homemaker, or whatever her title was, tapping away on her fancy silver tablet and ordering people around. Gone were her pleas over the phone for the people I'd rearranged and rescheduled behind her back after I snooped around on that fancy tablet, thinking that would be enough for her to call it quits.

Poppy was doing what she had to do for this project by herself. Everything.

She wasn't calling it quits. She wasn't leaving.

"What can I help you with?" She picked up her paintbrush so the paint wouldn't drop and stared at me, waiting for an answer. Her oversize sweatshirt slipped over her smooth, freckled shoulder.

I still couldn't understand why she was painting halfway out the front door, letting all the cold air in.

Every breath felt like ice stabbing at my lungs. "It's fucking colder than a well digger's ass in here."

For a second, I almost thought I saw a curve of her lips.

"Air flow. In case you haven't noticed since we haven't painted yet, there's no overhead lighting in the main areas."

I hadn't noticed. When I peeked over my shoulder, it was hard not to see the small, capped wires hanging from the center of the ceiling.

"It would probably help if you put on a shirt," she suggested.

I forced myself not to look down at my chest. I had a shirt on. "I would've layered up if I had known my newly heated house was going to turn into a freezer."

"I'll be done soon. I appreciate the patience." Poppy said her thanks like that was the opposite of what she could appreciate from me, turning back to her project.

"Can you turn that down?" I asked, swatting a hand toward the radio, which instructed to say merry Christmas in Hawaiian for the millionth time.

With a sigh, she paused her painting. The radio volume went down two bars, though until the song changed, it still sounded like nails on a chalkboard to my ears.

"Is that all?" she asked.

"No," I said before I realized I wasn't sure what came next.

But I was still standing here for some reason.

"Then, what can I help you with?" Poppy asked, reaching up with the back of her hand to brush a strand of strawberry-blonde hair away from her face.

A streak of green ran across her forehead.

I bit my bottom lip.

"What?" she said, a little more agitated.

Oh, now, she was getting angry with me.

I shook my head. "Nothing."

"Okay."

"Actually, that's not true," I corrected.

"Of course it isn't," she muttered, so low that I was sure she didn't expect me to hear.

Most of the time, after having gunfire in my ears most days for the past few years and being stupid enough not to wear ear protection from the start of firearms training, I wouldn't have heard anything that wasn't directed right at me, but my attention was focused on her now.

I couldn't pry my attention away from the tiny line that burrowed between her eyebrows, which were a shade redder than the rest of her hair.

"What was that?" I asked anyway, leaning in closer.

She shut her eyes. When she opened them again, a false sense of composure was plastered across her soft features. "What can I do to make this experience better for you?"

When I didn't answer, however, the homemaker shook her head with a sigh, setting her brush to the side, along with her gaze, as if she couldn't stand to look at me anymore.

"I know what you've been doing, you know," she said.

To be honest, if she did, I was impressed. I hated to admit it, but for the past few days, it had been hard not to be impressed with Poppy Owens once I finally stopped my rampage of messing up her project whenever I saw the opportunity.

There was little doubt that the homemaker was determined.

And a little ambitious if she still thought she'd manage to pull off whatever designer cabin dream my sister likely wanted her to make a reality in the house that had once been all of one room and not much else until my grandparents built on.

"And what's that?" I asked.

"You've been messing with my project and plans for this cabin," she said. "I'm not stupid. I figure you're just waiting for the right time when I'm almost ready to give up again so that you can rub it in my face for some entertainment."

"Am I that predictable?"

She didn't hesitate. "Yes."

I opened my mouth to reply that I had no idea what she was talking about even though she'd truly hit the nail on the head. She beat me to it, leaving me with my mouth hanging wide open.

"I get that you're in a rough spot here—"

"I'm not in a rough spot." Even though I kind of was. I was pretty sure living in your grandmother's old house with no job and no one to complain about it to, no matter if it had been rewired and had central heat now, was considered being in a rough spot.

Some might even say rock bottom.

But at least up until today, since Poppy had arrived, the place was somewhat warm.

"Look, you don't have to deny it. I understand."

"You understand?" I shifted on my feet. "Please then, enlighten me."

"I understand that you lost your friend and you're having a hard time this time of year—"

"What did you say?" I clenched my fists. The words hit me harder than the wave of air snaking through the front door and hit me in the back of the throat, leaving me breathless.

Homemaker must've had at least an ounce of sense because she paused. "I said that I understand you're grieving, but it's no reason for you to be rude to anyone who's trying to help here. I'm trying to be professional and polite, but I'd appreciate it if you let me do my work. I'm finding it extremely hard right now."

"To be professional?"

"Yes." Her eyebrows rose on her head as she stood in front of me like we were going to have an actual conversation.

Damn, I'd fucked with the homemaker quite a bit over the past two weeks, but this?

"Go on."

That line on her forehead was back. It was much less endearing this time. "What?"

"What else ya got, homemaker?" I asked her. "You ready to share your condolences with me? Commiserate or something over a fish or even a fucking dog dying in your life, and then we can run off into the renovation sunset together, singing Christmas carols?"

"I can imagine that whatever you went through is—"

"You can imagine?" I barked a laugh, feeling as if whatever pleasant ounce of emotion I'd had this morning might as well have been swept away and out the door. Good thing she'd left it wide open. "You have no idea what I'm going through, and to be honest, I don't need you to pretend to care."

"You're right. I couldn't imagine that trauma—" she tried to correct herself.

And failed.

"You think you have any idea how it feels for everything to be completely out of your control, all at once?" I asked her.

Sucking on the inside of her teeth, the homemaker turned pale. Either she was about to fall over or she wanted to scream and let it all out.

I kind of wanted to see that.

"And don't spout that *trauma is trauma* bullshit."

Homemaker swallowed. When she opened her mouth again, her lips hesitated around silence before she spoke. "Looks like I don't have to. You seem to have it covered."

She set her paintbrush in the container and brushed off her hands. I watched as her chest rose and fell with a deep breath.

"In fact ..." She wanted to continue.

"What?" I wasn't sure if I had spoken so loudly since I had

come home. My voice sounded like a gunshot, sending my heart into a hammering beat to run far away from wherever it had come from.

But now, I yelled.

I wanted her to yell right back.

Yet it wasn't happening. I had been an ass to her all week. I'd admit it. She knew it and then still tried to pull this kind of shit to get to know me.

"I don't want to get to know you or bond, homemaker."

"Trust me," she mumbled, "I know that."

"Then, say whatever it is you want to say, little homemaker. Maybe it will make me not see you as so pathetic."

"I'm … I'm not pathetic."

"Is that so?" I asked. She didn't answer this time, but she looked closer to telling me to screw off. "What if I told you that I didn't like that green color you painted everything?"

"Y-you don't like the color?"

"You would probably run out and get a new one, wouldn't you? It would throw you into a tizzy, but you'd do it," I said, immediately seeing that I was right. "You'd get new swatches and rethink the entire design if I wanted. You will do anything I want here and put up with it because you want to make a pretty little house, like there's nothing more important to do with yourself than be a people pleaser. From what I can tell, I bet you've put up with a lot to make people like you, homemaker. How is that going for you?"

"Could you stop being a jerk for five minutes?" she finally yelled just to get a word in.

"A jerk?"

She didn't pause around my exclamation. "I get that you're acting out like some kind of child because you're lonely."

"I am not lonely," I snarled, though that might not be true as I jutted my chin out to her, goading her on. This was my entertainment. This was what I had wanted when I came out here to talk to her, wasn't it?

Tell me more.

Tell me how terrible I am. Tell me I deserve to never speak again. Tell me to go to hell. It's where I belonged. I needed to hear it, and finally, I was sure I had someone willing to tell me so.

"I seriously don't understand what your problem is. There's mold in your bathroom. Mold! Do you understand what that means?" the homemaker snapped, reaching to shut the front door, shoving the edges of what she had been working on inside.

The door creaked on its hinges before slamming shut with a bang.

I flinched.

The air inside was still cold, and she crossed her arms as if she was finally feeling it for the first time. "Of course you don't because though you live here, you act like you couldn't care less if the walls fell around you and you had to live in a tent in the woods."

I snorted.

"Not only that, but all the stupid paint I chose, except for this green—which isn't even the color I ordered—is backordered for some unknown reason, though I'm pretty sure you know exactly the cause. Don't you?"

"I don't—"

"What a lie."

I didn't answer.

She took another deep breath, trying to calm herself down. "I see what you're trying to do here, but it isn't going to work. I don't need you to like me, and the best thing I think you can do is to leave me alone. I'll finish the house. Then, you won't ever have to see me again. Okay?"

"Huh." I followed her as she tried to walk away. "A homemaker here, in my house, trying to make everything perfect?"

"Yes," she agreed.

"Is that what this all is? Does your job give you some sick satisfaction, living in a fictional universe where everyone just prances through their homes, cooking bread, and spreads kind-ness through the world so that everyone loves them?" I asked.

"Can you stop? You have no idea what you're talking about. And in case you haven't noticed, I don't need *you* to like me, Aaron Hayes. I like myself just fine."

"Good thing since you must, at this point, be desperate—"

"This coming from the man who looks like he hasn't showered in days."

"Because let me guess what this is all actually about, home-maker," I ventured, egging her on.

"I already told you what this is all about."

"Maybe daddy left mommy one day? Is that it? Did your parents break your sweet little family up, or was it someone else out there who broke your princess fairy-tale heart, and now, you're trying to make it all better by intruding into other people's business? Trust me, sweetheart, none of this work is going to change anything in the end. You're still going to finish this project, if you force yourself to, and my sister will have her perfect family Christmas she paid for if she doesn't get wine drunk before the big fat man is supposed to come down the chimney. Then, you'll walk out of here, sad and alone, and go home to some empty apartment somewhere, I'm sure. You're still going to fail, and no one is going to want you—"

I didn't recognize the sting until after it happened, and I stared down at the homemaker, who was looking down at her palm, which was starting to turn red. Her lips parted. Her eyes widened as she realized what she had just done.

"I'm—" she stammered. "I'm sorry. I'm really sorry."

I touched my cheek, where her hand had slapped me.

Her lips quivered, and her breaths came out in short gasps as she finally took a step back, as if to flee before I could come up with anything else to say.

Maybe I'd said enough.

"Have a great time here." She shook her head over and over,

not meeting my eyes. "Have a great *life* here then. I hope it's worthwhile. Alone."

eight

. . .

Poppy

AARON HAD no idea what he was talking about. He didn't. Or at least, he hadn't known that he did. I was happy with who I was. I liked myself. I was strong and talented and healthy. I accepted that. I appreciated that, though it didn't mean I never hoped for more. I hoped for the life anyone might dream of with a nice home and a love that filled all the empty spaces, which I knew better than anyone that not even a perfectly designed home could manage.

Nearly four years ago, I'd thought I met the love of my life at a mixer Simon had convinced me to go to. Or rather, I'd met him *after* the mixer.

"Go! Just once," my mother encouraged after Simon brought up the opportunity. "It's a good chance to meet some new people. Not even like that. As a friend even."

"I have friends."

"Real friends. Outside of work and chat rooms, or whatever you call it online."

"Design blogs, Mom."

"My point exactly. It'll be fun. You get to dress up a little. Do your makeup."

I stared at her as she said these things before she quickly waved herself off.

Either way, she'd won, and I ended up going to the alumni event on campus. It was held in the art gallery displaying modern oil paintings. Simon was there as well, though we'd already planned on leaving separately since he'd had dinner with a few of the other professors. I was in the corner, drinking tiny plastic cups of cheap pinot grigio, while people glanced toward me, likely wondering if I'd wandered in from the street since I certainly did not look like an Ivy League grad.

Because I wasn't.

After finishing my third plastic cup and getting judgy looks from the student bartender behind the light refreshments and snacks table, I stood on my toes to wave goodbye to Simon.

The streetlamps started to turn on, and the air had taken on a chilly quality, though the students rushed around in tight minidresses as they headed out to start their night at whatever party was being hosted.

Crossing my arms over one another, I tapped my foot in my uncomfortable kitten heels against the sidewalk as I waited for the ride I'd ordered on my phone to get here. I was ready to go home and call it a night.

Something barreled into the side of my arm, but it was enough to send me off the edges of my heels and back a step.

"Hey!" I nearly yelped as I turned around to see who had run into me, gripping my phone tightly in my hand in case someone was going to grab it and run.

Instead of a poor pickpocket, a disheveled man with wavy brown hair that curled around his ears, who looked like he'd just gotten out of work, wearing gray slacks and a suit shirt, righted himself until he stood tall. "I'm sorry. I wasn't paying attention."

Obviously, I wanted to say, tired and irritable from my night. I held it in.

"Sincerely," he said with suddenly great manners. He glanced around before he turned his attention back down to me. "I apologize. Do you know where Albertson Hall is?"

"Oh." I paused since, really, I didn't go here, but I did know the building he was asking about wasn't far. "I think it's over that way, around the corner."

"Can you show me?"

I blinked.

"I'm sorry. My sister—one of her friends called, and now, I need to go and make sure she's okay and not a complete wreck. You'd be coming in as two people's hero tonight," he said.

I looked around again. There had to be someone better to lead him, and my ride was set to pick me up at any minute. If it ever started moving toward me again. I nodded, leading the way. I led him to different halls and department buildings before we came across one that looked more like a dormitory.

A college student, wearing a crop top and high heels, had her friend, who smelled of cheap liquor, slung over her shoulder.

"I'm so sorry," the girl still standing somewhat upright said. "She told me to call you."

The man, who seemed to have found exactly who he was looking for, rolled his eyes and scooped up his sister.

"Please, don't tell Mom."

"Just get inside and go to bed."

She moaned once more but did as asked. I was still standing with him. I should've probably left, but he chuckled, looking down at me, and shook his head.

"Thanks. I doubt that this is how you planned to spend your night."

I shook my head, really looking at him now—from the way he grinned, a little crooked, to the way he looked me up and down like he, too, was just noticing me and he looked pretty pleased about it.

"My name is Poppy, by the way," I told him.

"It's good to meet you, Poppy. I'm Lincoln." He smiled, and for the first time, it felt like someone was welcoming me in.

After safely seeing his sister back to her respective residence hall with her friend, Lincoln told me all about his sister and how she was usually good at keeping herself together—so he wouldn't be telling their mom about this little incident—but had gone through a bit of a nasty breakup.

He then asked me if I'd had anything to eat tonight, and because I didn't count the gross crackers and cheese from the alumni event, I told him no. We went to a small restaurant a few blocks away. He ordered me my own fries since he said he was a notorious hangry fry-eater and it was best to know this now about him.

I laughed and replied that I preferred my own fries anyway before I dipped them in mayo, which made him cringe.

It had been one of the best nights of my life, and it was so easy to fall into his hazel eyes that swirled with green-and-brown galaxies. I couldn't imagine one where we wouldn't end up together. I mean, he'd literally run into me. It was like all the romance stories said it should happen.

I should've known better. I should've made my usual contingency plans, like when I worked, in case something went wrong and I needed to take an escape route to make it all okay.

But I didn't.

I let myself fall from the first time he smiled at me to the first time he kissed me. How he fit against me sent sparks through my stomach. It was the most perfect, simple kiss. I could imagine myself getting that sort of kiss every day for the rest of my life.

My mother, as imagined, was thrilled.

"Things are finally going right for you," she'd said, squeezing my shoulders when I first told her that I had been on more than a single date with someone, and she learned that Lincoln lived on his own in the Finance District and worked as a contract analyst.

"Basically looking for typos," he'd said, attempting to brush it off.

And for once, I wanted to agree with her.

Even better, my mom liked Lincoln. So did Simon, though they couldn't find a lot to talk about together.

Finally, things were going exactly how I wanted them to and had imagined.

Lincoln told me how much he loved me first. I easily agreed that I loved him back. It was easy that way. Simple.

After that, I opened up to him more. Trusted more. I shared the highs of finding my passion at Home Haven to the low years of pain and confusion. I told him about the years I went through where no one believed me and my body. They said the pain was in my head. They insisted that I had low tolerance, or I just had to get used to the monthly cycle like every other woman when the pain struck worse than ever every month until, finally, I could no longer take the anxiety of going to university away from home.

I told him about how I'd been to just about every specialist. I'd taken every test. And then one day. It happened.

One doctor changed my life. He told me the chronic, debilitating pain and frustration wasn't in my head. Endometriosis wasn't in my head. The tissue constricting around my organs wasn't normal, but it could be fixed—and for the most part, it was.

Though it was hard to let go that I was "fixed." That technically, I could go on with my normal life. For the longest time, I panicked whenever I felt a minor stab of pain. I was terrified that one day, the endometriosis would come back. That my life would pause again, right as I was finally getting it all together.

Even if, I also admitted quietly to Lincoln, things like children might not be as simple for me. At least not compared to others. It didn't mean that having children couldn't happen or that there weren't still options.

Lincoln accepted me, and he said without a second of hesitation, "How could I not love every piece of you?"

My dream life had fallen right into sequence. My internship at Home Haven was ending, and Michelle Maven, my idol, called me into her office to offer me a full-time position, starting at the end of the summer.

By the following fall, Lincoln brought up moving in together when his lease was up. I was practically living there as it was. He gave me space in his wooden dresser that squeaked whenever you opened a drawer. He picked me up a pink toothbrush and put it in the bathroom. Slowly, Lincoln incorporated me into his every day as if it were the most natural thing in the world.

As if he couldn't wait, however, Lincoln pulled out a ring on the corner of the street where he'd first run into me.

He barely got the question out before I said yes.

I couldn't believe how perfect it all was. With him, I felt like I was living like I'd always imagined—not too late and not too soon. I wasn't just living in other people's dreams at work every day, coming up with wallpaper design plans or what the best countertop would be to match someone else's cabinets. I got to work on planning our apartment. More than that, I got to work planning our wedding from the second I could and never felt so alive.

We set a date before the end of the month.

One night, he came home to his apartment, where I was already setting up for what had turned into weekly movie night. We each took a turn picking our favorites, even though when he chose after a long day of work, I usually fell asleep. Though I often did that during my picks too.

I did this time, too, only I was gently shaken awake.

"Sorry, did I fall asleep?" I asked.

"Poppy."

I adjusted as I looked up at him. When I glanced at the television, the credits were already rolling. "Linc?"

"I, um, I want to talk to you about something."

"Okay," I said. Still, he didn't say anything. "Is everything okay? Are you okay?"

"Yeah. I mean, of course I am. This wedding we're planning—"

"Is it too much?" I asked. I knew it was. "We can scale back. Say the word. I got a little out of control with the plans, but the venue and dress aren't paid in full yet."

I had gone with my mom two weeks ago. At first, I'd wanted something big and poofy, but ended up with a simple, sleek dress with small, embroidered flowers that looked a little like poppies around the bust to the waist. Traditional with a hint of modern elegance. I loved it.

"That's … good, Poppy." Lincoln looked away from me, back to the television.

The movie started over again at the beginning.

"Tell me what you'd like. When I started planning, I told you that I get a little overzealous with things, but I want to make sure that you're incorporated," I reminded him. "What do you want at our wedding?"

"I think I want a break."

I pushed back to look at him. Was this a joke? My heart pounded in my chest while the rest of me felt numb as I looked at him.

"We're getting married, Lincoln."

We were getting married. Weren't we?

"I think we should see other people," he continued. "I think I want to see other people."

"But I thought …" *I thought you loved me.* "What happened? What's wrong?"

"Nothing is wrong, Poppy. I just don't think I can do this."

"Tell me what upset you or what's going on so that I can fix it." I could fix it after all. I was good at fixing things if I knew the issue.

"I just …"

"What, Lincoln?"

"I didn't realize how much I wanted kids until now."

I blinked. "We talked about kids."

"I know we did."

"I want kids too." I tried to let loose a sigh of relief, but it was like my body knew better than to let me.

"I know, but you even admitted it a while ago, and I thought it didn't matter. But the more I think about it, the more I realize it does matter to me. More than anything."

"What does?"

"It could be hard for us? Having kids. Together."

"Well, yes. But we won't know. There could be no issue."

"It could maybe not even happen, right?"

I stared at him, mouth open, dumbstruck as I watched everything fall around me like the glitter confetti I'd debated was too tacky to throw at our wedding instead of bubbles or rice.

"That's a possibility," I answered honestly.

Lincoln nodded, expecting it. "I don't see a life without kids. Ever."

"But what about the wedding? The plans we started and moving in …"

"I can't, Poppy. I can't wait around and hope and take the chance. I thought I could. I did. I wanted to, but I'm sorry. I can't commit to disappointment."

I was disappointment.

I wished I could say that I didn't cry while I packed up all the things I'd left in his apartment or that I at least held it together until after he dropped me off at the house on the west side of the city, where I had always lived with my parents. But I couldn't.

Tears tracked down my cheeks the whole time, and he didn't stop one of them until I got out of the car, reaching to close the passenger door behind me.

"Poppy, wait."

A traitorous part of me hoped when I leaned back in the car, he'd say he was wrong and that we could pretend all of this hadn't happened. Instead, he reached out, cupping my head, and kissed me with one of those simple, easy kisses one last time.

Hannah had taken me out for drinks after my breakup, if that was what you could call it, for one of the first times we ever went out together and then again after I found out that Lincoln had gotten married within seven months. He and his high school sweetheart had a small backyard wedding in the suburbs. She had a glittery dress and a flower headpiece. They looked like a sweet couple. She was pregnant by the time they came back from their honeymoon, from what I had seen in the announcements on social media, unable to bring myself to unfollow him.

And I couldn't stop from asking myself how happy he must've been now that he didn't have me. That he didn't have to wait and see for disappointment. Because I knew what the girl he'd married and could build a home with had that I didn't. And it was that she was, in all factual evidence and design, the perfect partner—better than me.

I got the drunkest I had been in my entire life after Lincoln and I broke up. Or that didn't sound right. Ended things? Split up? All the ways to put it felt inconsequential. I felt the hangover for days after passing out in Hannah's apartment, filled to the brim with four other girls she'd been living with ever since she had come to the city.

It was one of the few times I'd ever seen her apartment, cluttered with clothes and half walls to separate all the roommates you could always hear clattering around in the background.

"I didn't think you'd want your parents to see you like that." Hannah rubbed my calf as she looked into my dead eyes before declaring that she was making breakfast. She burned the pancakes but added enough strawberries and whipped cream that I barely noticed.

It had been then and there that I knew that Hannah was the best friend I could ever ask for, even if we only ever saw one another at work or in personal crises. We worked well that way, and she agreed. From then on, we encouraged the other's overworking habits while feeding and watering one another.

Only now, I wasn't sure how long I had left to work at Home Haven with Hannah. When Home Haven found out what had happened and what I had done, I was certain that it wasn't only the promotion I was going to lose.

nine

. . .

Aaron

I **PACED** through the empty cabin. The homemaker, interior designer, DIY mess of a woman I had started to see, had left.

Just like that.

It was what I'd wanted.

She was gone. She'd gathered most of her things up; she hadn't paused before she headed to her car and left like hell was on her heels.

My phone continued its overly loud ring from the night-stand. The obnoxious sound pulled me back out of my head. I pressed the cool glass to my ear and dropped myself on the mattress that remained on the floor. My legs stretched out in front of me.

"What?" I answered.

"Hey." The person on the other end didn't pause at my abrupt greeting. "How have ya been?"

I was halfway to clearing my throat when I froze at the voice. "Barrett."

"Yep."

Shaking my head, I took a deep breath. "You said you'd stop calling."

His distinct, terribly jovial laugh was another sharp sound

pulsing through my skull. "We both know I've never been the best at keeping my promises."

My jaw locked, hand curling tighter around the phone as I gritted out my next question. "Why are you calling me?"

"Not for any sort of courtesy call to see how you are—that's for sure. I'm back in the area, like I told you I would be. I was thinking 'bout ya."

"Isn't that nice?"

"It's bad for my goddamn peace of mind, but I do, so don't tell me I shouldn't. I figured I'd give you a call and see how you're doing back stateside these days."

How am I doing?

I swallowed. It would've been easier to gulp down sand. "When did you get back?"

"About two weeks ago. Most of us are on leave for the next month. Maybe anyway."

Most of us.

Might as well of been none of us.

"It would be good to see you. We should go out and get a round at the Bar on Main tonight," said Barrett.

I picked at my sweatpants as I sat. The homemaker was right. There was a stain on one leg. I had no idea how or when it had gotten there. "I'm good."

"Come on. You know you liked my stories while you were laid up. Who else would've talked to your grumpy ass?" Barrett paused when he noticed I still wasn't laughing with him. "Don't be like that, brother."

"I'm not your brother."

"Sure you're not." He wasn't deterred. "One drink. That's it."

I sighed, looking around the room I'd sequestered myself in. It was a wreck. "One drink."

"I'll be there at seven."

"Seven." I hit the End Call button.

Once, I would've answered that phone and immediately been in my car for Barrett. Now, I wanted to scream.

I clenched my fists as I shut my eyes and threw my phone on the bed. I started to pace again, my feet trailing back and forth over the cold floor that the homemaker had also helped the construction crew stain to meet their deadline before they left. Even they had been surprised at how good of a job she did.

"A real pro," the lead guy, Frank, I thought, had said.

I hadn't even thought to ask him for his name. Or talk to any of them at all.

I'd wanted to be alone. And I was alone now. Pacing. Walking. Because I needed to breathe to walk.

"Deep breaths," the psych had told me on base after I got back and was still in the hospital, ready to be cleared after they pulled about eight different kinds of metal from my leg and the side of my body. "When you're overwhelmed, that's all you need to do. You have no other assignment or post to worry about, but taking deep breaths right now."

They forgot to tell you that, sometimes, it didn't matter. Sometimes, you couldn't breathe anyway.

So, instead, I kept moving until my body took a moment to calm down. It was fine. I didn't need to do anything.

But the house was quiet.

My keys, which I hadn't touched in days, sat in front of me.

And, *fuck*, I never liked being alone.

The Bar on Main still smelled exactly like I remembered. It stank of piss, stale air freshener, and crisp French fries they always had arriving a little burned in a cardboard cup. The dive bar had been a staple in the town for years, and it looked as run-down as ever, yet still, for some ungodly reason, it was packed to the brim with people.

A few heads turned my way when I stepped inside. It took a crack of pool balls and other indecipherable sounds to fill my ears before I turned right back around to the humid heat outside.

"Hayes! Wait up!" a voice called out after me.

Stuffing my hands in my pockets, I stopped in the middle of the parking lot.

Barrett caught up with me, coming to see my face. I noticed the way his eyes scanned me up and down before once again meeting my eyes. There was a smile on his face. There was always some kind of smile on Barrett's face.

At one point, I'd thought it was because he was stupid, but Barrett always had an incorrigible personality and sense of humor, constantly looking for the bright side.

Reminded me of someone else who had been butting themselves in my life lately.

"What's going on?" Barrett cocked his head to the side. "I thought I saw you walk in."

I shrugged toward the place. Looking down at my feet, I kicked at the ice and dirt. "It's loud in there."

Barrett paused before nodding. "You're right; it is. I came to talk to you and won't even be able to hear ya. Let me go and grab two, and we can sit out here. Don't you dare leave before I get back out here."

"Isn't there some law against open containers?" I asked, meaning it to come out teasing, but my tone fell flat.

"I don't think the old sheriff will come to bother us in the back of my truck. Do you?"

Probably not.

Barrett smirked, knowing he was getting his way. "I'll be right back."

A minute later, he ran back out of the bar and put down the cold metal bed of his truck. I didn't even mind the thick and heavy sort of cold, and neither did he. We were both used to it.

He twisted off the cap with the corner of his shirt wrapped around his hand before he offered the bottle.

I dipped my chin in thanks, lifting it to my lips to take a swig. At least we didn't have to worry about our drinks getting warm out here. "Didn't think you'd turned into a rule breaker, Barrett."

"Eh, decided to stop sweating the small stuff."

"How's that working out for you?" That time, my voice sounded a little better. More like I was attempting a joke. I cleared my throat, dipping my head down before looking back at my friend.

He gave a shake of his head as he nudged toward a small paper dish, like the kind you got at football games—red-checker-patterned and always felt greasy when you held them in your hands. "Still working on it."

"French fries?"

Barrett took two at a time and ate them. "Looks like you could use some. Maybe more than that."

"What are you trying to say?" I asked. "Commenting on my looks? I always knew you thought I was hot."

He chuckled. "Letting yourself go. What happened to the gains?"

"Left me somewhere during when my leg was shot up," I said.

"Eh, excuses."

I stuck a fry into my mouth and paused. My forehead creased as I attempted to decipher the taste I was getting that wasn't just burned—

"The new bar guy who deals with the fries apparently got into adding spices to the fries."

"It sucks."

Barrett laughed, eating a few more. "Really does."

I took a few more and chewed, listening to the music that slipped through the cracks of the bar.

"How long are you back for?" I finally asked Barrett once I had about a quarter of my beer left. My fingers started to turn numb, but neither of us suggested moving, even to the cab of his truck, which perpetually blew hot air out of the vents, even in the summer.

Barrett tapped his finger against his bottle like he was nervous. "Actually, I'm deciding on that."

"Deciding?"

"Not sure if I'm ready to reenlist for another deployment for a while."

For a second, I wondered if he'd said it just to get my attention. Either way, it worked.

"You're retiring?"

"I wouldn't call it that. Too young and handsome to retire," he joked.

"You're going to leave?"

"Maybe. Just not … reenlist. Maybe I'll leave. I don't know."

"You have to be kidding."

"People do it all the time."

"That's …" *Fucked up? Perfect?* I didn't know how to respond.

"I'm tired," Barrett said. For the first time, I heard it in his voice. The happy-go-lucky man that usually sat next to me let his head sag as he held his beer in two hands. He sucked on the side of his cheek. "You know I love the Army. I was good at it. I liked the structure. The challenge. You assholes."

Another joke we shared that neither of us laughed at.

Because it was just the two of us, along with a few others who had never come to see me at the hospital but still had been part of our core group for the past decade. Some more, some less.

But still, I couldn't believe it. "We're all tired, Barrett."

"Like you're going to run back into where we left tomorrow." He chuckled.

I stared at him. I shrugged. "I'm sure going to try."

"Now, you have to be the one who's kidding."

I stared at him.

"Hayes. Come on now. You did your duty. You got a Purple Heart," he said. "You're not going back out there. I saw your file that day, along with you. They discharged you."

"They medically discharged me," I corrected. "If I show them I'm fit, I'll be fine."

"But you're not fine, Hayes."

That was his opinion.

It was as if he could read my thoughts.

"You nearly lost your life out there. You had internal bleeding. You could've lost your leg. Don't think I didn't notice that you aren't as steady on it as you used to be, ambling out of the bar like you did."

"I'm fine."

He shook his head, taking a deep breath. "What's your plan then?"

"I …" I didn't have one. God, my thrilling part of the day had been messing with the woman deciding how to dress up the cabin with fringe throw pillows. "I don't know. I'm going to get myself back in shape eventually. Find a doctor to clear me and my leg for service. Get back in the game."

"That's what you want to do?"

I paused. Yes. No. "Don't you? What else is there?"

"This can't be all there is," said Barrett quietly. He took another sip of beer. "Not for me anyway. Especially not now when my team is down. It's not the same as it once was when we were kids."

"You're serious."

Taking a deep breath, he sat up straight once more and dipped his head, as if he were deciding what the hell he was going to eat for dinner tonight after our now-cold taco-Tuesday-flavored fries. "Yeah."

"What are you going to do?" I asked him.

"I'm sure I'll figure it out." Barrett took another sip of his beer before he turned toward me. "You will too, ya know."

I already had it figured out.

"I have him too, you know," said Barrett.

I raised an eyebrow. "Who?"

"Oz."

At the name, my heart skipped a short beat. That didn't make sense. Ozzy … Oz was with Vassar. He was meant to stay with Vassar. Above ground or not.

"No, you don't."

"He was in rough shape. When they flew him out, they

weren't sure he was going to make it. He's doing well enough now though, like the rest of us," explained Barrett. "Didn't you see him at the funeral?"

To be honest, I'd barely even registered the funeral when it was happening. It was quick. Or at least, it felt quick. I barely came to terms with the fact that Vassar—

I'd seen him just before, when we were sitting in the truck overseas, hopping out like idiots after being cooped up for so long. He had been laughing as he twirled off the path like some little girl singing in the rain and …

Vassar was gone.

Vassar was dead and in the ground with a flag draped around his casket, which I imagined his mother had spent every penny she had that he'd sent home to her. It might've been steel or oak—the same color of his eyes, which he squinted up at the sun with every day that I knew him—but I wouldn't know. Not for sure. I was just out of the hospital and half dead myself on pain meds.

I remembered it had been sunny.

And the whole thing had felt like a joke.

"You should see him," suggested Barrett.

"No," I said.

"He's in good shape."

"No."

A few people wandering out of the bar glanced in our direction.

Barrett, however, didn't even flinch. He let his legs dangle over the back edge of his truck before he looked at me and shook his head.

Don't look at me like that, I wanted to tell him.

"I'm not going to stop reaching out my hand," insisted Barrett softly, his voice not holding an ounce of the thick anger that dripped off my own. "Not for Oz. Not for you. Not for Vassar."

"You shouldn't say—"

"Why not?" he asked. "Why not, Hayes? Vassar would be ashamed, you know."

"Why do you think I care about that?"

"Because I know I do. And whether you believe me or not, I live every day, thinking about him," he said. "Pretty sure you do too."

"Then … you must not know me that well anymore," I said.

Barrett laughed loudly. The sound rivaled the music. "Shut up, Hayes. You know I know you all better than I know myself half the time."

Swallowing, I didn't answer him. Being next to Barrett only served to stir up all the memories and thoughts that I'd pushed down the past few weeks and hoped had maybe disappeared forever, like I'd disappeared—or thought I could for a little while until I sorted myself back out.

Barrett didn't get the memo.

He conned me into another drink, though I barely tasted it before he yanked me into him for a hug. "I'll see you then."

"What?"

"At my party. After I get back from visiting a few other family members I promised I would see if I made it back in one piece, I'm hosting a party at my new place."

"You have a place?"

"You know it," he said. "I told you, I'm thinking about sticking around for a while."

"And I'm going to tell you again that I think you're going to get bored and reconsider."

"I don't think so this time. My house. Holiday party. I'll send you the address, and you're going to be there," Barrett said. "Bring someone if you want."

I made no promises. "Like I'm bringing anyone."

"Then, just make sure you bring yourself," he said. "Though I have a feeling I'll be seeing you sooner."

"I hope not."

He shrugged with another smile that I never liked on him.

"You better not mess with me, Barrett," I called out after him as I made my way back to my truck.

He laughed loud enough that it echoed against the dark sky. "Who said I was messing with you?"

I should've gotten out of the truck immediately. I should've shoved the door open and made my way inside the cabin a few feet away from the detached garage. Instead, I shut my eyes for a minute. My head lolled back against the passenger seat as I listened to the silence, feeling the oddest sensation of cold seeping through my layers until I was sure my bones would turn to ice.

When I blinked my eyes back open, I saw the small light was on in the mudroom—or what, according to the plans, would eventually become the mudroom if I ever called to get the washer and dryer back on the calendar to be delivered. Was the homemaker back?

I swore that she'd left after she yelled at me.

Told me I was a jerk and to leave her alone.

In the moment, I'd reveled in hearing the words I screamed at myself half the time. Now, I felt empty.

I slammed the truck door open and headed inside.

Poppy? I almost asked aloud.

It was silent.

There was no holiday music blaring or a small woman's shoes by the door so that mud wouldn't be dragged in over the freshly stained living room floor, which I still couldn't believe she had done by hand for the past week, turning it from faded to a rich darkness that, with the dark paint, made the entire space feel tight and cozy, but not in a bad way.

In a homey sort of way with the white snow reflecting outside the French doors that led onto the patio. I imagined one day, someone would enjoy using them to let out pets or watch their children run around in the backyard while hosting a party with their friends and family laughing together.

But not *mine*. That wasn't even a thought I could ever have.

I kicked off my boots, noticing the empty spaces of the house now more than I had before—from missing furniture and mapped-out spaces for deliveries that never came. I hadn't realized how much I must've pushed the little homemaker's timeline back with all my so-called harmless scheming.

I shut the door to my room behind me out of habit from when Poppy would stay late even though she wasn't here now. I shrugged off my clothes and reached for the pair of sweats I'd had on before.

She'd had a point. There was a stain on them, and they didn't smell the best, which meant that I probably didn't either, no matter if Barrett had been polite enough not to say anything.

Turning on the shower, I let the water run over the black granite like rain before I stepped inside. Everything was working now. More than that, the bathroom addition off the main bedroom was unrecognizable from what it once was. Even unfinished so far, the cabin was turning out nice.

More than nice.

And the entire place felt my style—even if I'd never realized I had one before. How well this Poppy Homemaker woman seemed to know me and this space without ever even meeting the people who lived inside of it almost made me angry. The place was … it could be perfect. I hadn't wanted it. Most of all, I didn't deserve it when I'd thought I was coming back home to a cold shack.

I ran my fingers through my hair, which was the longest it had ever been in my life, but didn't bother to brush it or the shambles of the beard that was also growing to new lengths as I got back into my room. My bag and clothes were tossed all over the floor, and most of the clothes on the floor needed to be washed.

It would've helped if we—*I* had a washer.

I shuffled a heap of the stuff to worry about later into the closet, listening to the crunch of the cardboard box sitting in the back. Pausing, I knelt in front of the wide walk-in closet. Also a new addition. I slid out the cardboard box labeled with my name.

Tearing open the flaps, I peered at the teetering stacks of books inside.

I grabbed one of the books off the top, turning the worn paperback over. Block font was stark on the cover, alongside wide eyes staring through a royal-blue background. I opened to the first page. I'd read this one before. Hell, I'd probably read the collection of war stories twice out of necessity for school or pure boredom. My old, tight handwriting was scrawled, almost undecipherable, in the margins. Words were underlined, and quotes detailing the Vietnam War were circled in blue ink.

Flopping back on my unmade bed, I fell back into the story I vaguely remembered. My eyes turned heavy after a while, the book balanced on my chest.

"Come on, Hayes. Let it loose. Best kiss."

"Best kiss? You gotta be kidding me. Gonna get your diary out next, Vass? Read about your first crush?"

He shoved me. "Come on. You go first then, bud. Share all the gory details."

I rolled my eyes, taking a drink for no other reason than I wanted to. "I was sixteen. Drunk off my ass and alone. My buddies let me disappear to where all the coats were, and I practically passed out. But then this girl showed up."

"You sure she was real, Hayes?"

"Shut up. She was there, and she … listened. Then, fuck." I remembered the strawberry lip gloss that had tasted like sugary candy. I remembered how her hair had been messy yet perfect to slip my hands into when her lips fit just right against mine. Of course, I'd passed out, and she hadn't been there when I woke back up. Maybe it had been some kind of dream. Teenage girl mirage bred from cheap liquor. "That was it, best kiss I ever had."

Everyone leered around me as the next question changed to something bigger and likely a lot more lewd, but Vassar smirked, leaning into me.

"Sounds like you found your true love, man," he joked.
I shoved him again. His dog, Oz, barked at me.

But then, as I forced myself to stop thinking of Vassar, of everyone, for some reason, there was another figure breaking through my clouded mind. It was as if the homemaker were back in front of me. With stupid, kind eyes, she brought me baked goods to try so she knew what to get on the big day—Christmas, when the rest of my family would come to terrorize me as well. Her sweet voice easily turned fiery when I got under her skin as well as she was getting under mine. Her scent seemed to trail through the house more than the paint, light florals and sweet berries sticking around even after she left.

"Have a great life here then. I hope it's worthwhile. Alone."

I shifted in my bed, trying to get comfortable. My book slid off my chest and to the floor. I had no idea what I was going to do and I hated it. The unease prickled in my chest for the first time in an overwhelming realization.

All alone.

It was too much.

Not enough.

ten

. . .

Poppy

I WAITED for a call for the next twelve hours, unable to sleep in the same bedroom I'd slept in my entire life, all alone. I created pretty spaces around me from plush pillows to quilts, but in the end, I only used one of the pillows and half the bed was always cold—just like Aaron had insinuated. I waited for Michelle to call me and tell me that I was off the project and out of the running for the promotion. Even more likely? Fired.

Everything I'd worked for was about to be gone, all because I'd slapped Aaron Hayes.

I'd never slapped anyone before. I still couldn't quite believe that it'd happened. I wouldn't if my hand didn't still sting from force or the memory.

Hours ticked by. One after the next. But I never got the call.

My entire night had been as quiet as the drive as I anxiously made the trip back out of the city and toward the cabin, unsure of what awaited me when I walked through the mudroom door, using my key.

My heart rate rocketed from its anxious stutter as I entered the house again to a full-on race. I'd figured that maybe Aaron would still be upset with me for some reason, still likely unknown to man, but I hadn't expect *this*.

This felt excessive.

For a second, I thought it was a wolf. A small, short-haired wolf, sure, but a very dark, menacing wolf. My eyes widened on the animal staring back at me.

His dark golden eyes pierced into my soul with a cock of its head, taking stock.

"Nice … dog?" I ventured.

The dog had a slight limp as it took another step forward, making a low sound from the back of its throat.

What did I do?

Run? Freeze? Play dead?

"Hey!" Aaron trailed around the corner and snapped, but not at me. He swooped his hand under the dog's metal collar and pulled him back a step, looking the dog directly in the eye and almost baring his teeth at the thing. They looked like twins, right down to the nervous hitch in their legs. *Nice. You're a goddamn house dog now. Get used to it."

I might've died and gone completely catatonic.

I blinked a few times before I found my voice again. "You have a dog?"

The dog stared up at him after being let go. Or maybe it was a glare.

If it was the latter, maybe I wasn't at a complete loss at making friends with the animal. I took my own time to look at Aaron, taken aback.

For a second, I could've been convinced that there was an entirely different man standing in front of me. This morning, Aaron was crisp and clean. He wore a tight shirt underneath— was that a green-and-brown flannel? His hair was fresh with loose waves that fell over his head, growing out from the short buzz on the sides it must've been before, along with his beard that he hadn't shaved yet.

Maybe he wouldn't. He didn't need to look presentable when he was hiding out here.

He was fitting the part of woodsy grouch rather well. He

looked like he was about ready to head outside and start chopping down a few trees for firewood, wiping his unkempt brow with the back of his flannel sleeve.

I snapped myself out of the vision.

"Where did you get it?" I asked.

"What do you mean, *where did I get it*?" Aaron responded with undisguised disgust, though I was still debating whether it was toward the dog or me.

I didn't know how I could be clearer. There hadn't been a dog in this cabin any other day I was here, unless he was hiding it somewhere.

Had he found it in the woods? Was it a stray?

Oh God. I looked around the freshly stained floors for any scenes of a new mess. Was the dog even house-trained?

It looked old enough that it had to know better than to do its business inside, right?

Aaron didn't bother answering any of my questions. He immediately started to walk away from me. With the dog. "The dog is none of your business."

"What's its name?"

Aaron never looked like he got much sleep. This morning, somehow, he looked worse than usual.

He looked quite perturbed.

"You didn't answer my first question so—"

Aaron huffed, reaching back to rub the back of his neck. "It's just a dog. Yes, don't worry; your precious floors are safe. No, it's not a stray. I'm watching him for a friend for a little while."

"Oh."

"Yeah, *oh*."

For some reason, I hadn't expected that answer. Mostly because, though I knew he had once had friends, the past week and a half had been quiet.

This Aaron Hayes still has friends?

The corner of his eye twitched. Turning on his heel, he made it halfway around before I stopped him.

I reached out a hand as if I was going to grab him. Both he and the dog stopped. Maybe I wouldn't have to worry about the dog after all. The unnamed pet appeared as if it was going to be officially attached to him from here on out.

"I'm going to use some of the power tools," I said. "It might be a little loud once I get everything set up."

Aaron glanced over his shoulder. "And?"

"I didn't know if the dog would be okay with that," I said.

"He's fine with loud sounds. He's trained to be okay with them."

"Oh." I eyed the dog I still didn't know the name of.

He slowly lay back down at Aaron's feet like the world's grumpiest foot warmer.

Grump and grumpier. This was a work dog? The scariness of this animal was quickly wearing off as he all but fell over to his side with a harrumph.

"Are you sure?"

"Believe me or don't," huffed Aaron. "Wanna test it out?"

I didn't, but soon, I was going to have no choice. So much for attempting to be considerate. At least he hadn't brought up if he'd called my boss. It didn't seem like he had. He didn't bring up what had happened last night at all.

Pausing, I waited for it. Only, like my call telling me I'd ended my career, it didn't come.

Aaron finally made his way back down the hallway and away from me, exactly where I'd thought we were both going to start our day—already thrown for another loop.

As I bent down in the living room to straighten the drop cloth over the floor, my phone beeped with my daily affirmation notification.

I am in the right place.

I wanted to snort. *Sure thing, app.* At this point, I was sure it was using an algorithm to mock me.

But I looked around the unfinished house one more time. If nothing was going to happen, I had no time to lose.

. . .

The hours trickled by. I kept my music turned down low as I finished cutting the boards for the bookshelves meant to fit into the back wall, making them look seamless, as if they'd always been there. I hadn't gotten to start them last night. I sanded the frayed edges and yelped with delight when they fit into place right where I needed them to.

I still have it.

The last time I had done something like this was before I'd met Lincoln, when I needed other side projects and hobbies to keep me busy, but it was basically like riding a bike.

All I had left was to push the shelves into place, fix up the paint on a few edges, and put together the shelf that would bracket into the back wall to create a cozy reading nook, just out of the way of the fireplace, which I could imagine seeping heat into the living room on Christmas Eve while everyone was curled up in their pajamas.

I was measuring the molding when the creak of feet came from down the hall. I tried to ignore it. Aaron was likely coming out of his room for food or water.

He remained standing outside of the hallway, looking at me as I marked my next measurement.

My eyes scanned from him down to his empty side. "Where's your new companion?"

I twisted the piece of molding around. I nearly knocked myself in the face with it, feeling him watching me.

"Do you even know what you're doing?" he asked.

I huffed, "Yes."

"Are you sure about that? You know, I'm pretty sure your fancy company hired those big, hairy guys who were here last week for a reason. Didn't plan on their little homemaker running around with a handsaw. They'd probably like it more if you stuck to the kitchen, baking sourloaf or whatever."

"It's sourdough."

"What?"

I stopped myself before I corrected him again. "I know what I'm doing."

"I'm concerned about your well-being."

I was sure he was.

"Also wondering how this luxury design, which I'm sure my sister is expecting, is going to pair with your ... DIY?"

Setting down my work, I looked up at him from where I knelt on the floor.

"Yes, I know what I'm doing. No, I don't need any more of your commentary," I muttered. "And to be frank, as I believe we have decided to be as of yesterday evening, if you haven't reconsidered calling my boss about what happened—which I truly appreciate you haven't and that you're giving me another chance —it would be best if you could give me some space right now so that I can do my job and what I set out to do here."

"Poppy ..." Aaron blinked a few times, as if taken aback.

I peered up at him through my lashes, but went no further to acknowledge him.

"About yesterday. I wanted to say ..."

I waited for these words with bated breath.

"I think it's best if we don't talk unless you, as the homeowner, are genuinely having a concern. Okay? From now on, I want to make it clear that while I'm here working, I am keeping this strictly professional."

"Professional?" he asked as if he'd never heard the word before.

"No more, no less."

"Fine." He clenched his jaw before he turned to look over his shoulder. "Right. Oz! Come on."

The sound of dog nails tapped along the floor, coming toward us.

Aaron glanced at me one time before he made it toward the mudroom and headed outside into the cold.

Looking out the back door, I watched the dog I now knew was

named Oz attempt to jump over mounds of snow. I'd noticed his limp before, along with the bent nature of his one ear, but he wasn't letting that stop him. He yelled expletives at the dog who ran further and further around the cabin.

I snorted a laugh.

Standing to pick up the piece of wood I had been working on, I lifted it to make sure it was going to fit at the end before I did anything else. I stretched up on the step-ladder until I was tall enough for molding to slip into place before running my hand down the stretch of wood until the edge touched the ceiling—

I swallowed the sound that wanted to screech from my mouth.

Slowly, I looked down at my hand. I blinked, nearly dropping the piece of wood. Everything around me turned silent as I stepped down from the ladder and over the nail gun that I was luckily not ready to use yet. I dropped the piece of wood I had been holding. I hadn't gotten to properly sand it down before its final coat of paint.

Red dripped against the green.

It was anything but festive.

eleven

. . .

Aaron

OZ STARED AT ME, waiting for his chance to pounce off into the thick, icy mounds of snow like the world's most uncoordinated reindeer.

What a little shit.

I'd woken up this morning to a working doorbell. It rang an obnoxious number of times before I finally tore the door open. Cold air hit me in the face, along with the image of Barrett shoving a leash into my hands before appearing to decide if it was too late to run.

It was the worst ding-dong ditch I'd ever seen.

"He'll be good for you," Barrett had said. "Come on. Don't you remember when you said you owed me a favor?"

"When was that?"

He paused. "I'm sure it was some time."

I glared before I glanced back at the dog. Oz had already roamed past the entryway to the living room before finding a space in the corner and curling up on top of a drop cloth.

"He's deaf now in that bent ear of his," he explained to me, coming back to pat me once on the shoulder. "But he's good, Hayes. Take care of him."

"Take him back."

"I need to leave him with someone. I have to go back to base to pick up the rest of my stuff. As well as revel in the party they'll probably have for me," said Barrett.

Anyone else, and I'd have figured that they were joking. Barrett, however, was, oddly enough, widely liked. A fact that I was more and more confused by every second I spent with him.

The dog looked at me with a dark face. Gray, which I didn't remember, painted a thick line around his muzzle.

"I need to leave him with someone," said Barret. "I can't leave him alone while I'm away."

"Are you talking about me or the dog?"

He laughed.

"Come back here and get him!" I yelled after him again as he made his way back to his car and drove off.

He didn't.

Now, I was stuck in the cabin with two unwelcome visitors—the one looking at me like he was reacquainted with his long-lost friend and the other who wanted nothing more to do with me after last night.

Not that I could blame her.

Barrett was right. I was a mess. I couldn't even apologize like a normal person.

I nudged my boot against the snow, running my hand up my face. I didn't bother making Oz stop his antics, trotting outside through the woods like a prize stud anymore. The stupid dog was smart in some ways, but in others?

As if to prove my point, the dog stumbled through the snow back in front of me, looking behind my frame, as if in search of someone.

I shook my head, taking a deep breath until I could feel the frosty air hit my lungs.

Vassar was Oz's handler. Those two were stuck at the hip, and Oz made sure everyone knew it.

He thought he was the shit.

And he was.

But I spent just as much time with Vassar. Though Barrett and I had been good friends since high school, Vassar became a part of our team soon after. He had been a scrawny kid, especially in the beginning. You couldn't count on him to have your back in physical training for the first year, but, God, he was always funny.

"Why do you think they gave me the dog, Hayes? Think they can trust you?" he'd teased me.

Oz twirled around me once more before coming back to stand in front of me.

I bit the inside of my cheek, shaking my head. "He's not here, Ozzy."

He continued to stare.

We'd had this conversation already a few times now. The first time, I'd tried to get him to stop looking around like he was missing something. The second time—maybe that was the real reason why the Army had given the dog to calm, cool, collected Vassar, who liked to do extra work and study strategy and best team habits in his free time.

When emotions came to shove, I never could keep a completely clear head.

Luckily, even when I'd screamed about how Vassar wasn't coming back after I got out of the shower and saw Oz waiting for me, the dog had looked at me like he'd expected nothing less.

Just like everyone else who seemed to know me better than I knew myself.

I was a broken soldier who couldn't handle anything anymore. I almost wanted to agree with them unless I was going to follow through with what I'd told Barrett last night. I was going to push through this and get out of this funk I was in. Then, I was going to get cleared. I was going to get back to being what I had been.

Who I had been.

When I had first joined the Army, I'd thought the service was my only option, but it quickly became all I'd ever been and wanted to be. I was no longer just Aaron Hayes, the kid who was decent at sports and could get by well enough in school.

My job. My position. My team had made me whole.

Even if I wasn't sure, without Vassar, I'd ever fully be exactly who I'd thought I was again.

"Yeah, I don't know how the hell you managed to survive when he didn't." I wondered the same thing about myself. Sometimes, if I thought for too long about it, I could convince myself that this all was all just some kind of fucked-up dream.

"Come on." I waved a hand for Oz. If he was done frolicking around like a bunny, we might as well go back inside, where it was warm. "Inside. I still need to go and get you some treats or something, bud. You're retired now, you know?"

Walking alongside me, Oz jumped into the mudroom and shook off.

I seethed. "You're going to make an enemy out of the homemaker, too, if she catches you doing that."

Oz sneezed.

I shook my head as I walked through, pausing in the kitchen when I heard the water running. I watched the homemaker stumble as she turned to the door outside.

Toward me.

Poppy stopped in her tracks as if caught. Her eyes were wide, like a deer in headlights. Her pale face dipped down to the towel she had wrapped around her hand.

Now, my eyes were wide.

I took two large steps until I was standing directly in front of her. "Are you bleeding?"

Her lips parted before pressing closed again, as if she was suddenly angrier than she had ever been with me. She didn't answer.

I gaped at the red on the towel she held.

Yep. That was definitely blood.

I pointed at Oz to stay. He didn't put up much of a fight. He shook out again.

I knew it was bad when the homemaker didn't say anything at the distinct notice of her mudroom about to be covered in snow droplets and dog hair.

"You hurt yourself with one of the tools, didn't you?"

"No, I didn't," she insisted, voice tight.

She was even more ridiculous than I'd thought.

"Forgive me if the whole *gushing blood onto one of my new towels* doesn't exactly exude the truth."

"I didn't hurt myself with one of the tools," she muttered, swinging around to face me, her eyes filled with watery anger.

"Let me see it."

"It's fine," she insisted.

"Yeah, that's why you're running away like a dog about to die," I said.

She squinted at me over her shoulder. "Dogs run away when they're about to die?"

"Sometimes." I took her hand, turning it over in the towel to see the damage. I kept my face neutral, even when I wanted to kiss the deep gash there. It didn't look awful, but it didn't look great either.

Far from it.

"I didn't know that," she whispered, starting to gently tug her hand back from me.

"They want to save their owners the pain," I said.

Or at least I thought that was what Barrett had told me. And though Vassar had been the one with the dog and I was his closer companion when we were on the job, working, Barrett was the real dog lover. He knew just about everything about them.

"Or something like that. They're considerate."

"Then, you should've left me alone. I could've been considerate too," Poppy argued before sighing, seeing that I wasn't going to give her hand back until I knew what had happened. "I slid my hand against the wood as I was putting it up, and I guess I forgot to sand that one well, and ..."

Her hand was completely tugged out of mine as she took

another step through the slush on the driveway. I'd been too lazy to shovel it yet. I'd figured with even more snow planning to come by the end of the night, it wasn't worth it.

"Where are you going?"

It was clear she was heading toward her car now. That wouldn't end well.

"You need to go to the hospital," I informed her, in case she was losing some sense to her brain by the way her hand was still bleeding. I thought that the homemaker was supposed to be the smarter of the two of us.

"What?" Her eyes widened. "No. I'm going home."

"You're going to drive home? By yourself?" I asked.

"I have a first aid kit in my car. I'll fix it better with some bandages when I get home."

"Your hand is going to need stitches."

It looked like she was going through all the different scenarios of what was happening right now in her head. Dear Lord, and to think I'd already seen her attempt to park in my massive driveway once. I couldn't imagine what kind of menace she'd be on the road if I let her go now.

"I think it's fine," she said quietly.

"You're coming with me to get it checked out. You're not going home right now."

"I'm not going to the hospital."

"What's the big deal?"

Her eyes were already brimming with thick, heavy tears.

A moment ago, she had been standing here better than most guys when they were vaccinated to go overseas. Now, she was crying?

"I ..."

I almost heard the petulant *I don't care what you say; I'm not going*—like a child. Any concern I'd had over her tears disintegrated into a smirk.

"Don't you dare smile at me right now."

"I'm not smiling," I told her.

"You are too," she insisted. "I told you not to bother me and to leave me alone so that I could work."

"And I can see that's going well."

"You're a big asshole."

"A big one?"

"Yes. You're probably happy I got my hand sliced open," she said.

"I am not."

"Are too," she argued. "Probably. Deep down."

Well, I was starting to find this a little funny as well as frustrating.

"Or not so deep down," she mumbled.

We stood out in the snow. Her legs started to shake. Who knew if it was from the cold or blood loss?

I raised an eyebrow. "Don't be inflexible."

She gasped as if I'd hit a nerve. "*I'm* inflexible?"

"Right now, yeah. What's it going to take?" I made my way over to my truck. I pulled the passenger door open and waved a hand to get inside. "Want me to promise to be cheerier so you'll get in and stop bleeding all over my driveway? Or do I need to get a tourniquet out here?"

Poppy blanched. "It's not that bad."

"I was joking."

"Well, it wasn't funny." She bit her lip.

"It was kind of funny. Come on. Into the car, or it's high and tight. Then, you probably won't even have to lose your hand." I swung my hand toward the passenger seat once more. "Let's go."

"Stop it."

"I'll get you food on the way back if you're good. But we aren't talking about this anymore."

"You think that's what it will take? You getting me food?" She scoffed as if the entire idea was crazy.

This whole thing was crazy, so I didn't think I was far off.

"I know that you usually bring snacks," I told her. "You eat about every other hour, but you haven't eaten since you got here—at least from what I've noticed—so you're probably hungry."

She continued to stare at me.

"Plus, that means if you pass out while driving, you're not just endangering yourself, but also all the other drivers out there," I reasoned. "Think about the poor ma and pa, trying to get their sweet babies home from college for the holiday, only for you to run them off the road."

"Urgent care, or I'm not going."

I doubted they could do anything at urgent care at this hour. We weren't in a city that was crawling with health-care professionals.

I threw my arm again for her to get into the passenger seat, and surprisingly enough, she listened. I slammed the door shut before trailing around to the driver's side.

"Fine. Let's go before I'm blamed for another person bleeding out on me."

The urgent care smelled like vomit and disinfectant wipes. The nurses looked freshly graduated from vocational technical school in their patterned scrubs and enamel pins that declared they were *Nurse Strong*. The one who brought us both back to one of the three rooms to be seen had one shaped like a cartoon pill bottle, asking, *Am I on crazy pills?*

By the way Poppy's leg wouldn't stop shaking, I almost hoped she was so that she had some to share.

"Would you calm down?" I muttered.

Poppy glared at me. "I am calm."

"If this is you calm, I'm afraid of what's going to happen when they stitch up your hand. You look like you're preparing for one of the nurse Barbies to come back in here and chop your entire arm off."

Dear Lord, did she just gulp?

"Can you … can you be quiet?" The usually authoritarian homemaker hugged the side of the plastic chair.

I leaned against the wall as we waited, crossing my arms. "You shouldn't be nervous."

"Wow, that helped so much. Thank you." She managed to keep her voice down below a whisper. Her polite venom was a talent. "I'm not nervous."

"You're not special," I told her, realizing how callous my words sounded, but at least it turned that fearful look in her eye into something a little fierier. "This kind of shit happens to tons of stupid people using power tools. We'll be in and out of here once the doctor or whoever we need to see gets in here."

We were the only ones at the small-town urgent care, yet for some ungodly reason, we still had to sit here and wait for longer than fifteen minutes.

After another two, I sighed, listening to her sneakers tap against the linoleum. "They aren't going to amputate, homemaker."

"I know that," she said. "I just don't like it."

"That you messed up and hurt yourself?"

"Hospitals. Doctors …" She drifted off, as if realizing that I was still the one standing next to her. "You don't care. And you know what? It doesn't matter."

Who said I didn't care?

I was here, wasn't I?

The curtain was awkwardly yanked away on the metal track.

"Did I hear someone is a little nervous?" The doctor on call stepped in.

"Nope. I'm good. Perfectly fine," Poppy assured yet another person in this room unsuccessfully.

The woman glanced down at the homemaker's hand. "I hear it's a home renovation wound. The good news is that it doesn't appear to need any stitches."

Poppy glared up at me. *See?* her expression seemed to say.

I rolled my eyes.

"We can glue you up to make sure it stays closed. Then, all you'll need to do is keep it clean. You'll be right back to finishing up any projects. Renovations are always stressful for new home-owners, especially with the holidays right around the corner. Hopefully, this is the only hiccup you two have."

"Oh, no," Poppy quickly corrected the doctor, waving her injured hand before catching herself. "We're not together."

"Oh. I apologize."

Yet she continued, "I'm working on his home. He drove me here. I told him that it was fine."

"It's not fine," I muttered.

The doctor looked between us, making a few more notes. I was pretty sure *obsessive protesting* was going to be marked somewhere in that chart.

"I'll get someone in here to finish up with you, and then you two can head out. Have a good night."

"Thank you," called Poppy. Peeking back up at me, she took a deep breath as if preparing herself for whatever came next.

I resisted saying, *See? You're going to be fine*, again.

Relief stretched from the center of my chest that it wasn't as serious as I'd thought. A flesh wound. It was good that was all it was. But I was sure to her ears, any more encouragement would sound like *I told you so.*

After her hand was sealed with what looked like a thick coating of superglue and gauze, we drove back to the house in near silence. There was a low hum of country music over the radio—holiday country once Poppy got her hands on the settings.

I hadn't even known that was a thing.

I pushed the car into the park. Most of the lights were still on inside the cabin from our hasty exit.

Home sweet home.

For now anyway.

I made my way out of the car and to Poppy's door before she could reach it.

Holding on to the sleeve of her coat, I helped her down the big step from the truck to the ground. She made a little surprised noise when her feet hit the slush of snow that was still slowly coming down in a flurry.

I wasn't sure if the snow around here was ever going to stop, though I couldn't say that I minded. It had been a while since I'd been home for snow, and this year might've broken records for it already.

"Thank you." She shrugged out of my hand. "I appreciate you driving me there and making sure that I was all right."

"It's fine." I started to walk toward the door, waiting to listen to the crunch of footsteps behind me to know that she was following.

"I guess I should really head home now."

I stopped in my tracks. She headed to her car, covered in a thick layer of snow.

She had to be kidding me. Again.

Poppy Owens was really turning into a pain in my side.

"What are you talking about?" I asked.

"I should probably go home."

I nearly barked a laugh. "You're not going home. You just got your hand hot-glued back together, and it's snowing out," I reminded her. "You're staying here."

"Here?" She looked behind me at the cabin, as if I were suddenly living in a run-down motel. Sure, the accommodations these days weren't much better, but at least she could pretend to be proud of her work.

"Yes, here."

People would probably blame me if something happened to the pitiful thing at this point, and to be honest, I didn't need my blood pressure to get any higher in the name of Poppy Owens.

"You're staying here for the night. The weather is awful, and you're down a hand. You want to go out and get into another accident today?"

She laughed lowly. Twisting on her heel, she took another step toward her car. "You're being ridiculous."

I watched as she climbed into the car and then attempted to buckle herself in with one hand. I also watched as her tires spun in the snow. Hands on my hips, I didn't move to help her. More heavy flakes were coming down. We were no longer in flurry territory. No way was she going to make it back into the city with those bare, bald tires. It was a wonder the little homemaker had even made it here when the roads weren't completely plowed earlier in the day.

Or maybe she almost hadn't.

When she walked in the house earlier today, she was a little shaken up and red-cheeked, and neither thing could've been just because of Oz testing her out.

She didn't give up though. She never did. Until finally, she closed her eyes and rested her forehead against the steering wheel.

Defeated.

Who knew that was a look the unconquerable Poppy Owens had?

Taking my cue, I wandered over to knock on the window. "Turn off the car and come back inside. You're not going anywhere."

She hesitated for another minute. Then, the car shut off. She stepped out.

I waited patiently before reaching to help her towards the house.

"Just don't touch me," she stammered with something akin to a whine, yanking out of my hand as if she was going to make a run for it. She gasped as she stepped on a slippery patch.

I reached for her right before she steadied herself.

"Grab my arm before you fall," I ordered.

She needed to stop whatever this was she was doing right now.

"I'm fine. Let me hold on to an ounce of my dignity for one day," she insisted.

Was that what this was? "Let me help you."

"I'm not going to fall!" She took a step away from me, looking much steadier on her feet than she had before. "See?"

I rolled my eyes as I watched her head to the house.

And listened to the sharp, momentary squeak, followed by the crunch of snow.

I pressed my lips together, swallowing and ending up coughing instead.

God, if there was ever a time to not laugh.

If there was ever a time *to* laugh.

Poppy was still on the ground, and no longer choking on my tongue, I cleared my throat.

"You making a snow angel, or are you ready to head inside now?"

Clenching her jaw, the homemaker looked to be one second away from at last cursing me out. "Slippery."

"Wow, imagine if someone had told you that." I reached out a hand. "I'd be laughing hard as hell right now, but I don't know if you're hurt."

"I'm fine," she mumbled.

Of course she was. Poppy Owens, Home Haven designer extraordinaire, was always fine.

I was beginning to see that, even though now, I was less sure if it was true.

"I'd better start laughing then," I said without a hint of humor.

She scoffed. "That would be the day."

"The day what?"

"Hell would rise, and the snow would suddenly miraculously melt," she pleasantly informed me.

I snorted, not quite a laugh.

I bent down and swept her up into my arms. She let out a small yelp. It echoed through the trees.

"The phrase is *when hell freezes over*, homemaker."

"I think Satan wouldn't mind this moment of creative freedom to describe you." She held on tight to my neck, but didn't argue with me as I carried her the rest of the way into the house.

"I'm Satan now?"

"One of his underlings maybe," she muttered. "This isn't professional."

"Too bad."

twelve

. . .

Poppy

"ARE you going to tell me how to build this thing or not?"

"You're going to put that piece together there." I pointed at what I was talking about as I walked Aaron through how to make a bookshelf that looked like it had always been part of the home, step by step.

"Did you ever think that maybe this would've been better if you had gotten them from one of those big-box stores?" he asked. "You know they have a piece of paper that tells you what to do and everything. Emergency urgent care run probably not included, however."

And have the delivery not arrive to this place, like everything else?

I instructed one piece after another as Aaron worked through how exactly I'd managed to put the first one together myself. Time and a lot of energy.

Both of which I didn't exactly have in truckloads right now.

I was never going to get this place done.

I shook my head. No. I was. I was going to do everything in my power to turn this cabin around into the most idyllic holiday getaway anyone had ever seen. For the promotion. For Aaron and his family. For me.

No matter what it took, I was going to make it happen, even

if my hand still throbbed from whatever disinfectant they'd put on it at the doctor's office and I'd already suffered through Aaron putting me directly into the shower after we got inside from my embarrassingly ill-timed fall. I couldn't even find it in me to care. The water was so warm it tingled on the bottom of my feet. When I got out of the shower, a folded stack containing a gray pair of sweatpants I had to roll over a few times to make fit and an oversized gray sweatshirt waited for me on the counter.

Aaron's attention locked on me when I reentered the living room. His stare roamed over the way my wet hair stuck to the shoulders of the heather-gray cotton sweatshirt. Only then did he meet my eyes, which should've let him know then and there that I knew how absurd I looked.

"Make sure you take care of that sweatshirt," he said. "It's my favorite."

Worried I was missing something, I looked down at myself. "It's plain gray."

"And?" he questioned.

"I'll guard it with my life."

"That's all I ask."

That was also why I was forced to have a large napkin unfolded over my chest by the time pizza was miraculously delivered from the roads I wasn't allowed to drive on.

Even if I was slightly grateful that I hadn't had to. And he was fulfilling his previous promise about feeding me.

"I got fries too," mumbled Aaron, dumping another takeout container in front of me.

He took one before shoving the rest toward me in offering. I hesitated before I took one with the perfect golden crunch.

Though with food came another issue as the dog, Oz, stared at me without blinking, sneaking a step forward every few seconds, as if trying to be sly about how he wanted to steal my pizza.

He looked at me. He came a step closer. Then another.

If Aaron noticed, he didn't call the dog off.

At least he wasn't growling this time. Neither the dog nor Aaron.

"Can I …" I reached out and petted the back of his neck. "Oh, you're a good boy, aren't you?"

Oz seemed to like that, bending his body into me closer, until he was nearly about to push me right over onto the floor.

"Such a good boy. Oh, you want more pets? Do you want me to pet your butt? Weird, but all right. What a good boy."

The dog looked much more pleased with me than this morning, lightly panting with his mouth open.

It almost looked like he was smiling at me.

There was where all comparisons between him and his temporary owner ended. That didn't take long. He was much better mannered.

I couldn't help but notice the way Aaron paused occasionally to check in on us, shifting from one leg and back to the other like it pained him. He shook it out like a runner getting ready for a race, seamlessly attempting to cover up an old injury.

He shifted on his feet again as he reached for another piece of the shelf.

"You okay over there?" he asked, catching my line of sight.

I slid my hand away from Oz and took another bite of pizza. "Yeah, fine. Ready for the next step?"

"I just slide the shelf in, right?"

"Make sure that the shelves are level and even with the tiny markers I made on the wood," I instructed.

He twisted around piece after piece to make sure they were the correct ones I was referring to.

"You've never worked with your hands much, huh?"

"Not in the way you mean," he muttered, just loud enough.

Was that a joke? "Professional, remember?"

"Was that before or after I drove you to urgent care and we agreed you're staying the night?" he asked. "I thought I'd already decided that we'd throw that word out the window."

"Not your decision."

He huffed.

"And I'm not *staying the night*."

At that, Aaron raised an eyebrow, looking back over me, lounging on the floor in his sweats that smelled like spring-fresh laundry detergent, eating yet another slice after I said I was done after number three.

I'd admit, it didn't look great.

"Not like that," I said, a bit more sheepish.

He knew what I'd meant. Even though the real question remained. Where was I going to end up sleeping when the time came? It wasn't as if I could stay over on his brand-new couch that hadn't been delivered.

My eyes caught on to what he was doing next. "No. Don't use that small of a screw. You want it to provide structure for weight. Those are for the molding when it goes up at the end."

Aaron dropped the metal in favor of the one I was rapidly pointing at.

He wasn't terrible at following directions.

"First time building something?"

"Sort of," he said. "I didn't have a father who was around much and did projects by himself. My family used to live closer to the city, where my sister still is. Whenever there was a leak or issue, you called it out to be fixed."

"That makes sense," I said, not letting on to how much I knew about his family.

"I know how to sew."

I raised an eyebrow. "Really?"

"In the barest sense of the word," Aaron clarified. Not that I saw him sewing ball gowns or anything in his free time, but still, consider me impressed. "Can't even call it a party trick really, though it sounds super impressive when a guy says it, doesn't it?"

"It's sexist, but yeah."

"We were encouraged to learn how to manage the basics in the army. You should at least know how to sew a button back on. Then, there were sewing patches and making things last as long as you could. I wasn't the worst at it—that was for sure," he went on, pressing the drill to connect the shelves into place.

I focused on the work and not him as I asked more questions. "You weren't close to your family?"

He paused as if truly thinking about it. "Close enough. My parents were busy a lot of the time. My sister got that gene. My unit in the Army became my family."

"That's nice."

"For a while," he half-heartedly agreed.

"Can I ask you a question?" I asked.

"Pretty sure you've already asked a few," said Aaron. "But go on."

"Before, when you were taking me to urgent care, you said something."

"And what was that?"

"You said you didn't want another person bleeding out on you," I reminded him.

He paused his work.

I was encroaching upon a topic that he likely didn't want to talk about. Who would? He hadn't even wanted to accept me telling him that I understood that he was grieving the other day, but I couldn't help myself.

"Did that happen before? I mean, I assume—"

"Yeah." He nodded, turning back to look toward the mess of screws lying around. The ones he needed were right there, but he ran his fingers through them anyway, sending one or two rolling to the side. "Sort of anyway."

"I'm sorry," I quickly tried to correct, seeing his attitude start to turn. "You don't have to say anything."

"I don't remember much of it." He focused on finding the next board that I must've put in the wrong spot earlier. "When I was deployed this last time, there was an accident. We weren't supposed to be there. There was an old mine no one was lucky enough to run over until we did. My buddy took a hit. I took a hit."

My eyes scanned over the puckered skin on his leg and under his shirt, where I remembered scars running up along his torso when he couldn't be bothered putting on a shirt. Perhaps there was a reason for that. Maybe he liked to see those scars every day, to be reminded of what had happened.

"I was still conscious enough to try to get to my friend. I tried to stop the bleeding, but he was … it was already too late. They told me that I must've been in shock when I tried to save him. I was trying to bring him back to goddamn life." He chuckled lowly. "The only sound after we hit the mine was his dog. He wouldn't stop whining or crying—I don't know."

Both of us glanced toward Oz. He was lying next to me, maw in his paws.

The moment Aaron turned away again, I reached down to feed him a piece of my crust.

He scampered up to his feet, waiting for more.

Aaron hadn't noticed as he continued his story, words soft and vulnerable, whether he meant them to be or not. "Then, there was my own heart, still beating like it didn't even know that anything had happened. That everything had ended in less than a second."

There was a beat. We sat in silence.

"Told you, not a good storyteller," said Aaron, his voice void of emotion.

I felt pressure forming behind my eyes. But I wasn't going to cry. Not for him. Especially since I was pretty sure that he'd berate me if I did.

I forced myself to hold it together. "What was his name?"

Aaron took a deep breath. He peeked over his shoulder at me. "Vassar."

"Vassar. And Oz was …"

"Yep." He got back to work, leaving us in the quiet.

I broke the silence. "You shouldn't do that."

"What?" he asked.

"You should stop doing what you're doing right now," I said, my voice coming out more teasingly than I'd intended, though I still couldn't look at him.

He dropped the tool in his hand before he glanced up at my small smile, not talking about the bookshelves.

"I don't want to like you."

"You don't have to," he said. "Professional, remember?"

"Can't we just get along until I finish this project? Because I do need to finish it," I said. "And now, you kind of did help me here."

"Why do you even need to finish this project?" he asked. "Why not move on to the next snooty homeowner's house?"

"Are you calling your sister snooty?"

He breathed a short sound that sounded a little like a chuckle.

"Because I can't let myself not finish it," I tried explaining. "This job has always been my dream, and at the end of the year ..."

He listened closely.

"There's a promotion," I confessed, testing the waters to see if he was going to use this as another piece of ammunition to shoot back at me somehow. "I was told that the promotion was set to be mine. Now though, there's a sort of last-minute challenge since there are two of us up for it."

"And what's this other girl working with?" he asked.

"A house in the city."

"Just a house?"

I took a deep breath, setting down my slice of pizza as I laid it out for him. "A well-off family brownstone in the city that also wants to be ready for the holidays this season. Historical integrity, mixed with modern, clean edges and silver trees probably. If I know Alison—the works."

"The works."

"Yes."

"What do *the works* entail?" he asked. "Seriously, what are we talking about here? A fake Santa squeezing his ass down the chimney on Christmas Day and a fancy plastic tree or ..."

"More like thousands of dollars strictly for the holiday, dedicated to one-of-a-kind chandeliers and hand-blown Venetian glass ornaments."

Aaron let out a low whistle.

"You know, to give it that special kind of cozy touch," I said, even though I would just about die to be put in the position Alison was in. I looked around the cabin. "I know I can make this place look amazing. Not in the same way, of course, but it could be the best place I've put together so far."

Aaron must've seen what I did. There was a long way to go—from the painting to the furniture that needed to be brought in to fill all the rooms. Then the most important part of all. Decorating. For the home. For the holiday.

All of it.

And we were already so far behind.

"I'm also making sure that I plan your holiday perfectly. That's why I'm here. The event. The days before and day of Christmas. Everything will be perfect by the time I'm done." I tried to maintain positivity, but I was beginning to think I'd misplaced it during the blood loss earlier.

"Will your boss see it to decide?"

Would Michelle notice all I work I'd put in for the family on Christmas Day alongside the big picture of the cabin itself? I wasn't sure.

"Sarah has two children, right?" I asked.

Aaron nodded. "Why?"

"I was thinking everyone could make gingerbread houses in the kitchen one evening."

"Gingerbread houses? You never turn that planning brain of yours off, do you?" he asked.

"It's a classic," I said, ignoring the latter portion of his question. "Have you ever made one?"

"No. I assume you have?"

"Once," I admitted shyly. Though I liked to think of myself as a holiday-event-planning extraordinaire, there were still some things that needed a little work. "I made one at an after-school camp at the rec center on Pine Street in the city."

Aaron paused. "On Pine? I think I went there once years ago."

I hesitated before saying anything else, not looking up at him when I could feel his eyes land on me. "Oh?"

"Small world. Who knew your entry into home design would start with dry after-school cookies in such a dump?" he said.

"Yeah, it wasn't my finest work."

"I would've thought yours would've won first prize for perfect icing lines on the roof," he muttered with a curl of his lip.

I laughed. It was easy once it started with little high-pitched giggles. "So, you do know your way around a gingerbread house. Mine had way too many gumdrops. Completely messed up the gingerbread feng shui."

He raised an eyebrow, as if sensing more than that.

"The roof collapsed."

Aaron barked a laugh.

My heart stopped in my chest as I listened to the deep, resonant vibrato that escaped him. The laugh wasn't loud or long; it lasted a second. But there it was. It was enough for my eyes to widen in shock, as if hearing something rare and precious for the first time.

I'd heard it before, in the hallway or gym class.

I'd forgotten how perfect it was. How his laugh was one of the things that had made me fall for him when he didn't even know that I existed. You could tell a lot about a person by how they laughed. If they were loud and carefree or if they guarded their happiness close to their heart.

He noticed my pause. "What?"

"Your laugh."

"What about it?" he asked.

"Just haven't heard it before." Not in a long time anyway.

"Renovation disasters bring it out in me," he said, monotone.

I narrowed my eyes, taking another bite of pizza. Ozzy was

still staring at me, waiting for his next treat. "Me, too, but I don't think we have the same reason."

"Probably not. Yours is probably from joy."

"Or not to cry."

He stopped his work to glance back at me.

I lifted a shoulder. It was a joke. And, it also wasn't. "You think this has been the best renovation I've worked on? Sure, it's my first on my own, but I've had to deal with an angry homeowner making the process … not ideal."

"That bad?"

"You or the project?"

"Poppy—"

I stopped him there, but this time, he didn't hear it.

"I think what you're trying to do here is pretty great. I had no idea it took so much work to make all this happen. Especially now that I hear it's a hell of a lot more than fancy place settings," he said, a bit contrite. "I mean, you have battle scars."

If I hadn't already today, I might've fallen over at the words.

"You're ambitious. Determined."

"Thank—"

"Even though, as of now, I think we can both agree, you're never going to fucking finish this place in time."

We'd see about that.

He paused before he got back to work. Lifting another screw for my inspection. I confirmed before he drilled another shelf in. He was turning into quite the bookshelf-crafting expert.

"You really need to win this competition of yours, huh?"

"I don't like to think of it as a competition."

"Sounds like one to me."

I wiped my face with the back of my fist, still holding the end of my pizza slice.

The dog, who had been waiting patiently next to me this whole time, on the other hand, wasn't having it, huffing as he tried to nip at my fingers again.

"Shh," I warned him as I tore off another piece. He gobbled it up in one bite. "You need to be quiet."

"I know you're feeding the dog," Aaron informed me.

"And?" I asked.

He cast a look between me and Oz. This wasn't a fight he was going to win.

Aaron stared from my eyes, down the side of my jaw, to my lips, where his gaze seemed to lock on.

My heart pounded in my chest as his eyes softened.

I swallowed, inhaling on my words, making them come out a little breathy and squeaky. "What are you looking at?"

He continued to stare. Maybe he wasn't looking at my mouth.

I looked down at my shirt to see if I had anything on myself.

"You got sauce." Aaron reached out toward my jaw. His thumb ran along a damp line. He pulled away, and as if he wasn't even thinking, he stuck his thumb into his mouth, sucking off the sweet herbs and tomato with a graze of his tongue before wiping his hand on his jeans, plywood dust streaked across the thighs.

He cleared his throat while I couldn't pull my eyes away.

Oz snatched the last piece of crust out of my hand as it drifted toward him.

"Where does this last piece go?"

thirteen

. . .

Poppy

"HOME HAVEN HOLIDAY HOTLINE, THIS IS—"

"Hannah," I cut her off. "Why are you not answering your phone?"

Hannah gasped over the line. "Poppy, you know you can't call the hotline!"

"At least I know you'll pick up," I said.

I switched to speakerphone as I drove home after another day of working on the cabin. The bookshelves were up and looked spectacular, if I did say so myself. The last time I had done anything like it was when I wallpapered my aunt's laundry room, which was all angles.

Everything was also, at last, painted with Aaron's help—and not just the living room. Somehow, the next day I had come to the cabin, all the paint I had previously ordered weeks ago had been delivered—or miraculously found on the property.

I didn't quite believe that one, but I didn't bother to ask questions.

I painted the walls. Aaron shocked me with how good his cut-ins were.

I insisted that for the bedrooms and shared bath, we should wait for the painters to come back since they were already rescheduled, but Aaron argued, "This is my cabin, homemaker. Are you honestly going to tell the paying customer he's wrong to want to paint his own house? I promise I won't make it look bad enough to show up on camera for your little promotion competition."

I relented. At least he was using the correct paint colors and not the horrendous orange I'd left out in the garage that I most certainly hadn't ordered. He was even following my directions for some reason even though I had been able to do a lot more work since my hand, though tender, was healing up nicely.

"You completely messed up my queue rate here, Poppy!" Hannah cried over the phone, stealing me away from my constant slew of thoughts of the cabin.

"I'm asking you to go out for drinks, Hannah."

"Wait." She paused her horrified rant. "What?"

"I'll meet you at the bar you like that's around the corner from Home Haven," I said. "The one with all the frosted mirrors and cushioned bar seats that make me feel like I'm in an Art Deco painting with the tacky gold trim?"

"Are you asking me on a date, Poppy Owens? I'm a highly in-demand woman this time of year, you know."

For once, it did sound like usually cool-as-a-cucumber-mint-mojito Hannah really did need a drink.

Maybe two.

And maybe I did too. "Something might've happened. I need girl talk."

She didn't hesitate. "I'll be there at eight."

Running my fingers over the stem of the tall white wineglass in front of me two hours later, I nursed a single pour of pinot grigio while I waited for Hannah to arrive. There were only so many glares I could take in the quickly filling bar over the seat I was saving.

Luckily, it wasn't long before Hannah dropped her purse into the seat and hopped up in front of me.

"Look at you, branching out. Is that an actual drink in your hand?" Hannah swiveled in her chair as if she could see better that way. Her lips parted in shock. "Oh dear. Have I rubbed off on you once and for all?"

I shook my head at her antics.

Compared to being with Aaron all week, quiet and rough around all the edges, Hannah was a hit of fresh air. Vibrant and sharp.

"I'm older than you."

"Exactly. You go to a bar, and I am praising you over ordering a glass of white wine in winter. You need to be corrupted a little."

"What's wrong with white wine in winter?"

"Nothing if you don't understand that white wine is chilled and automatically tastes better in the summer."

"I think that's personal taste," I said.

She shook her head. "No. Pretty sure it's universal understanding."

I shook my head.

I couldn't remember the last time Hannah had convinced me to go out with her. I was too busy, and to be honest, I usually sat at home in the evenings with my mom and Simon while they watched reruns before they declared how they were beat and went upstairs to bed for the evening.

Over the past two weeks, I hadn't been home as often. From the late hours in the office, to spending all my work time and spare time at the cabin or eating dinner with Aaron from the few groceries he picked up or had delivered, the only time I had been home to catch up with my parents like I used to were in the brief moments after waking up in the morning. Even that was sparse so that I could attempt to beat traffic.

I hardly remembered the in-between.

Sleep. Drive. Work.

And it was all coming together, oddly enough. I didn't mind it.

The person I was spending the most time with now was the man who, days ago, I'd insisted was my most insufferable enemy. The boy who didn't know of my crush on him years ago and likely never would. But it felt nice. Perhaps it was meant to happen. Maybe I still had unfinished business with the man who might not have known me or remembered me.

But I remembered, all too well.

He wasn't quite the same. But then again, neither was I.

So, we focused on what we could do to complete the cabin. This would be my final business with Aaron Hayes, and I couldn't help the way I watched him work alongside me.

Because who would've thought?

Of course, the more time we spent together, the more I noticed how warm his eyes were. When they collided with mine, the way I remembered them years ago, I felt my breath catch in chest no matter what we were doing. I questioned whether it was time that maybe I hinted to him that we'd known each other before, years ago.

I blushed with the embarrassment of what would happen now, if he ever realized.

Hannah's soft hazel eyes widened in apparent outrage.

"What?"

"I just asked you a question and you were looking off into la la land over there. Oh my god. Is this why you need girl talk?" She gasped. "You slept with your high school crush. I knew it! Ha."

I attempted to shush her as I forced myself back out of my head. A few heads behind her at the bar were starting to glance in our direction.

"You didn't know anything because I don't even know what you're talking about right now," I said.

"My work wife has been corrupted."

I had not been corrupted.

Hannah leaned over the bar to wave her hand and catch the eye of the person working. "Where's this bartender? I need to get myself a drink, stat. Something that's pink or comes with cherries, inspired by your bright red cheeks. Fill me in as I order. Tell me everything that's happening with you right now."

I resisted the urge to bring a hand up to the side of my face. "Nothing has been happening. Work, work, and more work have been going on. That's it."

Hannah ordered her cosmopolitan as soon as the bartender made his way toward us, giggling at how she was already strumming her fingers against the speckled black granite bar top before the martini glass was gently set in front of her with a clink.

She leaned in so as not to spill, slurping up a large gulp. She let out a sigh of contentment as the combo of cranberry and vodka hit her bloodstream.

Clearing her throat, she returned to stare at me with raised brows. "Now, tell me why I don't believe you."

"Because you're bored, sitting in an office all day, and looking for drama?"

"Trust me, I'm not." She sighed as if thinking of something else before rolling her eyes. "Try again."

"But you're always looking for drama," I countered.

She reached for her martini glass, turning away from me.

"Hannah, do you need to tell me something?"

"It's nothing. I have four other female roommates. There are random pots to stir, and I have drama coming out of my ears," she said. "Right now, I want to hear about yours."

I didn't think that was it. I narrowed my eyes at her and waited for her to break in the silence. It always seemed to work.

Hannah couldn't stand the silence after all. She needed to fill it. She liked conversation, music, and podcasts constantly. Oddly, she didn't rise to the occasion. The only sound that came from around me was the bark of a laugh from the table in the corner and the clamor of glasses being pulled out of the dishwasher behind the bar, blowing up a billow of steam.

"Stop looking at me like that. I want to hear about this hot Army man you have riling you up. I thought you said you were beyond a—what did you call it? *A little high school crush?*"

"I am."

Or at least, I'd thought I was. Aaron wasn't a high school crush anymore. And he wasn't little.

And it was hard to stop thinking about the cabin when I wasn't there. And him in it.

"Mmhmm." Hannah took another sip of her drink, waiting for more details.

"Stop it. Anyway, it turns out that I was right. It was him sabotaging the whole project."

"You're kidding," she said, totally unsurprised. "I still can't believe it though. That kind of pot-stirring to mess up your scheduling takes a lot of energy."

"Now, however, he's helping."

Her eyes widened. At least that shocked her as much as it had me. "Maybe you aren't the only one with a little crush."

"Neither of us has a crush. He is alone in the cabin. We are working together. Professionally," I told her. "He's been doing a decent job, and he takes direction well."

"We like men who take direction well."

"He's been cooperative lately. And nice." I stared at Hannah through lowered eyes, knowing what she was trying to insinuate —again. "We're not sleeping together."

She put her hand on her heart. "Poppy Owens! When did I ever say such a thing?"

I rolled my eyes. "Uh-huh."

"I would never." She sounded like a shocked Southern aunt.

"Make that assumption?"

"Well"—she dropped the act and traced her finger around the rim of her drink—"it doesn't mean you can't maybe act with your instincts a little in the future."

"He's a client, Hannah."

"Hidden away in the deep, dark woods, where he doesn't leave so no one will ever have to know. I don't know. Having that kind of secluded spot, decorated by you around the holidays, things could get spicy—and I'm not just talking about the cider."

I shook my head again. "We are professional adults," I repeated. "I'm sure having a romantic affair is the last thing on his mind right now when he's already been through so much. Plus, he still doesn't know who I am, which feels like ..." *A huge lie.*

"Sounds like you're starting to like him," my friend murmured. "Or like him again."

I was. That was a problem. When he wasn't being a complete ass, he was starting to remind me of the boy I remembered liking more than anyone else over a decade ago. Or maybe this all was some strange workaholic Stockholm syndrome.

"You shouldn't let him get to you." Hannah cut through my thoughts once more. "You're in control."

It didn't feel that way. Every time I went back to the cabin, I felt less in control. The place was getting done. I could almost see it coming together in time. But with Aaron there, I was slowly fraying like a velvet Christmas ribbon.

I wondered if I would ever feel fully in control and not like I wasn't a second away from becoming my teenage self again, ready to self-combust with silly, unprofessional feelings for a man I still hardly knew as an adult, even if that was slowly changing now and he wasn't such a complete pain in my side.

At least not all the time anymore.

"But ..."

I looked at her as I reached for my glass of wine, taking another hesitant sip. I didn't drink much, but it was nice, sitting and sipping as we chatted.

"It wouldn't be the worst thing for you to lean more into following your heart, would it?" asked Hannah. "It couldn't hurt to let yourself focus a little on not working."

"The promotion is coming up, Hannah. I need to focus on the project. You are supposed to be telling me to ignore men and to focus on me right now."

"And normally, I would. But come on, Pops. I have faith in you. This project of yours? It's going to be great, no matter what happens. You're going to whip Alison's ass."

"I don't want to whip her ass, Hannah. We are both good at our jobs and—"

"Buuut"—she pulled me back on topic—"you don't always let go. Live. Maybe you could have some fun. Step outside the routine a little more. I mean, you seem like your normal, on-edge self right now, constantly thinking about work, but you also seem … giddy."

"Giddy?"

"Happy."

"I'm always happy," I challenged.

"Are you?" Hannah asked, forehead creasing.

Was I happy? And more than my affirmation app telling me so?

"I don't want to step on your toes here, Poppy," Hannah said. "But ever since I met you, when you were with Lincoln, who I know I shouldn't speak of, I've seen you be focused and pleased and maybe even a little excited, but I'm not sure if I've seen you be casually happy. Being casually happy after all is a big deal. Not everyone gets to wake up and feel good. And I want that for you."

"I want that for you too, Hannah."

"Well, I am," she said. "Most of the time anyway, I let myself be. Let yourself be too."

If only it were that easy.

"I'm not trying to get him to fall in love with me, Hannah."

"Whether that happens or not—fine, I'll stop." She shrugged, reaching for her drink. "Hannah from the Holiday Hotline is officially clocking out for the evening. Thoughtful responses are no longer guaranteed."

For some reason, I didn't think Hannah had to try that hard. Unless she put on the overly excitable party-girl face just as easily as the polished problem solver at work every day. All of us were pretending to be the perfect people we wanted to be until we ended up cracking under the weight of ourselves.

"Thank you for wanting me to be happy, Hannah," I said softly.

"Eh, don't get sappy." She let her hand fall out to the side, effectively waving me off.

"I miss you and the office."

"I miss you too. And I found out you're the only one who ever cleans the microwave in the break room."

I rolled my eyes.

"But seriously, once the holiday wraps up, you'll be sick of me again," said Hannah.

Soon, I'd be back in the office with her, post-cabin and post-Aaron. We'd be able to put this entire holiday month behind us. My favorite month once again felt completely draining.

And also, suddenly, it was already ending too soon. It was all moving along too fast—and not just because of the holiday deadline.

"I did get the wildest call the other day," she said, changing the subject.

"Tell me."

"There was a guy with a ham that ended up on the kitchen floor of some bachelor pad on the west side."

I barked a laugh. "What did you tell him to do?"

"I told him to pour some cola over it and call it a day." She lifted a shoulder in nonchalance.

"You did not."

"I did. I'm pretty sure the poor guy would've believed me, no matter what I said, so it was the basics."

"Our vegetarian preparing a ham."

"Gotta do what I gotta do." Her head lulled to the side as she recounted the call. "He seemed more than a little stressed out, getting ready for some kind of family get-together. He has three sisters, which I can imagine would be hell enough, especially since they'd already thought that he was completely going to flop the meal. Whenever he started to lose it, he'd do this chuckling laugh sort of thing. That's when I knew I had to rein him back in off a culinary ledge."

Sounded like a long call.

"It was a good thing that he found the hotline number," I said.

"It was."

"And then what happened?" I nudged her. "With the guy?"

"Oh. Nothing. He must've pulled it together," she said simply. Though her voice sounded off.

I could tell she was keeping something to herself. But like earlier, before we got into my own issues, I knew better than to pry into Hannah's cards, which she always kept just close enough to her sheer hot-pink blouse.

"Are you getting sick?" I asked instead.

"What?" Her brow furrowed before she must've realized what I was talking about. "Oh. Maybe? I swear my roommates come home with something new every other week, especially with the one working at the little heathen school of booger pickers."

"Gross."

"Another reason I don't ever want children," she said.

"What number is that on the list? Fourteen or eighty-two?" I teased.

She tapped her finger against her chin. "Somewhere in between, I think."

"Maybe you'll end up having a holiday romance, but not me."

"With who?"

"Mystery ham guy?"

Hannah froze with her drink a breath from her lips.

"*Hannah.*"

"No, definitely not."

I waited for her to come clean about something, but clearly, my intense stare wasn't working.

She shook her head over and over again until when I caught her reflection in the golden-hazed mirror behind the bar, she blurred. "Stop talking and drink your wine."

fourteen

. . .

Aaron

"JUST LETTING you know I'm on my way."

I sat up from where I attempted another sit-up without much success after the first dozen. What was worse was when I tried to push myself up directly to my feet.

Oz scampered out of the way from where he watched me with minimal amusement. My leg wasn't having it. No matter how much I stretched before or after, it locked up on me or fell asleep whenever I attempted to push it past its normal limits.

Or limits now.

I grunted as I tried to listen again to the voice coming out of the phone I had pressed against the side of my head. When I'd answered, I'd figured that Poppy's high-pitched voice would greet me, telling me that she was coming in even earlier than normal today.

But that wasn't who was on the other end of the line.

"What?" I croaked into the phone.

"I'm on my way to your house to drop off the kids for the day." My sister, Sarah, rushed over her words. "I don't have any other option. It's last minute, so it'll be a quick drop. See you in a bit!"

"Sarah!" I yelled into the phone, but she'd already hung up.

What did she mean that she's coming to drop off the kids? Did she accidentally call me instead of her nanny? Or better yet, a day care?

I yanked a pair of clean pajama pants out from the basket—since we'd finally had a washer and dryer delivered. I'd called and made sure they understood that it would happen before the end of the week someway, somehow so I didn't end up having to go pick up the appliances and put them in myself like I had the strings of holiday lights.

I was pretty sure Poppy could tell that they had been done by an amateur rather than her fancy and expensive outsourcing, but she hadn't said anything. Every time something new was delivered, she'd gasp with delight, a gleam in her eyes telling me that she knew that it was me, but again, she never said anything.

We just kept working at our own steady pace. Considering I hadn't wanted Poppy in the house at all before, it was kind of nice.

More than nice.

I'd even been getting some good sleep from how hard we were working during the days.

I called my sister back and listened to it ring.

And ring.

And go straight to voice mail.

Outside the cabin, a car honked.

Oz rushed forward to the door as if he could see anything out of the window, cast in a hazy glow of morning sunlight.

Pajama pants tucked into unlaced boots, I watched as a monster of a black SUV pulled up in my snow-covered driveway. My sister never skimped when it came to safety, especially in her cars that had to make it through the harsh northern winters.

The tires rolled through the weather like a bright and sunny day.

My sister was out of the driver's seat while the lights of the car were still on and her children, presumably, were still in the back seat. She left the door open as she held on, careful not to let go until she was steady.

Snow lifted and clumped into the edges of my boots, soaking my socks with every step I made out from the mudroom door. "Sarah."

"I need you to take the kids," she said without greeting. "Just for the day."

"No." I didn't pause before I replied, "What are you even talking about right now?"

"Please." Sarah looked between the car and back to me again.

I looked at the car, tilting my head away and letting my voice drop in case my niece and nephew were listening. "I thought you wanted them to have some magical fairy-tale winter-wonderland holiday here."

"That was the plan."

"Well, this place still isn't your holiday dream home."

Her shoulders slumped with impatience before taking notice of my pajamas. "Aaron, please … are you okay?"

I narrowed my eyes.

She cocked her head down toward where I limped to the one side of my body, trying to get myself standing straight. "Is your leg—"

"It's fine," I cut her off. "Just fell asleep when I had to come bounding out into the snow for you."

She huffed. "This shouldn't be a big ask."

"It isn't?"

"You know I wouldn't leave them here if I had another choice. The nanny is off. My backup babysitter isn't available. Liana barely thinks that she even needs a babysitter anymore, which is a whole other issue. I tried to make this easy for you. They're all packed and everything."

I stared at her.

She stared right back. A quirk twisted at the corner of her lips. "I bet you wish you were at that retreat I signed you up for now."

I barked a laugh.

"I know you don't like kids—"

"I didn't say that," I grumbled.

My sister didn't bother to correct herself or elaborate. "You're their uncle. We have to leave for the night. I'll be back in twenty-four hours."

"What's going on?"

"Nathan's aunt fell ill. It doesn't look good," Sarah explained.

"Nathan …"

"My *husband*, Aaron."

I blinked. "Oh."

"Yes. *Oh*. Anyway, he was close to her," said Sarah. "We have to make sure we visit in case she doesn't make it when we go up to see his side of the family for the holiday."

"You could just go to his side of the family instead of coming here for Christmas, you know," I offered.

Her mouth set into a thin line. It was the signature look that Mom used to make at us. A face that said, *We aren't talking about this right now.*

Or ever.

I rubbed the back of my neck. "I don't know what to do with kids."

"They aren't that tricky, Aaron. Stick them in front of the television if you must. Their tablets are packed in their stuff, too, if you get desperate. Let them play games. They're self-sufficient— mostly. Except for Gavin in some cases."

"In some cases?" I asked.

"Make sure he doesn't wander off and that he doesn't stand too far away from the toilet bowl when he has to pee."

"You have got to be kidding me."

"Their pajamas are in the bag for when they fall asleep. They really shouldn't give you any problems." She bit her bottom lip. It might be the first time I saw the beginnings of my sister about to beg. "I'm not asking the world of you right now. Let the kids spend time with their uncle they've barely met. I'll be back in the morning to get them."

I heard the crunch of snow behind me. I'd forgotten that I hadn't closed the mudroom door.

I knew who it was by the way my sister's eyes widened. "You got a dog?"

"No," I said before promptly correcting myself. "Yes. I don't know."

She raised an eyebrow at me so high it would soon disappear into her hairline. "You don't know?"

"It's …" *It's Vassar's dog,* I was about to say. Instead, I glanced down at Oz. "Yeah. Guess so."

"Is he … safe?"

"No. You should probably take the kids and leave now before he starts going completely insane." Right now, Oz looked more likely to take a roll in the snow. I waved a hand at him, and he went frolicking to the closest tree to take a piss. "He's fine."

"Are you sure?"

I stared at her and raised my eyebrows this time. "Don't you need to unload your precious cargo and get out of here?"

Sarah glared before turning to the car, waving through the window. "Liana. Gavin! Grab your stuff and get out of the car and inside Uncle Aaron's!"

The side doors of the car burst open. Out tumbled a small glob of a boy in a navy-blue puffer coat. He nearly fell over twice before he tugged his overnight duffel bag, which was as big as he was, out from under the back seat. He lugged it through the snow by the handle before his eyes widened at the cabin.

The Christmas lights hanging from the gutters were on since it was still dark.

"Whoa!" Gavin exclaimed, dropping his things. He took off toward the house. "This is like Santa's house!"

Sarah picked the abandoned overnight bag up and brushed it off. She extended it to me.

Taking the bag, I hiked it over my shoulder, adjusting my stance for the weight, feeling the pressure down my hip. How much was inside this thing? Did this kid pack bricks?

My sister turned to her daughter, slamming the car door shut. I had met Liana a few times before. Now, she was twice the size.

Tall, with her dark hair twisted back into a complicated braid. She looked nearly identical to how I remembered my sister when we had been kids.

"Mom," Liana moaned.

"I'll be back in the morning," my sister repeated to Liana.

She swept her daughter up in a big hug. After she pulled back, the little girl pressed her lips together. The look must've been genetic.

"Be good," Sarah warned, then turned to look up at me. "You be good."

"I'm nothing else," I said.

Sarah glanced between me and the kids again as if she was already starting to regret her decision. "Keep them safe."

"Here I thought, I was going to take them out bear hunting."

"Aaron," Sarah warned.

"Go." I waved her toward her car as I turned around and headed for the cabin, where the other two kids had already hurtled inside.

With a short whistle behind my teeth, Oz was rushing toward me too.

Inside, the only positive was that the kids no longer had their shoes on as they fought over who was sitting where on the couch. And Gavin proved his screeches could ring to new heights. I swiped a hand down my face.

Oz looked up at me, sensing my unease.

I shook my head at him. "Don't look at me."

***

The kids might've been wild animals the way they ran rampant through the cabin. Gavin had a collision with one wall that made more of an impression on him than it did on the wall. Thank God. I couldn't imagine what the homemaker would do if she came in and saw a dent.

Not that she should come in today.

She really shouldn't come into the house today. Not with this mess or whatever else was bound to happen.

The two kids were watching some kind of video on the tablet Liana had pulled out from her duffel bag. Here I thought, with all the money and nannying, my sister would've raised polite, posh children, the kind you saw in expensive clothing ads.

Instead, I was dialing the last recent number on my phone in warning.

Poppy picked up on the second ring. "Hello? Aaron?"

Who else would it be? "You don't have to bother with coming to the house today."

There was a pause.

"I'm working today," the homemaker countered. It wasn't a question.

Why did she have to be so stubborn?

I put a hand to my head. "I know. I know you are."

"What's the problem?"

"You're not going to get anything done here," I told her.

"Why?"

I huffed. "Look. My sister dropped her kids here unexpectedly because her husband had some kind of family emergency. I have to take care of them. They're a wreck. At this point, the place is going to be a wreck. I have no idea what I'm going to do with them, so might as well wait until I can clean up the damage."

"Damage?" Poppy didn't sound convinced. If anything, for some reason, she sounded … amused.

"Stay home. I'll call you in the morning. Then, you can get back to work and stay on schedule. Right now, I need to figure out what I'm going to do with two kids that I barely know."

"I'm not a kid!" Liana called out, hearing me talking on the phone.

I moved further into the kitchen, which looked bright and clean now that all the cabinets had knobs and empty spaces were filled with shiny appliances.

"Are you asking me for a favor, Aaron?" she asked.

Not Mr. Hayes. Somewhere in the past week, her professional pleasantries had faded, and I liked it more than I should've.

Aaron.

"No. I'm telling you to stay home. Do whatever you do when you're not here," I insisted. "Take the day off. Get a manicure. It's fine. Everything will get done, but today, I have to deal with what is here. I'm sorry to let ya down, but this is what it is. Bye."

"Aaron—"

I hung up the phone.

"I'm bored. Can I go outside? Are there animals out in the woods? What about lions? Can we build a snowman? Do you have any snacks?" Gavin asked at least a dozen questions at once.

I fought to find the answers.

Already, I stared at him as he befriended Oz.

The dog was curled up on the floor, letting my nephew—who I thought I'd met once shortly after he was born—scratch the space between his ears, not bothered by the bent, tattered one.

Oz blinked at me, as if saying, *What did you expect me to do? Traitor.*

"Why is your house so empty? Don't you have a Christmas tree yet? My mom put up our Christmas tree after Thanksgiving. Do you not celebrate Thanksgiving? Do you not celebrate Christmas?" Gavin let his mouth drop open in shock.

"I celebrate Thanksgiving." Sort of.

I couldn't quite remember the last time I'd had a proper Thanksgiving like I was sure he was thinking about. Everyone at a table, talking and stuffing themselves with turkey and potatoes.

"Why weren't you eating with us then? My mom said that you're family. Doesn't family come to Thanksgiving? Even my aunt Portia comes to dinner sometimes. She brought puffy-looking orange flowers."

I smirked at the way Gavin said Portia, like *Porta*. I didn't know who the hell Portia was. I hadn't known that Sarah's husband, Nathan, had a living aunt either.

"I wasn't around," I said.

"Oh," said Gavin. "Where were you?"

"Uh ..." I glanced around the cabin. I doubted my sister wanted her impressionable son to know that his uncle was recovering from nearly being blown up. "Away."

That seemed to satisfy him enough. But he had a point about snacks. Soon enough, they were going to get hungry. I ate out most of the time and not three meals a day, like I was sure they were used to getting at home with my sister and her likely all-natural, organic diet.

I was so out of my league here.

Liana continued to tap away at some game on her tablet.

She didn't look up, glued to the screen.

The doorbell rang with a calm yet insistent chime.

"What the ..." I made my way toward the door.

No one was supposed to be here today.

The final shipment of furniture should be here tomorrow or the next day. The chairs by the bookshelves held the loose paperbacks that had previously been hidden at the bottom of my closet. The dining table would also arrive, so the home-maker could do whatever she wanted to make it look like the place had come out of a Martha Stewart holiday collection.

Not today.

Running a hand through my hair, starting at my forehead, I swung open the front door to tell whoever it was to go back and check their schedules.

The homemaker blinked at me standing in front of her. She had her tote bag she always wore looped over her shoulder. In her hands, she held more than a few boxes.

"Poppy." I looked at her and the way she grinned at me to form words. "What are you doing here?" I asked.

She adjusted herself to hold the stack of boxes in her hands better. "Sounded like you could use some help."

"It's fine," I said stiffly, turning around. I knew she was going to follow me inside anyway. "I don't need any help."

"Oh." There was a small slam of something falling to the ground. I forced myself not to flinch. "Are you sure?"

"Yes. You're not going to be able to get any work done today with them here. They'll be gone tomorrow, so you can come back then."

"I see," she said.

I didn't think she did.

"They're going to mess things up," I told her.

She cocked her head as her brow creased.

"Houses are meant to be a little messed up," Poppy said, patting me on the shoulder as she pushed past me into the living room. "That's how you know they're working."

fifteen

. . .

Poppy

A MISCHIEVOUS GRIN spread over Gavin's face. Aaron's nephew had been smiling the entire time since I'd arrived.

He introduced himself with vigor. "My name is Gavin. I'm six and three-quarters years old. I'm in first grade right now, and I've never been to this house before, but my mom says that we're going to have Christmas here!" he rambled loudly, as if he wasn't sure if I would be able to hear him.

Even Oz, who had been wandering the perimeter of the room, glanced over at him, wondering if something was amiss. His one good ear was keenly perked up.

I pressed my lips together to hold back my laugh at his excitement.

It was a sight with Gavin's messy hair flopping over his ears. He looked a bit like his uncle. Though I wasn't completely positive. His entire face was warm and welcoming, even with the cool eyes that must've been a family trait. However, they were bright, filled with a never-ending beam of a grin.

I was positive Aaron's face would crack if he tried to genuinely smile.

When he had called me before, telling me not to come over, I'd figured that it was just another loss of a day. Sure, I knew that the furniture people wouldn't be there today, and there was only so much I could do, but I was already ready for the day. I was dressed and prepared to go back and work, and … I wanted to go back to the cabin.

Plus, even over the phone, when he mentioned that the kids were there, I wasn't quite sure he'd sounded as sure of himself as he tried to insist that he was.

It was no problem anyway. So, the kids were here a few weeks early. They'd see the cabin in its final form then. For now, that didn't mean the whole experience couldn't start.

In fact, it needed to.

"What happened to your hand?" Gavin pointed.

I glanced down at the smaller bandage that was still on it. With a bit of rest and Aaron making sure that I changed the bandage whenever it got dirty when we were working, the wound was completely sealed, though it still needed to heal a bit more.

"Ah," I said. "I cut myself, making the bookshelves. That's why you have to be very careful when you're working with sharp things."

Gavin turned toward the shelves in question. His light-gray eyes were wide. "You built those?"

"Yep."

"Whoa," he said, aghast. Or at least as aghast as a six-year-old could be. "But you're a girl."

"I am."

"Whoa," he repeated.

It was pretty whoa.

"I have another activity that you can build for the house too. I think we need a little more Christmas spirit here, don't you?"

Slowly, I managed to pry Liana off the couch and away from her tablet, where it'd looked like she was working her way through a game. I pulled out one item at a time from the bags I'd brought, and both kids started to ooh and aah as I pressed the premade dough from the bakery near my house into the molds.

I slid the tray in the oven, and they were set to cook for fifteen minutes.

Aaron stood off to the side, watching the way I moved around the kitchen. Gavin narrated the whole time whenever he wasn't asking questions.

I let him mix the icing into a bowl for us. Liana carefully laid out all the pieces of candy to use for decoration.

Gavin reached up, smearing sticky white icing over my nose.

I gasped, head arching away from the attack.

Icing trailed down from my nose before it dropped onto the table in a lump.

Both kids paused what they were doing in the kitchen, which was previously filled with noise yet it wasn't too loud. Gavin smirked, waiting for the fallout. Liana's mouth parted in clear shock at what her little brother had done, hands hovering over her organization of glitter and peppermint rounds.

Blinking, I could still see some of the icing on my face; some of it was caught on the edge of my upper lip. My tongue snuck out to swipe it away, and I leaned closer to him with a smile. "You think that is funny?"

"It is funny," cried Gavin, bursting into laughter at the fact that I hadn't gotten all the frosting off my face.

"Oh, yeah?" Before Gavin could understand what was coming, I took a glob of the icing off my face and reached out, smearing it over his cheek.

He paused his laughter.

"You're right," I said. "That is funny."

Gavin howled with delight.

The new oven, which had finally been installed at the end of last week, beeped with the scent of ginger spice.

Good. The cookies should be done.

I skipped to turn the oven off with a press of a button. "I think our walls are ready."

"The walls?" Gavin cackled.

"You got it."

"And the roof?" Liana asked, leaning over the parchment-covered table, her elbows scooching up the edges. "I'm going to put the gumdrops on mine."

Gavin gasped. "I want the candy canes!"

Reaching into the oven with red mitts, I paused, looking down at the tray.

"They look burned!" Gavin stared between the oven and my hands, holding the tray filled with dark pieces of a gingerbread house.

"They're just a little …" For a minute, my heart ached at the sight of them, but I wasn't sure I'd fully expected anything different. I let loose a sigh before nudging the oven door shut. The tray clattered lightly against the top of the stove. "Well done."

They were definitely burned.

"Well done?" Aaron asked me from the doorway, arms crossed and eyebrows raised.

"Nothing a little extra icing won't fix," I insisted.

Letting the pieces cool, I smiled at the kids, who stood frozen until they caught my complete ease. I hadn't missed a beat.

Transferring the pieces to the table, I warned, "Be careful; some of the pieces are still hot."

"I thought you were a master homemaker there, Poppy." Aaron spoke up again.

I looked at him over my shoulder, giving him a small glare, though I was sure my eyes were widening enough to show my slight horror that I couldn't even follow the simplest of premixed gingerbread dough directions.

He bit the inside of his cheek for a second there, and I almost paused.

Was this Aaron Hayes happy?

Wow. And it only took my baking demise.

"Well, it's a good thing that we aren't going to eat them," I said to the kids. "We're going to be making gingerbread houses. We're going to cover all the bits with icing and gumdrops if you'd like to participate."

"And glitter?" Liana lit up, clasping her hands together in front of her heart.

"Absolutely," I agreed. "All the glitter."

"I'm going to make a princess castle."

"All right, but remember, these are the walls we have," I said, reaching for the radio playing holiday music and turning it up another notch. "This will be a turret-less castle."

"What's a turret?"

"A tower, Gavin," Liana scoffed.

Gavin glared but started to smear icing everywhere.

Liana looked less than impressed, barely noticing her brother's displeasure. "I'll just pretend I'm making the castle after a fire."

That was one way to look at it.

Looking over my shoulder, Aaron stood under the rounded archway leading into the living room. I thought I might've caught something there.

Something that looked like a smile.

sixteen

. . .

Aaron

FROM WHAT I knew of the homemaker, she was all business.

Only right now, I wasn't so sure if that assessment was correct.

I watched from the archway to see what the usually uptight homemaker would do. Every step of the way, Poppy managed to surprise me. She had come into the house and got straight to business, pulling the previously irritated Liana off her tablet. Then, she'd corralled the two kids into the kitchen like it was some kind of parade.

Now, there was a mess everywhere. Icing was on faces. Powdered sugar sprinkled the floor like a freshly fallen layer of snow. Would she immediately jump into action with wet wipes and try to wipe it away?

Before I could jump in, not for the first time today, Poppy shocked me.

Poppy opened her mouth wide, as if in horror. But instead of a scream, she laughed.

The laugh was high-pitched and rang with the utmost delight. The sound was like wind chimes or the bells playing in the background of Christmas music, echoing through the empty house.

The three of them continued to work on their gingerbread

houses. There was no time set for the activity. No one seemed to mind. The gingerbread houses were taking up most of the day, but if anything, the kids were all too pleased about it. Gavin stuffed another broken piece of cookie into his mouth, smearing white and cheery red and green icing over his face without realizing.

After a while, Liana pointed at her brother's face.

"You look like Rudolph." Liana giggled.

"No, I don't! No, I don't!" screamed Gavin across the table. "Rudolph has a red nose, stupid!"

I moved to step in even though I wasn't sure what to do.

Poppy put a hand down between the gingerbread houses before we had a disaster on our hands. "Hey, be nice. Gavin is right. Rudolph does have a red nose. He's clearly a rare Gavin reindeer."

Liana laughed loudly. I hadn't heard the sound yet today. I almost wanted to laugh myself.

Gavin's cheeks turned red, though that could've been from all the sugar he had been eating. He stuffed another gumdrop into his mouth, and his teeth practically stuck together.

One thing led to the next until two dilapidated gingerbread houses were set up on the edge of the new rustic-style kitchen table, as Poppy described it, while she easily swept away most of the mess. Oz wandered back and forth through the kitchen in a loop, looking for crumbs.

Liana gasped as she looked out the window, leaving the cleaning to Poppy entirely. Gavin had made his way back to the couch, flopping there until Oz noticed the change. He trotted over to lick at the little boy's fingers.

Gavin giggled until I waved off Oz.

"Get out of there," I warned him.

All of them were already looking all too pleased with themselves.

"Can we go outside?"

I almost couldn't believe the voice belonged to Liana. She was still at the window. Turning around, she pointed. Her eyes flicked back and forth between Poppy and me.

Poppy smiled, with a small nod before directing them to get their coats and to double-layer their socks. "Of course we can."

***

Liana stumbled forward, catching herself over the snow. The piles of white sparkled under the last seconds of the sun setting behind the thick pine trees. She started to build a lumpy snowman. Somehow, she didn't get frustrated when the second sphere fell from her hands. She picked it up and attempted to roll it on top of the other. She didn't even complain when the snow started to seep through her knit gloves.

Poppy bit her bottom lip as she watched. It was as if she was internally trying to cheer my niece on from where we sat on the back patio. I'd been silent most of the day, a fourth wheel.

Unless you counted Oz. Then fifth.

I walked up next to Poppy as she sat on the edge of the stone wall where she must've brushed the snow off. When I scooted in next to her, she shifted a little to the side before looking at me. I handed a bottle to her and popped off the top. I didn't have much in the fridge for the kids. But I did have beer.

She hesitated before she took it, but she didn't immediately take a sip. I did before setting mine to the side. Rubbing my hands together, I blew hot air into my palms before tucking them as best as I could back into my coat. Poppy's eyes flicked toward me at the movement.

I cleared my throat.

"Yes?" Poppy asked.

"You're good with them," I finally vocalized.

"Is that a compliment?" She raised her brows, though she continued to keep her gaze locked on Liana and Gavin playing.

I rolled my eyes.

"Excuse me if I don't know how to take one from you," she mumbled.

I narrowed my eyes. "Since when have I told you anything else?"

She shrugged, finally taking a sip of the beer I'd offered her. She cringed. "This tastes terrible."

"Didn't think I'd be hosting guests."

She let out a small breath of a laugh as we watched the kids tumble around in their puffy winter gear. Ozzy raced after them, shoving Gavin down face-first into a mound of snow.

"Ooh," both of us exclaimed at the same time.

Gavin popped back up, face red, and ran after the dog without pause.

Poppy was watching them with a smile, though her arms were crossed to keep in the warmth. Though she was wearing her coat, in this weather, it didn't look particularly warm. "Maybe Oz isn't one hundred percent ready yet to be a house dog?"

"He'll get used to it," I mumbled.

"It's not a bad place for a dog to get used to," she said softly.

It wasn't. If we stuck around. If I let Ozzy stick around even. I kept thinking about the party Barrett had said he was hosting when he got back from visiting family. He'd pick up Ozzy then. The thought of the dog not falling over himself in the snow or annoyingly trotting next to me like a shadow wherever I went in the house made me wonder if I wanted him to take him back.

But he wasn't my dog.

"Why'd you come out here?" I asked Poppy. "I said you didn't have to."

"I know I didn't have to," she said, as if that was obvious. "I already told you I *wanted* to."

"And you just happen to have all the stuff?"

"The stuff?"

"For the gingerbread houses. I thought you said you'd pick that stuff up for the holiday."

"And I think I told you the holiday already started," she countered.

"At this point, you might as well just be done with the whole holiday experience," I said.

"Who said I was done?" she asked, as if my questions were meant to be humorous.

"Seriously."

She shrugged once more, as if everything she did was no big deal. There was still a bit of the day left, but she had filled most of it. And … at least the kids wouldn't go running back to Sarah and tell her what a failure I was as an uncle.

A small weight I hadn't known was there lifted off my shoulders.

"I told you I was planning," she said. "I wanted to make sure everything went perfectly."

"But I thought that you were making sure everything was ready for the job?" I repeated. "For when your boss or whoever comes to take photos."

"The photos aren't my job, Aaron. Not even a quarter of it." Poppy sent a wave of her hand toward the kids. The holiday lights I'd haphazardly strung started to twinkle one by one, illuminating us in the snow. "This is."

"You put a lot of time and effort in today."

"I did."

"You didn't have to do all this already though."

She met my eyes, her brows lowering a half inch, as if confused. "You can't put a timeline on a perfect day. Things change. They'll remember this day as much as the actual one. They'll remember they had a great holiday season and got to spend it with their uncle."

"I didn't do anything. You're the one who pulled it all together with the gingerbread houses with the frosting icicles and sugar windows …"

"You should stop that," she said before I could add anything else.

"What?"

"The constant self-criticism."

My brows creased as I turned to the kids, and then back to her. I was finding it hard to look anywhere else but at her.

Poppy's eyes were soft and easy as she gave a small shake of her head. "I can't imagine that you deserve it," she whispered.

Then, maybe she didn't know me as well as she thought she did yet.

This time though, there wasn't as much anger in the thought.

Yet, I thought to myself.

I cleared my throat.

She shrugged. "And you could've done all this. It just takes some thought."

"I would've ruined it."

"Like I didn't?" She giggled. "They're kids. That's what's great about planning for them. They won't remember whether they baked the cookies perfectly or if they came out with burned edges. They won't remember that their mom dumped them here."

No, the two kids wouldn't remember how crazed I was when they first arrived or when they sat looking like they were being punished in my living room. They'd remember the way they laughed whenever the gingerbread house fell and they had to piece it back together with more icing, like an unshapely shack. They probably wouldn't remember how the entire thing had looked so unlike the ideal holiday vision I had seen jotted down and displayed through the homemaker's plans. They would, however, probably remember how clear it was that the perfect homemaker couldn't bake, charring the gingerbread to a crisp.

I wondered if she could even cook anything besides boiled water.

I smirked, oddly pleased at finding some kind of flaw in this woman who had infiltrated my life over the past few weeks. Before, I thought maybe it was her stubbornness or that she was constantly cold and wearing cheery, ruffled socks. I thought it was how she was dramatic nearly all the time, but especially when she was excited.

Yet, every time I thought I found a flaw, I decided, in the end when the room was completed to her exact specifications or when she plopped down on the couch in the afternoon for a snack that she never cooked herself looking the picture of cozy, it wasn't one.

I couldn't find one flaw.

"At least there wasn't another tragic ginger cookie roof collapse."

She smiled. "There is that. I can't say I had hoped it would have gone better. Can you?"

A truck pulled up into the driveway. Another delivery? I swore there wasn't supposed to be one today.

"What's going on there?"

Standing up, she brushed herself off. "Tree."

"A what?"

"Well, I figured they couldn't start celebrating without a tree." Poppy shrugged as if it was the most obvious thing in the world. "And you aren't the only one who can pull some strings to make this house come together."

I stared, walking after her. The kids noticed the delivery, too, and rushed back toward the house, where a man was pulling out a large pine from the back of his truck.

"How?"

She pursed her lips. "I have my ways, Aaron Hayes. Did you really underestimate me on this?"

I shouldn't on anything. Ever again.

"The decorations are in the hall closet," she said, a minor direction I easily followed as we raced to head inside.

For the first time, I didn't think any of us were unhappy to be at the cabin.

"Come on." I motioned for Oz.

His head was cradled between his dark paws on the edge of

my bed. I threw the fresh comforter back as I got it ready for the kids.

He grumbled at me.

I tried to make him get off the bed to start when he started to climb in with me most nights, but after so many days of working with Poppy the past week, I wasn't willing to exert any more energy, fighting a battle with him. Now, he thought all the spaces were his.

I was surprised Poppy didn't mind the dog staking his claim. Instead, she took out a lint roller from seemingly nowhere and started silently swiping away the fur Oz left behind every time he moved.

That was entertaining in and of itself.

By the time everyone was here for the holiday next week, everything would be in place, including the two, small guest rooms for my sister, her husband, and the kids to share. For now, I wasn't letting the two of them on the couch.

Oz didn't move.

"Come on, Oz. You can't sleep here tonight," I told him, bending down to look at him. "Time for bed. I know I've been nice, but the kids are sleeping here. You can't."

Breathing in, the dog let out a heavy huff. He still didn't budge.

"Please don't make him go, Uncle Aaron," said Gavin, climbing up onto the bed. "I want to sleep with Ozzy. He likes me."

Gavin slowly petted a long line from between the dog's ears and down his back. Ozzy—*damn him*—leaned into the touch. His head was basically in the kid's lap, wet tongue hanging out of the side of his mouth.

Dangerous, terrifying K9 indeed.

I knelt in front of the dog's face. "You'd better be nice, and if you do anything wrong in here, you're out. Got it?"

Oz stared back at me like I was the most absurd individual

he'd ever laid eyes on. Sometimes, I was sure he could understand me beyond what a dog should.

"You're out of here if you mess with my family," I repeated.

My family.

I blinked a few times at the thought. I hadn't really thought of it all until today. My sister and I were never what could be considered close. Today felt different. The cabin was quiet yet full as I took my time to tuck Gavin in under the thick duvet. Liana rubbed her eyes before climbing into bed next to her little brother.

"Please, Uncle Aaron?" Gavin asked again. "Can you let him stay for the night?"

"You tell him to get down if your sister wants him to or if there isn't enough space. He has a bed on the floor he can use."

"There's enough room."

I cocked my head at Gavin.

He sighed, much like the dog. "Fine."

"Good. Good night."

"Night, Uncle Aaron," both kids called after me.

I listened to the kids whispering behind me inside the room before I walked out into the living room. Poppy tossed pillows off the couch before she extended them into a much more luxurious bed than I remembered couches ever being able to be turned into.

Honestly, when the couch had first arrived, I'd expected it to be something out of a fancy catalog that you'd never want to sit down on, let alone sleep on. Another surprise.

A second one? The way my eyes were attached to Poppy, who was wearing nothing but an oversize shirt that trailed down to her knees.

My shirt again.

"I'm sorry." Poppy fluffed a wide bed pillow before setting it toward the back of the makeshift bed. "All I have is clothes for tomorrow. I have no idea where my sweatpants went, and I didn't want to go searching in your room for anything if the kids were already down. This was on top of the wash bin."

"It's fine," I said.

It had been my idea anyway that she stay the night again. The final shipment of furniture would be coming tomorrow, and she needed to be here. Not to mention, it was much later than she'd ever driven home back to the city before.

I didn't want her on the road.

"I'll still be sure to take extra-good care of your favorite sweatshirt." She offered a small smile.

I shook my head. "Looks better on you anyway."

She snorted, looking down at herself. "I doubt that."

It was true. I shrugged.

"Are the kids asleep?"

"They're winding down. Llana finished brushing her teeth." I swung a hand back toward my bedroom. "The dog didn't want to leave Gavin."

A small smile curled at the corner of her lips. "That's adorable."

"Yeah, I worry about the dog being alone with them, but …"

"You don't think Oz would do anything, do you?" Poppy asked.

"No, but he's still a dog. He's an animal."

"But he loves those kids."

"Still doesn't mean he wouldn't accidentally do something to the people he loves and who take care of him," I said. She parted her lips, but I cleared my throat before she could speak up, jutting my chin toward the tree positioned in the corner by the fireplace. "You're not going to leave the tree like that, are you?"

The tree was decorated as one would expect a tree decorated by overexcited kids would be. Ornaments were clumped in certain sections. Tinsel was thrown here, there, and everywhere.

She bit her lip. "Don't tell them."

"Wouldn't dream of it."

"Say the elves redecorated or something," she said. "I figure, if they want to, they can redo it when they arrive again next week for Christmas."

I snorted a laugh.

Her eyes snapped open wide. "Wow."

I hit the one lamp, leaving on the light in the kitchen, and I waved for her to climb into bed. With me. We slid between the sheets as if it were the most natural thing to do between us.

Just last week, we'd barely been speaking.

Now, I goaded her with a shake of my head, knowing exactly what she was referring to ever since she first seemed so astounded when I actually let myself relax enough to laugh.

"Another laugh. I'm just shocked." She met my challenge. "Didn't know you had it in you."

"This how you win men over? You insult them?"

"More like teasing. And especially if they deserve it," she said before she blinked a few times, her eyes drifting away from mine as she realized that we were both getting comfortable, lying next to each other with one pillow separating the space between us.

"Your Mr. Right must be something."

"If you think I have a Mr. Right and I'm lying with you on the couch right now on a weekend and after I spent most of the week here, you are crazy."

There were the insults again. The *teasing*, I mean.

"There is no Mr. Right. There is no mister … no anyone, for your information. But now, you're breaching the code," she whispered.

"The code?"

"The professionalism code."

Poppy shifted under the blanket as if struggling to get comfortable. I pushed a little extra toward her to wrap around her shoulder.

"Oh, well, I didn't realize there was an entire code now, Snow Angel."

Poppy inhaled at the new nickname I'd given her. "There is," she insisted.

"I find it hard to believe that you don't have some sap running after you, taking you to some kind of Christmas concert or something," I said.

"You think I live in some cheesy holiday movie, don't you?" she said. "No. I'm all alone."

"Tragic."

"Truly."

"You scare them off," I said.

Her eyes narrowed. "No, I don't scare people off."

"You are pretty intimidating."

"I am not," Poppy argued.

I shrugged.

"I'm not intimidating," she repeated.

"You know what you want. You go after what you want. You enjoy what you're doing ..."

"And that makes me intimidating?"

"It makes you rare."

Again, there was that narrowed stare, as if she was deciding if she should glare. Unless that, too, was against her professionalism code? Being combative was a no-go, wasn't it?

"I'm pretty sure that's a synonym for odd," she settled on saying.

"It makes you unique," I rephrased. "To truly love what you do—not everyone gets that opportunity or to keep it when they find it."

"Did you find what you loved to do?"

I opened my mouth to respond. To say, *Of course I did*. I loved the Army. I loved the family I'd made there.

But I paused, thinking about it.

I'd groan in the morning when I had to get up, and sometimes, when I closed my eyes, I'd beg that I would wake up anywhere else but at work, at training, or overseas. When the days got long, I thought to myself, *I could be happy if I never had to see another minute of this work ever again.*

"It's who I am. I'm going to go back. I'm working toward it," I informed her. "Every day, my leg is getting stronger."

Though, that wasn't exactly true.

"But do you still enjoy it?" she asked before seeing I was at a loss for words.

Did I still enjoy it?

"Either way, I mean, you'll have a lot more excitement ahead of you. Even if it's scary."

"Scary?"

"Yeah, it's scary going into the unknown," she said. "But, my step father, Simon, once told me that life is meant to be a little scary if you're doing it right. Life isn't supposed to be frilly all the time; it's a battle."

"You think life is a battle?" I asked.

"We all have our own."

Here we go again. "I'm sure everyone does."

She rolled her eyes.

"Go on," I gave in. "Tell me your battle. You held whatever sad backstory you have in you in long enough. What, two weeks?"

"Three. But no."

"Why not?"

"I'm not going to tell you. Why would I when it's clear that you don't care or don't want to?" She raised an eyebrow, which I could just see through the dimness in the room.

I shook my head. "Because you've already surprised me more than once today."

Poppy blinked, as if unsure what to say to that. Maybe I surprised her too.

"Go on," I encouraged.

"Okay," she whispered, gathering her thoughts. "At the end of high school, I developed pretty terrible chronic pain. At least, that was what the doctors called it. They couldn't figure it out. I would curl over myself; it was so bad, and no one seemed to care."

"Are you in pain now?" I asked.

She should her head. "Not like I was. Sometimes, I can forget about it. But not long enough not to ..."

"Not to what?"

"Remember," she said, honestly. "And worry that it'll come back. Eventually, the doctors found out the chronic pain wasn't some mystery. But it took about five years. Too long, yeah, though some people go longer without that kind of diagnosis, which almost feels like a godsend. People finally started to look at me like I wasn't insane. I had—*have* endometriosis."

I'd heard the word before, but the look of confusion on my face must've been plain to see.

"It's basically when uteruses attack."

"Doesn't that happen every month?" I asked ignorantly. Immediately, I wanted to correct myself.

I didn't get to. Poppy giggled.

"Sort of. But more. It's when the tissue sort of invades other places, and around that time of the month or even other times, the tissue sort of"—she squeezed her hands together in a little fist between us—"contracts."

I cringed.

"Yeah. Not the best feeling." Poppy swept her hair to one side, casting it out of her face. "After I got my diagnosis, I found a doctor who specialized in treating it. I had surgery for it to go away for good. It's never guaranteed though … but that's it. I doubt you want to hear any more of the little details."

She was wrong. I wanted to hear more.

"But you're not in pain now?"

"Like I said," she whispered, "not like I was. But that doesn't mean it won't come back one day. Or ruin other things. You don't have to pretend you want to talk about it. Not your kind of trauma, right?"

I felt like she might as well have punched me in the chest. "I …" *I had no idea.*

She slowly nodded, as if she knew exactly what I was thinking. I hoped she did because I couldn't find the words. They disintegrated on my tongue every time I tried to think of a phrase that would somehow make up for how horrible I had been to this woman, who was trying her all at something she loved so that other people could love it just as much.

"And getting to the point, it wouldn't be the first time a relationship ended because of it. So, maybe that's why I brought it up," she confessed.

"Ended because of what?"

"Because"—she shook her head—"with the diagnoses and the treatment, there's a risk of infertility issues. Men often want children. Among other things. And they want simple. Even if they say they don't care or it isn't important to them … it is. And I'm not. Simple anyway," she said. "No one wants someone already preprogrammed to disappoint you."

Who told her that?

"Anyway, now, I'm okay with that. I have realized that I'm just not good at it anyway."

"Good at what?" I dared to ask.

"Relationships. Every one I've ever had ended horribly, and I've come to terms with that. I'm dedicated to my work. I won't let myself down, doing it. You're right. Home Haven has always been the dream. I'm content that it will be my love. And I refuse to disappoint myself in the relationship I have with it," Poppy said with a small huff, the same way I imagined she said her little mottos that popped up on her phone every morning.

I noticed them a lot. At first, I'd snorted at them.

I am strong.

I am capable.

I was almost certain at some point I was going to see an affirmation that went something like, *I can handle another day of working with this walking asshole who makes life hell.*

"It sucks that you had to deal with all that. That you had to deal with other people who made you deal with all that," I said. "I'm sorry."

Poppy paused, studying me. It was as if she was unsure, or shocked I'd said anything at all.

At some point, we'd gotten closer to each other. I could almost feel the breath of her words on my cheek when she spoke. "Thank you."

"Don't thank me."

She stared at me through tired, half-lidded eyes. "Thank you for taking my pain seriously. Thank you for taking *me* seriously."

"Anyone who didn't would be a fool."

I would know. I had been one.

Maybe I still was one. I couldn't stop myself from looking at her. I couldn't' stop thinking about how soft her skin would be if I reached out and brushed my thumb over one of her rosy cheeks, which I'd thought was from her embarrassment or the cold, but it was just her.

And now, I didn't move as my eyes turned from her jaw toward her mouth.

God, I had been looking at those lips for days. When she laughed and then opened wide to reveal her perfectly pearly teeth. When she pressed them together as she shook her head at me or, even better, when they pursed just so—not quite a pout, but not quite *not* one either—and her cheeks got all red in a way where I was dying to know what was going on in that head of hers. What in the world would this well-behaved little homemaker have to say to me that made her face so scarlet?

So angry.

Right now, her cheeks burned in a different way, a heady pink, as I leaned in closer. Her breath caught, parting those plush lips.

"You know what, Snow Angel?"

"Huh?" She looked down at my mouth.

I knew I shouldn't do it. I wasn't a complete idiot.

But I was starting to think, *For Poppy Owens? Oh, yeah. I am an idiot for her.*

"Being professional is overrated."

So, it was no surprise when I leaned in that final inch and kissed her.

seventeen

. . .

Poppy

THIS ISN'T HAPPENING.

I'd said it more than once in the past few days. But this time, I meant it more than ever before.

This cannot be happening.

But it oh-so clearly was.

Just like that, Aaron Hayes was kissing me.

Again.

This time was so different from the last kiss, when he had been slightly drunk and I was not. Now, we both tasted like the bubbly bottled beer, which I normally hated, but currently, I felt like it was everything I'd ever wanted and more. Shifting forward, he angled his lips over mine to take the kiss deeper. His hand cupped the other side of my face, keeping me still for his mouth to continue its delicate exploration.

I was all too willing to give him full access. Through my lashes, I watched the way his lips parted and slid over my mine, heavy with want. But I wouldn't miss this, not for a second.

Aaron Hayes is kissing me. This is real. This is happening.

And I realized it might've been one of the things I'd wanted so deeply for far too long.

Aaron let his mouth trail down toward my neck, skimming over the sensitive skin there before he pulled back. There was a single moment, giving us each a breath, before another kiss came down again—less teeth, more tongue.

He lavished me with this kiss, and I didn't want to break away.

I didn't want this to end. Once it did, I knew all too well that everything up to this point could all come crashing down. It would be just like it had been when I was in high school. Everything and then nothing. A grand reveal, only to feel like a certain spot in my chest was being yanked out and crumpled up.

Like it would with my plans for this stupid cabin, which was also now becoming one of my favorite places to be.

But it would end. It had to.

Did it have to?

Common sense taking over, I shoved him back. Or maybe he shoved me back—gently.

It didn't matter so long as the kiss ended quickly.

Maybe not as quickly as it should've.

"We shouldn't," I gasped, trying to be quiet. It was only us in the room though, not another sound other than the heat kicking on.

"Did I make a mistake?"

"No. Don't worry; you didn't make another mistake," I said.

This one was all on me.

It was all on me and yet …

Aaron pulled back as he looked down at me. "Another …"

My chest heaved forward, back arching, as if I could make it the rest of the way back to his mouth.

I wasn't ready to let go yet.

Aaron's brow creased with confusion.

"Poppy …" He said my name. A little strong. A little surer.

He didn't call me homemaker or the bane of his existence. Not even teasingly, like the way he whispered the name Snow Angel

—angel coming out like his last breath escaping his lungs, breathless for me.

"Poppy."

Were my lips that memorable? They couldn't be. They were just lips. Pink and a little chapped from being outside in the cold.

I couldn't help it. I reached to touch them. Aaron watched me closely as I ran my fingertips along the bottom. They were damp and swollen compared to before.

Before Aaron kissed me.

And I didn't want to let go.

Dropping my hands, I slid them up Aaron's arms. They felt amazing. He felt amazing. I didn't know if they were so toned because he had been helping me work and carry things all week or if they always had been and I was noticing because I was finally touching him, feeling the smooth blond hair over his forearms and higher, around the curve of his biceps.

When I traced up the side of his shoulder, Aaron was still staring at me. Waiting.

Honestly, so was I.

You know what? Maybe he was right. Professionalism? I really couldn't see its virtues. I could barely see my own.

My hand cupped the back of his neck, and suddenly, there was no longer any hesitation. His mouth was back on mine. I hauled him as close as I could get him.

Where I was timid, Aaron didn't hesitate. My hands glided over his neck and all through his hair, messing up any sort of effort that he'd put into it. He shifted himself further toward me, moving the couch that didn't creak. It was good stuff, durable yet classy. I'd chosen it for that reason. I hadn't chosen it for this, but everything was multiuse in the cabin.

I thought my nervous system might overload from all the sensations I was feeling right now. His hips were heavy against mine, and his chest was pressed flat on me. When I leaned my chin forward for a little more, a sound emanated from the back of his throat—a moan that rattled my bones—as he deepened the kiss.

I had never heard Aaron Hayes like this. Not in his laughter. Not in his glares. Not in his anger.

This was pure want and pent-up desire.

I'd never wanted anything more. At least, not that I could think of when he was holding me, kissing me.

The only thing I could think of was, *Please don't ever let this be over.*

There was no space between us to spare for any other worry or anxiety that usually coursed through my head.

Aaron moved with a peck at the corner of my lips until he was peppering my jaw with tiny, wet kisses. His mouth trailed over my jaw and under my ear, continuing what he'd teased at before. I gasped, and his hands slipped to my hips, pulling mine against his.

"You look so good in my shirt," he murmured huskily and almost a little mischievously.

For a second, he almost sounded like the Aaron I'd once overheard with his friends. Only he was older now, and I couldn't help but think that maybe I liked Aaron better now than the one I'd held like a tightly kept secret in the corner of my mind. I liked his messiness he used to hide behind the golden boy persona. I liked the gruffness, surrounded by edges so sharp that I sometimes questioned whether I'd cut myself if I got too close.

All of him.

I cried out against his mouth from how much I suddenly wanted. Heat grew under the thick knit blanket that was tangled over us, making everything even hotter until I was sure I was about to break into a sweat from our feverish touches.

"Shh," Aaron warned me, breathless. "God, why do you have to be so sexy?"

I had never been called sexy before in my life. Not ever. The idea of it made me bold.

I slid my hand up his shirt, feeling his muscles contract. I could feel the scars and puckered skin I had seen from a distance before. Aaron's hands held me tight, gripping me against him. He pulled away again for air and came right back, as if he needed me to breathe as much as I felt like I needed him right now.

For so long, I'd been alone. Going from project to project. Working and combating problems, like mold or unruly clients. But now, like that night years ago, on top of a pile of coats, when I'd first kissed the boy that I convinced myself I was madly in love with at the age of fifteen, I never felt less alone.

But he hadn't known that. He still didn't know.

Something in my chest yanked hard, and it wasn't from the lack of air.

When we pulled away the next time, my nose grazed his. Our eyes flickered toward each other's and then back down to our damp, swollen lips. Mine parted, but not to kiss or quietly beg him for more.

Should I tell him?

I swallowed. What was the point? This was just a kiss. This was just a little more than a kiss. But that was all. That was all it could ever be. Right?

He was still going to leave. I was still going to be done with this project and—

Aaron's hands loosened from around my waist, sliding over my hips until he released me altogether.

Our breaths were deeper as I stared at him. He stared back at me, though the room seemed even darker than before. It was kind of perfect. The room. The scent of gingerbread. Him.

Aaron's eyes started to close. I couldn't tell if he forced them to or if they were simply too heavy to remain open any longer.

"You're pretty good with them too, you know," I whispered.

His eyes opened again, blinking a few times until he seemed sure that I'd said anything at all. "Huh?"

"The kids," I clarified softly. "I think you're good with them whether you realize it. I think you could be a pretty amazing uncle. You're … you're doing great. You're a good man."

And it was quiet again.

"Good night, Poppy."

My chest was still heaving as I nodded repeatedly.

"Good night, Aaron," I whispered.

eighteen

. . .

Poppy

IT COULDN'T HAPPEN AGAIN.

I shouldn't want it to happen again.

That kiss haunted me through the night until I couldn't keep my eyes open. I fell asleep, and then I still imagined it in my dreams. The feeling of his hands gripping my hips tight, as if he was afraid of me getting away. The scrape of his tongue against my bottom lip.

When I got up in the morning, it was the first thing I thought of, bringing my fingers back up to hover over my mouth as if I could still feel what had happened last night there.

Aaron was already awake. When I looked out the back windows, he was outside with Oz, leaving me time to get the couch back in order and get dressed for the day in another pair of jeans and a loose sweater.

I shook my hair out in the mirror before loosely braiding it back. There. It wasn't great, but when had I ever put my most fashionable self forward since the first day I'd arrived anyway? At least now, I was presentable when the final load of furniture arrived, which I still had to get the cabin ready for, double-checking that the rooms were cleared and the spaces I'd planned for each piece were marked for easy delivery.

Everything moved easily in the morning. Aaron came back in. The kids were packed up and getting ready to go.

The thing that wasn't easy? Aaron was avoiding me.

We'd kissed last night.

The man who had become one of my biggest challenges ever, and I'd kissed him. My heart still hammered in my chest every time I thought about it. He, on the other hand, couldn't look any more unruffled.

The kids were eating dry cereal when he passed me again.

"Good morning."

"Huh?" He glanced at me as if he'd forgotten I was standing there. "Morning."

A honk sounded outside.

"Mom's here!" Gavin screeched.

Both of them gathered up their stuff before Aaron ushered them toward the mudroom for their boots, which, at some point, he must've gone back out to unlace so neither of them struggled to pull them back on.

I followed Aaron outside, the early morning sunlight casting a golden glow on everything it touched. The air was crisp and cold, sending a shiver up the back of my neck.

Aaron was busy loading the kids' bags into the car, his movements smooth and efficient. I stood awkwardly by the side, unsure of what to say or do. Part of me wanted to bring up the kiss, acknowledge it and maybe even talk about it. But another part of me hesitated, afraid of what his reaction might be.

He didn't want to talk about it. Or look at me.

I caught Aaron as he walked by me. "Aaron—"

Just as I was about to open my mouth, Aaron straightened up and turned to face me. His eyes held a mixture of emotions that I couldn't quite decipher. There was something like regret, but also a hint of longing.

He glanced over his shoulder, raising his eyebrows. Nothing passed between us. As if nothing had happened.

Did it happen?

Of course it did.

Yet I shook my head as I watched the kids raced toward a large SUV.

Sarah had gotten out of the front seat, looking over the place now in the sunny daylight that hadn't been here yesterday. "Wow. This place has come a long way, hasn't it?" Sarah looked around her, eyes wide in awe. Her eyes then landed on her little girl, leaning into her side. "You look tired."

"Gavin stole the covers."

"I did not," argued Gavin, standing on the car's footrail, handing off the handle inside. "Ozzy did."

"Ozzy?" Sarah asked.

"The dog!"

"Oh. I see. Well, we can nap later when we get home. Did you two have a good time?" Sarah asked, likely not expecting an answer from her kids. Certainly not the one that came from her youngest.

"We love Uncle Aaron!"

His sister's eyebrows rose in clear shock. She glanced between her brother and her child again, as if making sure they were talking about the same guy.

"You do?"

"We made gingerbread houses and went out in the snow. I never got to go out in the snow before since you said the snow was dirty," Gavin muttered.

"Well, on the street, it is. That's why it gets all gray." Sarah tried to explain the slush of the city's winter weather.

Liana shrugged, making her way to the other side of the SUV to get inside. "Poppy was cool."

"Ozzy and I made snow angels out there. We didn't go past the trees since that's where Uncle Aaron said he couldn't see us. I followed the rules," Gavin went on, relaying the events of the past twenty-four hours. "Then, at night, we watched Christmas movies and decorated the tree. I made an ornament out of a cookie that

Miss Poppy said wasn't really a cookie, so I couldn't eat it, but it was awesome."

"Wow," responded Sarah. "Sounds like you had a good time."

It was only then that Sarah seemed to notice me standing there. "Miss Poppy, I presume?"

"That's me."

She extended her hand. "It's good to finally meet you. I wanted to go over your plans for finishing the renovation and design of the house for the holiday. But as you can see, nothing in this family often goes to plan. This past month has been so busy—"

"It's all right. The renovation was off track, but everything is moving on schedule now." I looked back at the house, my eyes catching on Aaron, who hugged his nephew before shutting the back passenger door. He shoved his hands in his pockets, kicking gently at the snow stuck to his boots. "Things are going a lot better than I could've expected actually."

Sarah followed my line of sight before cocking her head at me. She certainly couldn't tell what I was thinking or what had happened between us, surely. "Glad to hear it. We appreciate all the hard work you've been putting into this project."

I smiled, grateful for her understanding. "It's been a pleasure working on your family's home. I think the final result will be worth all the effort."

Aaron approached us, a faint smile on his lips as he joined the conversation. "I have to agree with Poppy. The house is shaping up."

Sarah clapped her hands together. "Well then, let's head back home and let you two get back to work. The kids are exhausted from all the fun they had with Uncle Aaron," Sarah teased her brother.

Before she got back into the car, Sarah met my eyes one more time, giving a small wave.

Thank you, Sarah mouthed toward me.

I shook my head, hoping it conveyed what I wanted it to. It wasn't me. It really was him. Mostly.

Sarah looped an arm around her brother. Aaron tried to escape before giving in. He gently hugged her back.

There was a tension between us now, unspoken words hanging in the air. But he only watched as his sister get in the car, start the engine and pull out of the driveway. It was just the two of us again.

It took the rest of the day before I could be somewhat content with the furniture. It was all in the house. At last. I couldn't believe that I was so close to the end. But now, the sun was starting to set, and I had a feeling that I shouldn't linger for another night.

Aaron hadn't spoken to me beyond the normal pleasantries all day or when he occasionally helped me shift bigger items in each of the rooms to get them to the right spot. He didn't bring up anything about last night, and I was starting to think that I had dreamed up the entire thing.

Clearing my throat, I moved toward the kitchen, where Aaron was unloading groceries.

Actual groceries. Beside the snacks and leftovers we accumulated from eating takeout, I had never seen him go to the store for real ingredients until now.

"Everything is good to go for now," I said. He shut the freezer door at my words. "I guess I should head out for the night."

"Yeah. You probably want to get back," he said. He didn't look at me.

"Okay. I'll be back ..." Tomorrow. I would be back tomorrow, just like I was every other day.

Again, he dipped his head. I repeated the motion.

It wasn't until I put on my coat and was halfway out the door that Aaron's eyes flared. It took until I got to my car for him to come the rest of the way after me. "Hey, wait up a second."

I paused, halfway into the driver's seat. His lips parted as if to say something, and I waited for some sort of explanation. Something.

He leaned into the side of my car as I looked up at him. If he kept leaning in, then he'd maybe kiss me again. We were at the perfect angle, and his lips fit so perfectly against mine—

He tapped the edge of the door. "Call me. Let me know when you get home."

I blinked, freezing in place at the gentle request. It still wasn't what I had expected. "Oh, okay. Sure."

With another nod, I shut the door. He took a step back. I twisted my key in the ignition and waited for the air to warm a step above a tundra.

We had spent the last two days together, but it almost felt like we were right back to where we'd been when I first came to the cabin weeks ago. Now, there was something between us.

A spark. A fizzle.

And it was being stomped out.

It was probably for the best. I mean, like I'd told Hannah, one word from him, and I would be out of here. The small chance I had at the promotion would be wiped away. I could probably even be fired. I was so stupid.

It was good he was acting like I was nothing to him, just like before.

It had to be *professional.*

Again.

My heart leaped into my chest at a small knock on my car window.

I rolled it down. "Aaron?"

"Snow Angel."

He had to stop calling me that. When he did, it felt like a thousand butterflies started to flutter in the pit of my stomach.

"Hey. I, um …" He took a deep breath, though it didn't seem to settle him in the slightest. "There's a holiday party coming up.

A friend is hosting it. I know you're busy, but do you want to go to the party? Get into the spirit or whatever?"

"A friend?"

"The one who dropped off Oz." He waited. For me. "Wanna go? Think of it as a … thank-you." Even if he couldn't say *thank you* outright.

"Okay. Sure."

"Good." He swallowed as he turned back around and walked away from me again. "Good."

nineteen

. . .

Poppy

AT THE SOUND of the doorbell, I sped down the steps to the front door in my robe. No other time was I ever running late, except, for some reason, when it came to Aaron Hayes. Luckily, Simon didn't beat me there; in fact, he had been oddly quiet so far this evening.

Catching my breath, I threw the front door open, startling Aaron on the other side. I opened my mouth, words dying on my lips.

He raised his eyebrows, but his eyebrows weren't what I was looking at.

He'd shaved. His jawline was visible and much more angular than I remembered.

"Are you all right?" he asked.

"Yes! Of course. Give me one minute, and I'll be ready," I said, out of breath.

Aaron looked me up and down. "Nice duckies."

I glanced back down at my old robe. It was soft and fluffy, but I'd also had it for the past decade, if not longer. Feeling my face heat, I swiftly turned back up the stairs to finish getting ready. My dress was already laid out on the bed. Slipping it over my head, I checked my phone one more time, trying to see if Hannah had called me back yet.

Ever since I'd agreed to go to this party, I wondered if it was a huge mistake. It probably was. This wasn't usual. Then again, nothing of this project had been.

My phone shook in my hand, but it wasn't Hannah.

I trust my decisions.

I used to find the affirmation notifications on my phone to be my favorite part of the day. Now, I was pretty sure they were listening to me.

Setting my phone aside, I turned back to my mirror, fixing the way my dress lay before reaching for the small red jingle bell earrings I'd set out. With little plaid ribbons above each one, the bells even jingled, though it wasn't the same ring my phone would make if Hannah managed to call me back.

Hannah had definitely been keeping something to herself lately. We were both busy. I was consumed by the cabin, and I'd heard that there had been an uptick in Home Haven Hotline calls since the Holiday line had been promoted.

I would have to find time to talk to her soon and get to the bottom of whatever was going on. Because Hannah always said she was okay, whether or not she was. She smiled, even when she was raging.

But I had never seen Hannah quiet.

One thing was for sure: I knew what Hannah would tell me anyway if she did call back.

Live! she'd very likely scream at me. *Look right at that man in front of you, who looks at you like you're the most brilliant thing since sliced bread, and take him to bed! Live and forget that lowlife, balding assbag who hasn't reached out to you in years and is probably having horrible sex with that chick from four counties over. Do it for all of us, Pops!*

Or something like that, I'd imagine.

Walking down the stairs, I could already hear a new conversation, along with the jingle of my holiday earrings. I fixed the back of one of the earrings that hadn't quite clipped. Once I got it, I let it hang with the tiny trill it made.

"It's nice to meet you, Aaron. Officially, that is." Simon chuckled.

"Yes," my mother agreed. "We've heard enough about you."

I cringed, and from what I could see, so did Aaron.

"I was going through a few things. I acted a bit childish."

I scoff-laughed, and it echoed down the steps.

Aaron's eyes caught on me, scanning over my face and down to my simple flat shoes with the bows.

"What?" I asked. "Am I overdressed?"

Aaron shook his head quickly. "No. Sorry." He coughed.

"All right there, Aaron?" my well-meaning yet socially awkward stepfather asked, reaching out a hand as if he was more than willing to pat him straight on the back.

Aaron put out a hand to stop him before he could manage it. He turned back to me. "You look great. I was telling your parents what an ass I'd been, but they'd already heard all about that."

Heat rose to my cheeks.

"Honestly, for a while there, messing with Poppy was a highlight of my day. Though, I admit, I could've been a bit more *professional* about it," Aaron said, using my word.

At this rate, the word would have no meaning. There was less and less intention behind it every time one of us said it, broken down into letters and sounds, as if we were tramping all over it.

"And not ruined most of my orders," I added, as if a joke, though it came out much more serious than intended.

"Not my best choice," he agreed.

"Are you doing better now?" Mom cut in. "My daughter hasn't come home with nearly as many complaints as of late. Then again, she hasn't been coming back home most nights it seems with your cabin keeping her busy."

"Mom," I whispered, though was certain she heard me.

"That's good to hear," Aaron said, unconcerned at the subtle insinuation.

"Family is so important. It's nice that you were able to come back to the area," my mother went on.

"Ah, yeah. My sister has been making sure to check in," Aaron said. "It's been good to have the company at the house, whether or not I thought so before. Poppy's been a real … great friend. I'll be sure to repay her for the kindness that she has shown me, even when I haven't been the most gracious host to her."

"That's very nice of her," said my mother, albeit a little stiff, not expecting such an answer.

"The holidays can certainly be lonely. This was around the time Marylin and I met." Simon smiled, reaching to take Mom's hand.

She rubbed the back of his hand with a smile at him.

"It's game night, you know," said Simon. "If you don't have to leave for your party, I could break out the Scrabble for a round."

My mouth dropped open before I could stop it.

Aaron somehow beat me to find words. "We could—"

Reaching for the edge of his jacket, I attempted to pull Aaron back to the front door for a hasty exit. "We're going so we aren't late to Aaron's friend's party that he planned specifically for tonight. Aaron can't miss it."

"Too bad," said Simon. "Thought I'd offer. Maybe another time."

Aaron paused before he nodded, though I had a feeling we both knew that wasn't true. Soon, I'd be done with my project, and we'd go our separate ways.

Since when wasn't that the expectation?

Then again, when had the professional expectation included accompanying the client to a holiday party on your night off?

"I appreciate the invite," Aaron replied.

I slipped on my long wool coat that I never got to wear on the job, for fear that I would get it dirty.

Mom hugged me tight. "Have a wonderful holiday party,

sweetheart," she said before letting her voice drop lower. "You call if you need anything."

"I'll be good. Love you, Mom," I said into her shoulder before she finally released me. I turned to Aaron with a nod toward the door. "Let's go."

He looked at me once and then again, doing a double take at the look I gave him by the time we got to the truck. He opened the door and waited for me to get in. I was still looking at him with a combination of suspicion and concern when he buckled himself in and started the car. Warm air immediately started to blow out of the vents.

"What?" he asked me, glancing up at the rearview as if he thought he had something on his face.

"Nothing," I said with a shrug. "I was just wondering, since when do you have manners?"

"I'm not an asshole all the time."

"Just to me?" I asked.

"You're a special case. Your parents were nice."

"Since when was I not nice to you?"

"Not the same," Aaron said, glancing at me again. He chuckled, and for a moment, the tension between us dissipated. "I can't help it if you make it so easy."

I raised my eyebrows. "Oh, is that so?"

His eyes glanced down to my lips, painted a glossy red.

My breath hitched, wondering if he was thinking about the same thing I was—the last time we had sat this close to one another. Our lips touching, fitting so perfectly against each other's. So soft and smooth like—like—

"Can't decide if I like the duck robe or this better."

"Right." I shook myself out of it. I forced a laugh. I reached for the dial on the radio, turning the volume up before I looked down at the gearshift, still in park. "Ready to go?"

twenty

. . .

Aaron

"OH, LOOK, IT'S THE LOVEBIRDS!" Barrett swung open the front door toward us.

I was about to throw a swing at my best friend. If not for the comment, then for the ridiculous oversize Christmas sweater he had on with a huge reindeer with light-up antlers.

Poppy stepped inside the house without a word, slipping her coat off to hang off the edge of an armchair that had a pile of others.

"What the hell, man?" I nudged Barrett in the shoulder.

He chuckled, already red in the face, likely from too many cups of holiday punch. "I thought it was funny."

Maybe it would've been a few weeks ago. But this past week … everything felt … different.

I couldn't even pinpoint what kind of different. Just different. And it was no wonder.

I'd kissed Poppy Owens.

I kissed the homemaker. I kissed the interior designer. I kissed Snow Angel, who still made the corner of my mouth twitch like I wanted to smile for some stupid reason.

I kissed Poppy Owens, and the moment I did, I felt like I'd

been transported back to ten years ago, when everything was okay and right and felt good.

No, that wasn't right.

It felt *fucking amazing.*

I'd kissed her.

Now, after days of forcing myself to maintain my distance — knowing if we got too close, I would be ready to bend her over the counter and kiss the hell out of her again— my heart hammered in my chest in a way it hadn't since I had been overseas.

Hours ago, I'd almost considered backing out on this whole thing. What was I thinking, inviting her along to Barrett's party? She wouldn't have been surprised if I'd canceled. No one would've been. Not even her parents, who had looked at me like they couldn't quite figure out my problem.

Consider that a universal problem.

But now, I couldn't help myself. I couldn't take my eyes off Poppy to look at the over-the-top holiday lights or decorations Barrett's mother must've helped him put up at his new house, which looked a little on the run-down side.

I watched as Poppy wrapped her arms around Barrett in a hug. He nearly took her feet right off the floor.

"Thanks for inviting us. Or Aaron. Thanks for letting me invite myself, basically." She smiled good-naturedly.

"Don't even start with that." Barrett pulled back to look between us again. "I figure it was all you that got this guy here tonight."

"He invited me," she said honestly.

"You're kidding."

She shook her head.

Barrett beamed at me, flashing his one chipped tooth that he never got fixed after whacking his face off the rappel section of our training course either the second or third year. "You big softy, coming to my party."

I stuck my hands in my pockets. "Just wanted to make sure I saw your ugly mug before I got out of this place once and for all."

"I'll take it." He waved a hand around his new old house. "Food is in the kitchen. Everyone's hanging out. I think we have some games around here somewhere. You like the place?"

"It looks great."

"Thanks. Figured it was time to set down some roots."

"I thought you always said you'd go west," I said, partially joking.

He shrugged. "Things change. I need to tell you all about my plans."

"You have plans now?"

"Tons." Barrett paused before he hit me on the back. He walked backward, away from us and toward the kitchen. "We'll talk in a minute. I need to go check on a few things. Be right back. Get some food!"

For some reason, it still astounded me how well Barrett exuded the kind of charismatic energy I could never seem to understand, let alone emulate. Joyful. Happy.

Someone you want to be around.

Somehow, he always managed to pull himself together. He was the one of us to put on the brave face when times got tough in our trio, even when he looked insane doing so. All because, as he'd told us, "I refuse to go out any other way."

It seems he'd meant it. Even back in the small town he had grown up in.

He still laughed loud enough that you could probably hear him a town over and threw parties like he had done back on base. With the minimum supplies we'd had, he'd stock up on snack crackers and booze whenever he could, saving them for a night when we looked like we could use a pick-me-up.

Even when we were back home, Barrett was always there, so we didn't lose touch. He was always the happy one. For some reason, I'd forgotten about that.

Barrett was constant. He was consistent. He was the one who had taken care of us all and never let any of us down.

I looked around the small yet already-homey house that Barrett's mother must've decorated, if I had to guess.

Barrett was an only child and close to the woman who'd raised him. His mom had always invited me over for dinner during high school and it was there that I got a mom again too, for a short time. That woman acted like I was a genius for passing my classes and being a decent friend. Even if she wasn't too pleased with me when her son enlisted with me.

Poppy nudged me. "You all right?"

"Thanks for coming with me tonight," I mumbled quietly.

She smiled softly. "Of course. I wanted to be here with you. *Here*, I mean. I can never pass up a good holiday party. But you made me worry when you told me to prepare myself to meet Barrett. He's nice."

"Because he's too nice," I said. "All the time."

"Must be so foreign and frightening to you."

"You have no idea."

"I feel like he and my friend Hannah would get along," she said.

"I'll have to meet her sometime."

Poppy barked a laugh, which frightened me more than anything.

"What?" I asked.

Pressing her poppy-red lips together, which I kept staring at, she shook her head. "Nothing. Just envisioning it. I'm going to go and get something to drink," she said. "I think I see some kind of fruity punch. Would you like anything?"

"I'm good."

"I'll be back in a minute."

After she walked off, I couldn't help but wander off after her.

I watched as she scooped a cupful of whatever everyone was drinking, which looked like cranberries. Everyone continued their conversations around us. Some people were draped over the couch or sitting at the table, surrounded by snacks, grazing.

"Aaron." Barrett's mom turned the corner, immediately waving a hand at me. She greeted me with a wide smile, similar to her son's, though that was where the resemblance ended. "It's wonderful to see you."

"It's good to see you too, Ms. Barrett." I accepted the hug she wrapped me in. I didn't remember her being so short.

"Barrett mentioned that you might be coming." She let go to take a better look at me.

I ran a hand through my hair, glad I'd shaved.

"I hoped so, but I wasn't sure. I heard that you were in an accident?"

I almost wanted to deny it for some reason. Though it wouldn't have mattered. It was clear from the dip of her head to the side that Ms. Barrett saw right through me.

"Yeah, I was. Better now though. Slowly getting myself back in working order."

"I was so worried for you. And you have no idea how sorry I am about your friend," she said softly. "Barrett might put on a brave face, but … he hasn't been the same since he came back with all of you boys."

Barrett was leaning back on his heels across the room, laughing with someone as he downed another cup of punch.

"Seems to be doing well."

"He keeps himself busy. Always has. I know I shouldn't worry so much anymore, but like I said, you all will always be boys in my mind, running off into life, guns blazing, literally." Her voice drifted off. "I'm sure he's told you he's leaving the military?"

"He mentioned it," I confirmed. "He said nothing was set in stone."

"He apparently put in his leave quite some time ago, not long after he came to visit you in the hospital. I mean, he says he has a plan with this house and land he purchased out here. See if you can squeeze out any more details for me. He hasn't been telling his mother much of anything these days, though I want to pry, I won't lie. I'm happy he's safe."

"Absolutely, Ms. Barrett."

"I want to see you all happy," she said, squeezing my wrist. "And please, you know better, call me Sheryl. And feel free to come by to the old house anytime you need. Don't let me get lonely now that you boys are back and so close. Stop in for whatever. If you need a warm meal or just some company. I'm still a mom. I've always thought of you as one of my own since you started spending time with my Barrett in school."

"I appreciate it."

Catching me before I moved away, Ms. Barrett cleared her throat. "Also, I wanted to say, your grandmother would've been proud of all you've accomplished."

I blinked.

"She would've," she said once more. "Look at you—turning into a kind, strong man. It's all a mother could ever want."

And yet I still didn't know if it was what my mother and father would've wanted for me, let alone my grandmother, who I was pretty sure hadn't even recognized me by the time she left us.

"Thank you, Ms. Barrett."

"Sheryl."

"Sheryl," I said before she turned and headed off to another person she'd caught coming in the front door that I didn't recognize.

I didn't recognize most of the people here, save for Barrett, Poppy, and—

My head swung back to face the guy coming toward me with his arms wide, looking as shocked as I was, recognition flaring across his face before it did my own.

"Aaron Hayes?"

"Isaac?"

"Yeah." The man in front of me smiled, wearing a tight maroon sweater. Still, he looked just like the guy I'd played football with since I had been in elementary school until I left. He was holding two cans of soda from the bucket in the kitchen. "You want one? My wife didn't want what I'd grabbed."

"Oh, sure." I took one, popping the tab. "How are you?"

"Good. Real good. I just got married to Fiona a year ago. She's Barrett's cousin. We live a few hours west but drove in for the weekend. Fiona has also been looking at some houses this way for a better school system—so she says. We both miss family. Glad I did come in for the party now too. Small world."

It really was.

"Been a long time."

"It has been," I agreed.

"You know Barrett?" he asked before shaking his head. "Of course you do. Army brothers. That's right. I hadn't put the details together until now, when he mentioned you. Man, I never thought you'd go into the Army though. Weren't you up for some kind of award or something in English? You put my essays to shame. I'm pretty sure that's why the teacher graded the rest of us so harshly."

"Nope. Military ended up being the best choice I made."

"That's awesome," Isaac said. "How have you been? I didn't even ask."

"Just great," I said.

"It's crazy, too, that you're here with Poppy Owens," Isaac said.

I twisted to look over my shoulder, noticing Poppy was still in the same spot, though now, she was talking strictly with Barrett by the fireplace. Her hair was tucked behind one ear, showing off one of her obnoxious jingle bell earrings that trilled with every movement she made.

"You know Poppy?"

Isaac cocked his head to the side. "Of course I do. We went to school together," he said. "Don't you remember?"

"I ..."

"You were only there for a few years though, I know. Yeah, Poppy was in school with us all through middle school and those first two years of high school before you transferred out," said Isaac, still watching as I fought to figure out what he was talking about. "I can't believe you don't remember that."

"I think I do. Maybe."

"She had this huge crush on you sophomore year. Honestly, I feel kind of shitty about it all, looking back to when word got out. Kinda tortured her a bit." Isaac sighed as he started to remember more. "We sucked."

Poppy had a crush. On me?

I cycled back through my memories, trying to place her. Poppy never told me anything about that.

She never said—

"Right," I said. "Sorry, took me a second."

"No problem, man. It's good to see you. Maybe if you stick around the area, we can catch up sometime?"

"Sounds … good."

I turned back and stared at Poppy again. This time, it didn't take long before she glanced back toward me, eyes narrowing while Barrett was still talking. She was too polite to turn her attention fully away from him. She went back to the conversation while I continued to stare.

Poppy. Poppy Owens.

I'd kissed Poppy Owens.

I kissed Poppy Owens.

And it wasn't the first time.

Something seized in my chest as everything came back to me. I remembered our kiss—comfortable and soft. Like when I was breathing. How easily we'd come together when nothing else had felt as good in my entire life. And how I hadn't felt that for the first time the other night.

It all made sense now. How it'd felt like that last piece of home that I'd thought I lost long ago.

Because Poppy was the last piece of home I'd had before I moved out of the city. That night at the party, I barely remembered anything. But I remembered that kiss. I remembered her and the kindness she showed me. I thought maybe, I dreamed it all, because it felt a little too good.

And … she hadn't said anything.

Why had she not said anything?

I started to walk toward Poppy, unable to take my eyes off her. Until a much broader, less appealing form stood in my way. I stopped before I ran face-first into a knitted reindeer.

"Barrett"—I leaned around his shoulder—"I need you to move."

"Hold up a second." He put up a hand.

I attempted to get around his hand, though I didn't know exactly why. What did I plan to do when I got to Poppy? Confront her? Ask her why the hell she didn't tell me that she knew me?

"I plan on opening a kennel."

My eyes snapped back to Barrett.

He raised a golden brow. Just one. "You didn't hear a word I said to you, did you?"

I sighed, and my shoulders slumped. "No. I'm sorry. What did you say?"

"I wanted to let you know that I put in my final letter to the Army. I'm out. Officially this time," he said.

"Wow."

"I'd been turning things around in my head for a while now, but after everything that happened and seeing maybe that you'll be around, I'm moving forward with those plans."

"And what are they?"

"I bought the farmhouse here to fix up. And once the weather warms up, a kennel is going to be built on the property," he said.

"For dogs?"

"Yeah, of sorts," he explained. "Retired K9s specifically, but we'll see how long that lasts. I didn't get this land out here for no reason. It'll be a rescue."

"That's—" I usually joked at his expense whenever I got the chance, but now, I watched the calmness settle over my friend's otherwise tired expression. "I'm happy for you."

"Thanks. Like I said, I don't know what your plans are—"

"I'm"—I didn't know either—"sticking to the plan."

"Well, if that plan doesn't work out, know that I'll still be here. How's Oz doing, by the way? I figured when I hadn't heard anything …"

"Good. We're doing good."

Barrett glanced over his shoulder toward the living room, where Poppy was talking to another woman with curly hair pinned back on either side of her face. "It looks like you are. I'm happy for you too, Hayes. You deserve this."

"What?"

"Peace."

I shook my head.

"You do," he said. "Hope you see that someday."

"Now, I know you drank too much punch."

"Eh. Think whatever want. She seems like she likes you, though." Barrett shrugged. "Who knows why? But I wouldn't mess around if you want to do anything about it."

I watched her across the room, sipping her drink and making small talk. The picture of ease. So perfectly put together.

Oh, I was going to do something all right.

twenty-one

. . .

Poppy

"ARE YOU A FRIEND OF BARRETT'S?" the woman who had complimented my earrings asked me.

We stood next to the tree and window, where we could see out into the piles of snow, frozen from the cold. She had tight, bouncy curls and soft pink lipstick that made her skin look amazing.

"I'm Fiona, by the way."

"I'm Poppy," I told her. "One of Barrett's friends invited me to come with him."

"Oh, that's so nice."

"It is. I love a good holiday party. Usually, I'm busy working."

"What do you do for work?"

"I'm a designer."

"Fashion?" Her eyes widened.

Did my jingle bell earrings not say enough? "Home and interior. I work for Home Haven," I corrected.

Fiona gasped. "You're kidding!"

I shook my head.

"I love Home Haven! I have followed their social media for ages. Such stunning work, and now, they have a website and everything."

"They do," I said. "It's really exciting how it's all expanding."

"I can imagine. You must feel so lucky to be a part of it," she said.

"I love my job," I agreed.

"All the opportunities around here in the city are another reason I want to move back to the area. My husband, Isaac, is from near here, and I just love it."

"Your husband?"

Fiona motioned across the room toward a man with gelled hair that stuck up near the front. "He's right over there. Maybe you can convince him how great this area is, though I think I'm already wearing him down. His parents are still around, too, which helps. Plus, I mean, Barrett and my aunt are here, too, and it would be nice to see them more."

I narrowed my eyes at the man she'd pointed to across the room. He looked oddly familiar.

"Where in the city is he from?"

"Isaac?" Fiona thought for a second. "I'd have to ask again. I'm not good with all the little neighborhoods. But I know that he went to Oak ..."

"Oak Bridge?" I filled in.

Immediately, Fiona nodded. "Yes, that's it. Oh my goodness, did you go there too? Now, we'll have to steal him away and see if you remember each other. I imagine, in the city, it's a big school."

It was, but I was starting to remember him already—and not because Isaac had been someone exactly memorable to me, but the person he'd hung out with on sports teams and in the hallways had been. He spent enough time with Aaron that I was certain that he'd remember him.

"Enough about him though." Fiona laughed. "I'm sure he'll come over at some point. Are you ... on anything exciting now?"

"Huh?" I'd missed part of what she said.

"For Home Haven," she prompted. "Are you working on anything new and exciting right now?"

"Oh, yes," I said. "The friend who invited me here actually—a friend of Barrett's—he has a small home, more like a cabin, not too far from here. It was expanded. I've been working on finishing the renovations there and making sure that it's perfect for a family holiday coming up."

"That's amazing. Can't wait to see the final pictures."

Neither could I, and that reminded me how soon the photographer would be coming to take them for the magazine.

Fiona's brow creased as she looked to where Aaron was quickly approaching. "It looks like he's more than just a friend of Barrett's."

Aaron was coming toward me and only me, not looking at anyone who paid him any attention.

"Looks like a conversation I want to overhear but should probably go. I'll see you around, hopefully. I'll be looking for your work on Home Haven's socials!" Fiona said. "Happy holidays!"

"Happy holidays," I responded, unable to look away from Aaron. He stood directly in front of me now, brows low and eyes hard. "Aaron, are you all right?"

He grabbed my hand. I looked down at it. I wasn't sure if he'd ever grabbed my hand. Ever.

"Let's go."

"What?" I asked, confused. "We just got here."

"I'm ready to go."

I didn't want to be rude. I looked around for Barrett, who must've been talking to Aaron before he stormed over here.

Barrett raised a hand in a wave. I waved back as Aaron gathered our coats from the chair we left them on, but I hadn't managed to shout out a thank-you.

"Aaron, did something happen?" I asked.

He didn't answer.

"That was so rude. You can't storm out of a party a friend invited you to."

Though clearly, he had and didn't seem to care. He barely even looked at me as walked all the way to the truck. He climbed into the driver's side and turned the key. It rumbled to life.

"Buckle up," Aaron instructed.

"Did Barrett say something? Are you not feeling well? I don't understand here—"

I stopped myself from continuing. Aaron wasn't going to respond. I was baffled, yet unable to figure out what else to say when he was not going to talk. His jaw was hard, though his hands remained in control on the wheel, though he did start driving until I clicked my seat belt into place.

The rest of the ride home was silent. Not even the radio was loud enough to breach the uneasy tension that made the space feel uncomfortable and thick.

What had happened back there? Had Aaron not had a good talk with Barrett? Was he upset with me?

I mean, he still could be after the other day that we still hadn't talked about. The kiss.

Us.

Even if there was no us.

We were back in front of the cabin before I could let myself spiral down into a pit of puzzlement. Aaron turned off the truck and got out. After another minute, trying to stay calm, I followed.

Opening the door to the mudroom, Aaron kicked off his shoes and walked in without looking back at me. Tiny nails pattered toward the door, and I watched as Oz attempted to jump the best he could to greet Aaron.

"Chill out, Oz," Aaron mumbled, smoothing a hand over the dog before sending him away.

He still wasn't looking back at me. I froze there in the mudroom. Usually in here, I looked around to make sure everything was in its place, that this room was complete. Dark blue paint and wallpaper were perfectly aligned. I had nothing left to do with my design. But I wasn't focused on my work. My entire focus was on Aaron and the heavy pulse thudding in my chest.

Aaron continued to walk through the house. He slowly took

off his jacket as he went through the kitchen and into the living room with a sigh.

One step at a time, I walked in after him. I looked at the back of his head. He'd pulled himself together once and for all tonight. I had seen it happening slowly with clean clothing and consistent showers and making sure that he was eating while we worked to fill out his frame. But now, he was clean-shaven and crisp, rolling back his shoulders to stand tall.

I wasn't sure if I would've recognized the man as the same one standing exactly where we'd met a few weeks ago. But I knew Aaron now. I'd known him for over a decade. I knew the good he had in him. I knew the sound of his laughter. I knew his anger, and I knew what he looked like in tears.

But this kind of Aaron, pacing and quiet as he searched through his head for something—I was still unsure what—I didn't know. Not yet.

"I'm sorry," I said.

Aaron twisted around to face me. I stood behind the couch in the living room, dropping my purse on the cushion so I could wring my hands.

Now, he was the one who looked confused. "You're sorry?"

"Yes," I said.

"About what?"

I swallowed, gathering up some ounce of courage. I knew I had it. I just needed to find it somewhere in myself. "The other day, I shouldn't have even come to the house after you told me not to. I should have been more considerate and not pushed your boundaries, which led us into inappropriate behavior, and I truly apologize that this has made you uncomfortable."

He stared at me like he was looking at some sort of alien in front of him.

"You think this is about how I kissed you," he said.

Wasn't it? "Yes."

"Because I kissed you? That's why you think I'm acting like a crazy person right now who can't even string together a stupid sentence?"

This time, I didn't answer.

"I kissed you," Aaron said, leaning in closer to me. "I kissed *you*."

His lips were a breath away from my own.

"You did." I blinked rapidly, forcing myself to keep eye contact with him. "You didn't have to do that, and I'm sorry it happened."

"You're sorry?"

"Yes. I put you in a position where—"

"What if I wanted to?" he asked.

I stood still.

"Haven't thought about that, have you?"

I shook my head, still not quite understanding how we'd gotten here. One minute, we had been at the party, and now, even Oz had skittered away to a cozy spot near the fireplace and out of this strange exchange.

"No," I said. "You don't have to say anything or lie. I get it. You haven't cared about what I'm trying to do here. You haven't even wanted me here at all for that matter."

"Since when, Poppy?"

"It wasn't a mistake. I won't say that about it. The kiss. And I'm sorry. I know you don't even like me, especially not like that. So, I've been trying to keep my distance and be respectful and *professional*."

God, he was making me start to hate that word.

"Yet I've been failing," I admitted, putting a hand on my forehead. "Clearly."

"You really think that I don't like you? Care about you? Damn, Poppy." Aaron ran a hand through his short hair, which was starting to puff out on the sides.

"You're giving me whiplash here, Aaron. I don't—I don't know what you want me to say to make this better, and everything is almost over. Either let me do my job or …"

Or?

I didn't even know anymore.

I let my hands fall to my sides in defeat.

"You don't get it," said Aaron gruffly.

"Get what?"

He nodded. Once. Twice.

"Fine then. Here." He shrugged as if what he was going to say was simple. "For the past few weeks, you've been digging under my skin. Trying to find all my buttons. But then I started to watch you work, and I saw your passion for what you do, and I talked to you—"

"Whoa, don't sound so pleased about spending time with me."

He put up a hand to stop me. "I tried not to like you, Poppy, but sometimes, I can't help myself. It's like you're constantly sitting in the back of my brain. When I'm not thinking of anything else, I'm thinking of you. You're always there, in the corner of my mind. Your face. Your smile. The way you laugh before covering your mouth with your hands, like you think no one wants to see your teeth. I think about you all the time, whether you're standing right in front of me or late at night, when my mind won't turn off and I'm in bed. Then, I'm only with you."

I stared at him.

"So, when I found out tonight that this wasn't the first time we'd met, that we had known each other from over a decade ago, it dawned on me. That the girl with the hesitant laugh and concern always written on her face … and the lips that had tasted like strawberries that night I was at a party, wasted off my ass and cursing the world … it was you."

He knew.

"How did you—"

"Why didn't you say anything?"

I took a deep breath. "It was clear that you didn't remember. I couldn't think, what was the point to tell you? Especially after a while. I mean, I'm a different person than I was back then anyway. So are you."

"Even without knowing the reason, I wanted to be angry that you hadn't said something. Poppy Owens, the girl with the crush on me that I'd barely even met once until the night before I left," said Aaron. "But I'm not angry."

"You're not?"

Aaron slowly shook his head back and forth. "I was alone for most of the night, you know. My sister was supposed to be watching me, but I snuck out of the apartment. My parents had been in an accident a few nights before. They died, and my entire family was up in arms, trying to figure out what they were going to do about me. I couldn't stand being in that house anymore, so I left. I wanted to go to the party. So, I did. I went to the party and got a little drunk, and yet I still felt so damn awful that I crashed on a pile of coats in the guest room. Then, you walked in."

I looked at him.

"You came to the party with your friends who were always awful to you at school, and yet you were always smiling for some reason. I could never figure out what you could be smiling about. Whose life is so good that they're always happy, right?"

"I wasn't always happy."

"Then, why the fuck were you smiling?"

I shrugged. "Because I was always told to. 'Smile to make everyone else wonder why you're smiling,' Mom used to say. As if that would help me make more friends. Better friends. It didn't, but at the time, I was willing to try just about anything. So, I did."

"And was smiling and pretending to be happy easier?" he asked.

"Sometimes." Other times, it'd felt like my smile was slowly eating me away from the inside out.

"Yeah, I didn't have that advice."

"Clearly."

Aaron breathed a sharp laugh. "Yet, I'll admit your smile sure made me feel better. Especially that night at the party."

"It wasn't a big deal."

"It was though, Poppy. It was a big deal. You made that night bearable for me. You were the only one who stuck around, and years later, I didn't recognize you, and you didn't say anything."

I waited for it. I waited for him to finally get angry and kick me out.

But he didn't do that. Instead, he took a step forward. I took a step back until my back was flush against the bookcase.

"And when I figured it out, for some reason, there was only one thing I thought."

I swallowed, feeling the pressure from the lack of space between us. "What?"

"I regretted not kissing you again sooner."

He didn't pause now before he kissed me again.

It wasn't like our last kiss, hesitant and brushing enough that it could've been an accident. This kiss was deliberate. It was hot. It was us. I breathed and bent into him, unable to help myself. Neither could he. His hands felt as if they molded to my body, his mouth lavishing me.

I gasped, angling my chin back until my head leaned against a shelf and I was able to stare up at him.

"What?"

"Just making sure this isn't a body-snatchers situation," I said softly before shaking my head again. "We need to stop."

"Why?"

"Finding out—it doesn't change anything here, Aaron."

"It changes everything." He stood there in the silence, given the light snow falling outside could be heard if you listened close enough.

"You're being dramatic."

"I am?" he asked.

"Uh-huh," I said. "You might be the most dramatic man I've ever met in my entire life. Listen to me."

"I'm listening."

"We're still exactly where we are. Let's leave all this at that. We have all of, what? Five days left? We made it. Congratulations to us. Let's just be happy with what we managed here." I looked around at the nearly perfect home I managed create here. "We can pause. Then neither of us will have to worry about ruining any of this."

"Who says anything about ruining?" He pushed the shoulder of my dress down with a smirk. "I think that us together do the exact opposite of ruining."

I was transfixed by the way his lips curved. He took a gamble —or maybe it was already obvious what was going to happen between us by the way our chests touched and our eyes wandered to exactly what we wanted but were too afraid to say. He reached out to tilt my chin back down, aligning my lips with his. I didn't resist.

Aaron Hayes was holding me the way I'd always wanted for years, and I'd let him do it all night if he'd allow it. Just like this.

"I don't want to be alone anymore," he whispered. "I've realized I really suck at it."

"Then ..." I took a deep breath. The words were perched on the edge of my lips, ready to slip free, but hesitant.

Aaron reached up, running his thumb along my bottom lip, as if it would coax them out.

"Then, don't be," I whispered. "You don't have to be alone."

Not anymore, I corrected. *Not for now.*

The words made his breath go uneven, which was good because I wasn't feeling so steady myself. Even less so when he was kissing me.

I felt the power of it, my lips opening in a shallow gasp. Aaron took the moment to sweep in, tasting me, claiming and teasing all at once.

I arched. I didn't want any space between us other than the fabric of our clothes, which felt thick and overbearing.

"Yes?" He asked me, making sure we were on the same page. His hands were already trailing back and forth over my body.

"Yes," I whispered, leaning back in to tilt my mouth over his skin.

"My little homemaker wants to devour me."

"More than anything."

I let my hands drift down from where they stalled against his chest. My palms slipped over his navel where his shirt had ridden up. I gripped the hem.

He grumbled, looking down at me with pained desire. "I think I want to let you."

"I want to see you," I whispered against his mouth.

He scraped his teeth against my neck as he finally found the small white ribbon holding together my wrap dress. He toyed with it, waiting to pull and let the fabric fall away.

I shivered.

"You're still dressed," I whispered.

He breathed into my ear, "Then, undress me, angel."

twenty-two

. . .

Poppy

MY ENTIRE BODY shook with the anticipation of what was happening.

This cannot be happening, my brain screamed.

It was though. It really was.

My gaze was unwavering from Aaron as he took a few steps back to give me a better view. Lifting my hands to my lips, as if to hide my amusement of how we were going about this whole thing, I barked a laugh that did not sound dainty in the slightest.

But I didn't tell him to stop.

I wanted the exact opposite of him stopping.

"Waiting, Snow Angel," he teased with a curl of his lip. "Are you all talk, or are you going to ravish me?"

"You've been reading too many of your grandmother's old bodice rippers." I shakily took a step toward him.

"That's not true," he said, though we both knew it was. "If it were, I'd be the rake."

"I can see it."

"And you'd be the sweet debutant I'd compromise. You, of course, wouldn't know any better before the devilish rake exposed you to a world of desire and pleasure at his own hands."

I giggled, reaching out to him. He grabbed my hand, pulling me in.

"I think you should get new books."

"I don't know. I think you'll like what they taught me."

His skin radiated a golden warmth, highlighted by the soft glow of lamplight in the room. My eyes traveled down his bare chest, admiring the hard muscles and defined lines, while I also felt a sense of nervousness and longing.

I wasn't used to playing this role—the seductress. I was always just Poppy.

Safe.

Boring.

Often, I was a disappointment, which I never wanted to be ever again as long as I had the choice and capability.

Fingers lifted my chin until I looked up, meeting Aaron's cool eyes, half lidded with obvious desire. Desire for me.

I gulped.

"I sure hope that look isn't about me," he whispered.

"No," I said immediately. "Me. Only ever me."

"Don't be nervous. I've waited for the girl who made me feel whole for over a decade. You take your time with me."

My heart took off in my chest. My fingers trembled slightly as they grazed over the skin of his neck. He arched it to the side so I could have better access, gently running my fingertips back and forth until I was cupping the back of his head and sliding over his back.

Even with his clothes on, I never realized how strong years of intense workouts and training had made him. Not only that, but it was as if he was emanating warmth, seeping into me through my skin like a poison—or maybe a salve, igniting a small fire, smoldering on embers for so long. Since Lincoln, I'd never thought I'd feel this kind of way ever again. Or maybe it had been since I'd met Aaron for the first time.

Finding the buttons at the top of his shirt, I slowly undressed him. Each piece of clothing fell away to reveal more of his taut body. He didn't stop me as I took my time, marveling at the sight that felt much different from when I'd accidentally caught him coming out of the shower or when he'd openly walked around the house without a shirt.

This was given, and Aaron's breath picked up as he watched me.

I traced the curve of his muscles, the strength in his frame. All of it was mesmerizing. And the way he looked at me, with such intensity and desire, made me feel like the most beautiful woman in the world.

Aaron's own hands, as if unable to help themselves any longer, reached up to touch my shoulders and down to my waist.

He looked at me. "May I?"

I nodded.

He gently pulled on the tiny white ribbon holding my dress together, letting it fall open to reveal the lacy slip beneath. His chin dropped to his chest. He chuckled softly, the rumble in his chest sending a shiver down my spine. "So many layers."

He pushed my velvet dress back over my shoulders, helping me to step out of it before he took over, picking me up and carrying me down the hallway that was gently lit with lights that kept the historical integrity of the home, but now flickered, washing his bare frame in gold.

"You amaze me," he whispered, voice barely audible, but perfect for me to hear as let my toes skim back against the bedroom floor before I was standing front of him on my own feet.

And it was us.

I swallowed hard, feeling the sincerity in his gaze. "I've wanted this," I admitted, my voice trembling.

I reached up, feeling bold as I pulled his head down until our lips met again. This time, there was no hesitation, no uncertainty. Maybe both us wanted and waited for this much more than either of us could say with words.

Every touch was electric, every kiss searing.

We collapsed onto his bed, kicking away the smoothed and

folded comforter and perfectly selected sheets that not even I could care about. Our bodies remained moving, hungry for more.

I felt the weight of years of longing and desire wash over me like a tidal wave. I was drowning in it. The passion. The intensity. All of it. It was overwhelming, yet it was all I had ever wanted but would never admit.

We continued to move together, our bodies entwined, our hands exploring every inch—from the smooth swaths of skin to the puckered scars we'd each accumulated over the years, though he certainly had more than me.

I whispered his name, a prayer, a promise.

"I don't want this to end," I gasped, feeling my breath catch in my throat as I held him to me.

"Then, I'd better make this worthwhile," Aaron said with another small chuckle.

The sound made my heart soar as I laughed with him.

His eyes locked with mine, a fire igniting between us. I could feel the force of his desire, the electricity of his longing. It was intoxicating.

Yet even as we drove each other to the brink of pleasure, I couldn't help but feel that hint of fear that I wished would shut up but wouldn't.

He would go back to his plan of rejoining the army and I would finish up the project.

And this was it.

That was that.

My thoughts were cut short as our lips met once more, and his hands tangled in my hair, pulling me closer. The warmth of his body enveloped me, and at that moment, I knew I really didn't want this to end. Not his whispers, telling me how beautiful I was as I melted into him. Not the gasps escaping our lips, adding to the enticing soundtrack.

Everyone was right about me. I got in too deep.

Too easily.

As we collapsed beside each other, our breaths ragged and our bodies still shaking, I held on to this feeling.

Let it consume me.

If only for now.

I had right now.

"Don't think like that." Aaron traced my features.

"Like what?" I whispered, not trusting my voice, which came out scratchy from use already.

The sound seemed to delight him.

"Like it's already over. It's not. It's only the beginning."

And as if he had something to prove, he showed me so.

twenty-three

. . .

Poppy

WHEN I WOKE UP, I knew exactly where I was. Still, my heart seemed to beat straight through my chest. I rolled over and stared back into the light eyes of Aaron Hayes.

He was lying there, right next to me, and all I could do was breathe. He chuckled at something.

"What?" I asked.

"Just looking at you." His voice was a husky whisper that sent shivers over my skin. I remembered how that voice had sounded, passing over my skin, and I squirmed.

"Something funny?" I asked. "I thought you were going to find a new source of entertainment other than teasing me."

"Eh." He shook his head. "I think I already found that."

His hand dipped lower, tracing the space between my breasts.

My skin burned with renewed heat for him. Goose bumps? Gone.

"I wonder what my friend Vassar would say about this."

"And here I was, thinking you were imagining me in bed."

"The mouth that's forming on you. Is this confident Poppy?"

He was bringing it out in me.

He smiled with one corner of his lips. "Vassar always joked

that I would never fall in love. That, out of all of them, I would be a bachelor for life."

My heart stopped before picking back up a second later.

Fall in love.

I wasn't sure what to think of the words.

Aaron shook his head as if it meant nothing. Maybe it didn't. It couldn't have. It had been a slip of the tongue.

I cleared my throat. "Would your friend be shocked right now or disappointed?"

"Vass? Never disappointed. If anything, he liked the drama. He was always around for a good time, but not exactly a long one. Honestly, he was one of those guys who would do anything for you. No questions asked. Probably would've come home on leave at some point and gone to a casino in Vegas and accidentally gotten married."

"He sounds fun."

"He was." Aaron paused, letting his fingertips skate away from me as he rolled over and out of bed.

I watched the cords of his muscles unclench and stretch up to the ceiling as he raised his arms over his head.

He yanked on a pair of sweats from the floor before making his way to the door. "Hungry?"

"Always," I whispered. I needed to savor every slice of him.

For the rest of the day—strike that—for the rest of the week we had left leading up to the holiday, I felt like I was living in a sort of daydream. I'd never had this kind before though. I'd trained myself not to. My daydreams were of crown molding and the perfect kitchen appliance you wouldn't mind having out on the counter all the time.

But all my thoughts now were attuned to one thing and one place.

Aaron and the cabin.

The cabin and Aaron.

Aaron and home.

Home.

Aaron.

With the extra hours, I packed myself a weekend bag and ended up staying for most of the week until I had to leave again for more clothes, practically living in Aaron's oversize gray essentials most of the time anyway.

We'd go to sleep late after he pried me away from whatever section of the house I was working on, finalizing until I couldn't find any more holiday details to adjust or furniture to move. One room at a time, everything suddenly started to come alive.

Sometimes, Aaron would lead me to bed and tuck me in. He'd kiss me until I was drunk with his touch, and my eyes would flutter closed, even with the lamp on so that he could read another chapter of a well-worn book off the shelf before drifting off himself. The dark circles under his eyes started to disappear.

We'd wake up in bed to a dark morning from the way the trees cut us off from the rest of the world. We'd have a slow breakfast of coffee or tea—whatever I had left in the cabinet from the past few weeks. Sometimes, he'd make eggs. He was pretty good at scrambling. They were never too dry or runny. At one point, Aaron even surprised me before I got back to work one day, picking up fresh produce from the grocery store after I mentioned wanting to make a simmer pot of cinnamon and cranberries. He arrived with some of the best oranges I'd ever had, so ripe that the fresh juice dripped over my fingertips, which he licked clean.

I started to decorate the house for the holiday. Here, there was going to be no minimalism. Only maximalism, until the place was warm, cozy, and full. I could smell the citrus the whole day as I worked.

Often after getting lost in the process, I'd peek over my shoulder and find Aaron looking at me, checking in between his walks with Ozzy or making his way through his small library. He'd run his hands around my waist as I made him dance in the living room to the holiday music he hated but knew I loved, even when it was clear he had two left feet. The dog would try to join us, and I'd laugh so loud that we couldn't hear the music anymore.

It was just us as I put the final touches on the garland. I fluffed the pillows on the couch, teaching him how to do the perfect center chop to make them look cozier and less showroom. I set the dinner table with white and green candles of different heights and a plaid table runner, which Aaron admitted didn't look as bad as he'd thought plaid could.

It was all coming together. The perfect holiday was in sight.

It was hard for me to believe. More than that, I had a feeling that I shouldn't. If I did feel that feeling after all, the one that meant being comfortable and happy, I'd let myself fall too far into all over again and…

I wasn't a naive girl anymore.

But the week was ending, and I was starting to worry—

It was too late.

"Are you worrying that pretty little head of yours again?" Aaron leaned over my shoulder to get a better look at me. His fingertips ran a featherlight trail over my cheek.

I sat at the bottom of the tree, making sure that the popcorn garland was the right blend of traditional and vintage. Though the kids had done a good job, I needed more than that for when the photographers got here tomorrow. A few more layers would do the trick.

I tilted my head up to look into Aaron's eyes, half hooded and at ease. He held me right there, cupping my chin in his hand. Everything was perfect once more.

"Your oven beeped a minute ago."

"Oh!" I was startled out of his touch as I stood up and made my way into the kitchen.

When I opened the oven door, for once, the cookies weren't completely burned. A little extra golden around the edges, but they would do.

Hastily, I slid my hands into oven mitts and pulled out the tray.

"Who are you making them for?" Aaron asked. "The photographers?"

That wasn't a terrible idea, but I'd rather pick up a few than make them. Though the photographers weren't going to make the promotion decision, it could never hurt to schmooze them with baked goods.

"They're for Hannah."

"Doesn't your friend know you can't bake?" He cocked his head, staring at the cookies as I pushed the oven door closed and set the tray on top.

They weren't *that* bad.

"It was a bet," I explained, slipping my oven mitts off to give the cookies another look. I placed my hands on my hips, feeling Aaron step closer behind me.

"A bet?"

"I bet her …"

Aaron's mouth trailed up the side of my neck.

"I bet her …"

"You want me to guess?" he whispered against my skin.

Seemed like he already had an idea.

"You."

"Me?" The pads of Aaron's fingers trailed down my body, turning me around until I was backed against the counter. He scooped me up and deposited me there. His touches moved lower. He bent at the knee.

"Yes, you. Me giving in to you."

"Is that what this is?"

"Mhmm."

He knelt in front of me and the brand-new countertops, eyes bright but mostly hungry.

I told him so.

"How can't I be when I'm looking at something so delicious?" He wasn't talking about the cookies.

He pressed a kiss to the inside of my thigh, and I fell back onto my elbows to look down at the sight before me.

My eyes widened. I couldn't help it; I laughed, the sound bursting from somewhere in my chest, and I pressed a hand over my mouth.

Aaron grinned again. Such a pretty, devilish grin as the side of his face scraped up the inside of my calf, my knee, my thigh.

"I can't help myself," he groaned. "I think I need a taste."

When I got up in the middle of the night, the floor was cold. Oz tipped his head at me, catching to see who was up. His collar clanged against the floorboard before I returned from the bathroom.

The poor dog hadn't quite picked the spot to sleep yet. He always ended up somewhere between the doorway and wherever was closest to us.

When I walked past him in the hall and onward to the kitchen, he followed me, keeping watch.

"You can go back to sleep," I whispered to him.

Oz didn't move to turn around, watching me as I took out a fresh glass from the cabinet and filled it with water from the filter. Taking a sip, I looked around the house.

"I'm not going to disappoint myself," I said, looking back at the dog.

Oz continued to stare at me, as if listening to my every word. He slid down on his paws until he was stretched out along the hardwood.

"I'm not." Even though I wasn't sure. I was basically setting myself up for disappointment, no matter how many cozy late nights on the couch I spent with Aaron, knowing full well that this wasn't just sex though neither of us broached the topic. It wasn't just the heated moments, where he seemed determined to take me in every room as I completed them to make them even more ours.

"You like it here, don't you?" I asked him. "I'd like it here, I think, if I were you. Lots of space outside. Bet you never thought you would find a home in the middle of the mountains, did you? Even the snow is nicer here. It's a good thing that Aaron gets to keep you, huh? He seems like a pretty good guy, and you'll get to stick around and enjoy the place, I think. Or travel to wherever it is you two are going soon. Is he going to sell the place still? Do you think you can make him reconsider?"

Did I want him to? I realized that when we'd started all of this, if I were anyone else, walking away might've been easy. It might've been fun even to have the fling. But I wasn't anyone else. I was me. And if there was anything I should've known better, was to think I could do fun or casual.

"Do you know what's going to happen once this is all over?" I asked Oz.

He raised his gray eyebrows at me.

I sighed. "Yeah, I don't either."

The house was coming together. I should be happy. Ecstatic even. That was what I should've been focused on now and not anything else, but I couldn't. Not when I was already itching to get back into bed and feel the weight of Aaron's arms hold me, molding me into his side like I was meant to fit there. The place was nearly done with time to spare.

It was a miracle.

My first solo project was almost complete. It was all over.

I washed my glass and set it to dry. I tapped the one light off, and I maneuvered back down the hall in the dark like I knew this place like the back of my hand. As if I'd never been more comfortable in any home I'd ever been in before, even my childhood bedroom, where I whacked my shins on the side of my platform bed more often than not.

Aaron was splayed out in the middle of the bed. His arms were stretched to either side, like he was a star. But he wasn't relaxed. His cheek twitched. Little sounds ripped through his chest, whimpering.

I took a step toward the bed, pausing before taking another.

"Aaron," I whispered.

He didn't seem to hear me. He was asleep, dreaming.

"*Aaron*, you're having a nightmare."

Nothing.

I reached out, gently touching his shoulder. "Aaron."

His hand swung up, grabbing on to my wrist.

I was startled as he rapidly blinked his eyes open, staring right at me.

"You're dreaming," I told him.

Swallowing, gasping for air, he nodded. Reaching out, his arms looped around me, pulling me into bed with him.

"Sorry," he whispered.

I shook my head against his chest, where he held me tightly, like I was some sort of comfort to him. A shield.

"It's okay," I whispered. "I'm sorry I woke you up. I … I didn't want to leave you there."

Aaron gave a low, tired hum and kissed my shoulder.

"Poppy," he murmured.

"Yes?"

He froze in the middle of whatever he had been about to say. It was easier to talk with someone at night, in the dark. But sometimes, you still couldn't get it all out.

"I'm glad you're here," he said.

I opened my lips, unsure of what to say.

"I'm glad I'm here too," I said before we fell asleep for another day.

Another morning closer to the holiday.

twenty-four

. . .

Aaron

I HATED the way the paper crinkled under me as I sat, waiting for the doctor to come back in. But that quickly changed when I realized how much more I hated the way he sauntered into the room with a small too-happy smile on his face as he looked over my records. He hummed as he jotted down his notes.

I tapped my fingers against the side of the table. I'd made this appointment what felt like ages ago when I got back to town. Now, I was here to be told whether my life was over, and I didn't get to go back to the one thing that I was good at and loved.

Or at least, that was what I'd thought the appointment was going to tell me when I made it. It felt … less important now for some reason. Less intense. Even if I was just as impatient.

"You look good from where I see you were a few months ago," the doctor said, glancing back down at my file once more as if he was going to see something new there.

"Great. I guess you can sign off, and I'll be out of your hair," I said.

He glanced up at me for less than a second. "I'm not signing off."

"What?" I asked. "You said I was doing well."

"And you are."

Not good enough.

The doctor folded his hands on the desk, a wedding ring flashing on his finger. His gaze remained steady. "But you still have a ways to go, Aaron," he said. There was no reason he wouldn't use my first name, but for some reason, knowing I would never be called Hayes again according to him, felt like a shot to the gut. "You're mentally and physically fit from what I can see here, but …"

"But what?"

"This is only the first step. You know that. First is my signature. Then you'll go back through the entire induction process, including a physical, fitness test, and anything else they need to declare you fit to go back into action."

"You don't think I can do it."

"My medical advice is that you're unprepared to return," he said. "You had a TBI less than a year ago and an honorable discharge. That's not going to hold you back from finding new work or whatever you choose to do."

"I'm going to go back. It's what I am meant to do."

"I'm sure you'll be able to find someone to write you off on this," he said, closing his computer. "I'm just not going to be the one to do it."

I hung my head between my shoulders.

"Talk to me, Aaron."

I shook my head. He wasn't going to sign it. I wasn't going to be able to reenlist. For some reason, I'd expected to be angrier or more upset. I should've been. Shouldn't I?

I glanced up at the clock above the door. Poppy was probably finishing up with the photographer who was supposed to stop by two hours ago. After making sure that he was decent enough, I'd put Oz in the mudroom and left them to it. She had been fretting about where everything was in the house for the past day and a half now, mumbling to herself about needing to make sure everything looked perfect as she adjusted trinkets on the edge of the bookshelves, filled with my and my grandmother's books until she took a step back and smiled at her hard work.

When she smiled, her face lit up.

In my opinion, the cabin had turned into more than her unreasonable need for perfection. What she'd done was amazing. I honestly couldn't believe it myself—from the way the lights sparkled on the tree with ideally spaced ornaments, to the gas fireplace that was as homey as true woodfire.

It felt like home.

"Aaron," the doctor interrupted my train of thought.

"I'll find someone else then."

The doctor let out a deep breath. "Determination is a good quality. But, do you really want me to sign off on this and send you back to your commanding officer who might or might not accept it to get, what? Another year or two? Less than that?" he asked. "Don't answer. Think about it. I'm sure being home has reminded you that a lot of people love you. Your family. Maybe a significant other who would be happy if you stuck around."

Poppy's face flashed in the front of my mind. I shook it away.

"Do you want me to be honest with you?"

"You haven't been?" I nearly scoffed at the man.

I stood up from the table and slipped my coat over my shoulders.

"I don't think you're getting back out there. You had internal bleeding. Your leg is likely to produce chronic nerve pain if you keep pushing it. Having a medical discharge isn't the end of the world, but people rarely reenlist after it, Aaron. You and I both know that. Make peace with it. Consider yourself lucky. Consider this a second chance for you to do whatever you want with your life and your future."

But what if I had no idea what that meant anymore? Weeks ago, the future had been planned with getting back to where I had been. Where I was supposed to be. That way I'd be sure that I didn't forget. That way, I'd make sure Vassar's life—his sacrifice—was worth something.

I sucked on the inside of my cheek as I offered the doctor a single nod.

His sincerity followed me out the door. "I don't suggest living in the past."

twenty-five

. . .

Poppy

"THIS PLACE?" The photographer breathed out heavily as he looked around, stretching after he finished up his final shots in the living room with his camera that nearly took up a good section of the room.

Peeking over his shoulder, I watched the images come through. The place looked even better than I could've imagined with the lighting.

The fireplace was working and roaring with a quiet hum. Outside of the French doors, I couldn't have choreographed the snow falling any better myself. The flakes glowed from the outdoor lights. The tree somehow was the ideal amount of muchness without being overwhelming.

I didn't know how it'd happened, but I'd pulled it off. The renovation. The decoration. Every piece. It was everything.

And if possible, it was more.

Would it be ridiculous if I cried right now? Because I felt a little choked up.

"If I had to choose a place to live outside of the city?" the photographer went on as he started to pack up. "This would be it. It reminds me a bit of the area where I grew up. More trees, fewer farms, of course, but I'd certainly not mind a winter if I could stay here."

Pride swelled in my chest.

I cleared my throat. "Thank you."

"One of the better places I've shot," he commented.

"For Home Haven?"

He agreed. "You could probably keep the place and rent it out for the holidays every year and have a wait list."

I breathed out a small laugh. "Not a terrible idea."

I hadn't heard anything from Aaron about not selling the place. However, I hadn't heard him mention anything about selling the place either since I'd started to spend more time here. So, who knew? Maybe the next people who took over this place would have the same idea.

"The owners are lucky they had this kind of land and were able to fix it up."

"They are."

"Especially with you at the helm," he said. "You're good."

"I appreciate that," I said. "What's your name again?"

He swiped his hands together, a simple wedding band on his one finger catching the light before he extended the other hand to me. "I apologize. I'm not sure I introduced myself. I'm Jack. I should have a business card in this bag somewhere."

His cropped dark hair fell to one side of his head, and his striking blue eyes managed to seem casual and unruffled as the rest of him. He didn't seem like the normal preppy photographer I'd seen from Home Haven, trying to sneak in as many bylines as possible. A last-minute freelancer, likely.

"Thank you."

"I wish you the best of luck. They'd be crazy if they didn't keep ya around," he said, catching my surprise. "The other designer let me in on the secret competition between the two of you, though I was curious why only one set of my photographs were contracted to the magazine specifically."

I corrected him. "I won't be fired or anything. It's a promotion."

"My mistake."

"Sometimes, things just don't work out."

He shrugged. "Eh, sometimes, I learned you have to go after the things you want."

Pausing, I nodded. "Do you need help with anything?"

"Nope. I'm all good to go. These cameras are practically my children."

I opened the door leading outside for the photographer, nonetheless, watching as he headed back toward his car and loaded everything up.

This was it. There was no more to do but complete the job.

The competition was over. The promotion would be chosen by Michelle, likely sooner than later.

It was all out of my hands now.

I held a tentatively bright smile as I watched a truck make its way up the driveway. My contented expression faltered at Aaron's. Catching me standing on the front porch, he turned to walk up to me.

"What's wrong?" I asked immediately.

"Nothing," he insisted, though his voice was tight. "Everything's great."

"Everything went okay at your appointment? How's your leg? Did the doctor say anything?"

He cleared his throat. He nodded for another moment, as if he was debating something.

"Do you need to do more physical therapy or ..." I drifted off, unsure what else I could say.

He stopped me from having to search for another option. I didn't want to say the one I knew he didn't want to hear today.

His leg, though he hadn't been struggling as much with it as I remembered at the start of my project here, would never be the same.

"Nope. It's healing up fine. Should be able to return to top shape soon enough," he said.

For some reason, it felt like a hit to my stomach. But it shouldn't. I should be happy for him. I should be happy.

"That's great."

He'd be back where he belonged. Just like he'd said. We talked about it, and I knew that his life wasn't going to keep him here in the area or with me, but for some reason, I couldn't fully let myself believe it.

He looked around the front porch, where I'd set up rocking chairs with pillows that matched the holiday theme of the rest of the house. "The cabin looks fantastic. Your boss would be crazy not to see the good work you did here. It looks like an entirely different place. Give yourself some credit."

I would when I got the promotion, and then I'd know it was all worth it and everything worked out how it was meant to be.

"Thank you," I whispered, looking up at Aaron through my lashes. I'd managed to put makeup on today, knowing that the photographer was coming and wanting to look professional.

Aaron stared back at me with a small, tight smile. He wasn't telling me something.

"Wait there!"

I turned back toward the car, where the photographer had paused packing up, looking at us standing here to see him off. Before he managed to put it away, his camera was back in his hands.

"Stay right there for a minute," directed Jack. "I want to get a photo of you both standing on the edge of the porch there."

"Oh, you don't have to—"

"It's a great shot."

I glanced at Aaron. He shrugged. Nodded.

"All right."

Before I could turn to look back away from Aaron, the photographer had already taken the photo.

"Perfect."

"We look all right?"

"Like a holiday card. You could use the photo for one if you're late getting them out."

I blinked a few times. "I appreciate that, but we … we aren't together. This is his cabin."

"Ah." Jack paused. "Sorry 'bout that. My mistake. I'll send it to you after I edit through the batch. Never know when you might make a memory you'll want to remember."

"Thank you again!"

The photographer left us both on the porch. Neither of us made a move to go inside. After a second, I turned toward the front door.

Aaron's hand circled my wrist, gently guiding me back toward him. "Hold up. I've been thinking about this all morning."

He tilted my head up to meet him, and his mouth sank into mine for a kiss, slow and heavy. It was just us in our hidden little winter oasis. We didn't hasten to move as he peppered me with one or two more short pecks.

I could already feel the heat I'd come to know well over the past week brewing low in my stomach.

His lips hovered over mine as we broke apart.

He hummed, as if in thought.

I cleared my throat. "Your appointment went well?"

"It went as expected," he said.

I stared at him, unsure of his diplomacy. It was unlike him, even though his body language remained loose.

"Are you sure there isn't anything you want to talk about—"

My phone rang, buzzing loudly from my back pocket. Michelle's name lit up the screen.

"Excuse me."

"I'll be inside."

I watched as he went, and I walked off the porch, crossing my arms as I realized how cold it was outside. Life was slowly leaking through the cracks of the home we'd built in the middle of nowhere with this project. And it was all rushing in too fast.

I pressed my phone to my ear. "Good morning, Michelle."

"Good morning, Poppy. How are you?"

"I'm …" I looked over my shoulder at Aaron before taking a few more steps away. "I'm doing great. The photographer just left."

Michelle gave a small squeal of delight over the phone. "Is it everything you hoped for? I hope you're happy with the result of your hard work. I know you put a lot into this project. A lot more than anyone could've expected."

"Yes, I'm … overjoyed with how everything turned out," I said.

"Poppy, are you sure everything is all right?" Michelle's voice held a tinge of concern. "You sound a bit off."

I glanced back at the house, at the closed front door that separated me from Aaron. "It's probably the connection out here. And I'm a little tired. It's been a long week."

"I understand. You've done a wonderful job, Poppy. Both with the house as well as with the Hayes-Preston family. Ms. Hayes-Preston already reached out to let me know impressed she as with your work and professionalism."

Professionalism. I bit my lip as I swayed from foot to foot on the walkway.

"I can't wait to see the final photos and show the world what we've accomplished here."

"I'll make sure everything is ready for the holiday," I assured Michelle.

"Wonderful. I expected no less," she said. "Be aware that I'm hoping to call a meeting to discuss some important things, as you know, before the new year."

Of course, she was talking about the promotion.

"I can't wait."

We said goodbye and ended the call.

Taking a deep breath, I walked back toward the house, feeling the weight of uncertainty settle on my shoulders. As I opened the door, Aaron was nowhere to be seen.

It was all going to work out.

I shook my head in disbelief, taking in the sight of all that I had accomplished. It was nothing short of a miracle that everything had come together within the tight deadline I'd been given. Despite the constant rush and physical strain, I hadn't collapsed from exhaustion even once.

Every muscle in my body ached—a reminder of all the work I'd put in. As I took another step forward, Oz came bounding toward me, excited to see me after being cooped up while the photographer was there. His wagging tail and playful barks echoed through the room, adding to the sense of chaos and accomplishment that filled the air.

It's all going to work out.

It was as if I was striking a deal with the universe.

Please let this happen.

Let the affirmations be true.

Let me be happy.

Let me be healthy.

Let me be strong.

Let me get through this. Let me have good things …

My heart clanged in my chest.

I was staring at Aaron. He smiled back.

I didn't ask for anything more.

twenty-six

. . .

Poppy

"IS THIS FULL HOMEMAKER MODE?"

I didn't bother to answer Aaron. I bustled through the cabin, adjusting pillows and placing throw blankets over the back of the couch. I twisted holiday figurines on the bookshelves and double-checked that the oven wasn't too hot to warm the cinnamon rolls that I'd bought premade from the bakery.

The warm scents of cinnamon sugar and orange were supposed to be inviting. I didn't need Sarah and her family to walk into another gingerbread disaster.

"What? Not making anything this time?" Aaron leaned against the doorway to the kitchen, the picture of ease as he continued his relentless teasing.

Nothing he said was going to stop me from continuing to make sure that everything was perfect for his sister and her family when they arrived though. I should've been done a while ago so that I could make a quiet exit after going over everything with her, but I wanted to wipe down the counters one more time.

He chuckled, watching.

I playfully swatted him with a towel, shooing him out of the kitchen. "They're going to be here at any minute."

"I'm dressed, aren't I?"

The doorbell rang.

I hopped once, unable to contain the nerves and excitement. They were here already.

Aaron looked me up and down and chuckled.

"Go answer the door." I waved him off.

This was it. This was the culmination of the days I had put into this house over the past month. It'd all come together—not only for it to be cozy and livable, but also for this holiday, which I hoped they'd remember for a long time. And not because I was still worried about accidentally burning their morning rolls.

Every detail had to be right for today. And tomorrow. But today especially.

My last day in the cabin.

"Uncle Aaron!" Liana called, her voice carrying through the house.

Oz rushed past me from where he was sitting, hoping I'd drop something. He raced toward the action. I brushed off my hands on a towel, turning the oven off, but leaving the buns inside. I peeked around the corner to the living room.

Sarah entered behind her daughter, her face breaking into a wide grin. Behind Sarah, the rest of the family spilled out of the car, each one radiating a mix of holiday cheer and relief at finally arriving at the cozy cabin.

"Whoa! This is ah-mazing!" Gavin screamed as he raced inside, straight into Oz, who was more than excited to greet him. Gavin responded with a shout and a bubble of laughter. "Down, Ozzy. Ozzy!"

Sarah shook her head, peering around in complete and utter awe. She covered her mouth with the top of her hand, unbelieving.

Her husband, Nathan—with perfectly groomed hair swept over to one side of his head and glasses that reminded me of Simon's pair, but Nathan pulled it off much better—walked in behind her. His arms were full of duffel bags and a tote of presents.

I took that as my cue to rush forward, easily taking them from him.

"Oh, thanks," he said, not seeing me first before handing a few things over.

"Not a problem in the least."

I moved everything back to the two guest rooms, the smaller one for the kids. I dropped all the bags into the larger one until they could figure out whose stuff was which. However, I had a good feeling the race car bag was Gavin's from what I remembered from the kids' last visit.

By the time I made it back out into the main area, I was able to watch Nathan's eyes widen, along with the rest of the family's. Each of them slowly turned around the space as if they needed to take it all in, all at once.

"Wow, they really managed to fix up this place."

I smiled, listening to their amazement at how the place came together as I stuck the bag of presents in the hall closet. I'd let Sarah and Nathan know where they were before I left so they could sneak them under the tree before morning.

Hugs were exchanged, much to Aaron's obvious chagrin. Soon, the front door was shut, and everyone was inside, savoring the warmth. Sarah's eyes continued to sweep over the carefully arranged decorations, the twinkling lights around the tree, and the spread of treats on the table.

I really should get those cinnamon rolls out of the oven. As I carefully moved past everyone toward the kitchen, Aaron's sister caught my hand.

Did she grab the wrong person?

Sarah looked directly at me.

"It's perfect," Sarah whispered, squeezing my hand once.

My heart swelled in my chest. I smiled, glancing at Aaron. Was he smiling as well?

I beamed.

Sarah watched the exchange.

I turned my attention to her. "If anything is missing, please let me know. I'll head out and be out of your hair in a bit so that you can enjoy your family holiday together."

Sarah's brows lowered as she looked again between Aaron and me. I mean, I knew I'd been here the other day when she picked up the kids, and she might've assumed that something irregular was going on between us, but I didn't want her to think—

"Nonsense," said Sarah, still holding tight on to my hand. "Stay."

"I couldn't." I shook my head. "My job is complete, though I'm glad that I was able to see how you all liked it. I hope you have a wonderful holiday here in this home together."

"We'd love to have you here for the day, Poppy. The more, the merrier. Unless, of course, you have other plans for Christmas Eve?"

Pausing, I didn't want to lie. I shook my head. I'd promised my parents that I would be home to spend all of tomorrow with them, knowing that today would be full of to-dos, unable to think about anything else, even after I left.

"Plus, the kids are excited to see you again," reasoned Sarah.

"Stay." Aaron's soft command broke through the kids' cries of delight over the few small presents I'd helped Aaron wrap for them, already tucked beneath the tree.

They continued shouting, begging to see if they could open one early.

I hesitated, staring at Aaron and the softness in his expression, even as he stood across the room from me. Not bridging the gap.

"Okay."

Sarah at last released my hand. "Amazing."

"I'm Nathan. It's good to meet you, Poppy," Nathan introduced himself properly with a polite smile. "Seems you've met the rest of the family already."

"It's good to meet you too." With everyone standing around, I started to feel the nerves creep back in. Casually, I addressed everyone. "There are cinnamon rolls for a late breakfast."

The kids raced me into the kitchen. Oz quickly followed behind.

The morning, full of sugar and icing, melted into the afternoon, and then everyone gathered around the fire, sharing stories and laughter. A symphony of happiness echoed through the walls of the cabin as the kids played the games that I'd stacked in the reading corner. I refilled snacks and empty glasses of wine for Sarah and Nathan, who were impressed I'd managed to get their favorite red for dinner.

As they gathered around the table, perfectly catered in a way that looked like it had been homemade, following the family preferences, they appreciated my honesty that, though the cabin kitchen could handle a full holiday meal, this one was not my doing.

Especially not when the kids laughed, outing my gingerbread mistake.

At the sight of my face turning as red as the Christmas decorations, Sarah admitted she wasn't much of a cook either.

The kids were also happy to share the story of her burning mac and cheese on the stovetop.

Aaron reached out next to me where we sat at the table, running his thumb back and forth over the back of my hand to soothe my embarrassment as much as my laughter that I was unable to hold back.

Soon, the kids had changed into pajamas, printed with candy canes, and nestled on the couch to watch classic holiday movies with the throw blankets wrapped around their shoulders. Nathan fell asleep between them within the first twenty minutes. The glow of the Christmas tree bathed the room in a soft light, casting a warm and inviting atmosphere over the cabin.

I was unsure if I'd ever felt more content than when I watched the family bond and enjoy each other's company, every soft smile and comfortable adjustment as they made themselves at home pulling on my heartstrings.

I took a second to capture it all in my mind. All day, it felt as if I was meant to be here, in this home I'd helped create for these precious seconds.

Aaron followed me back into the kitchen, where I started to rinse plates before organizing them into the dishwasher.

A few weeks ago, none of it had even been here.

Arms wrapped around my waist from behind. "You look happy," Aaron murmured into my ear.

"Everything is just how I wanted it to be," I stated, standing up straight to lean back into him. He smelled like fresh pine and some kind of spice. "Do you know if Sarah is happy with it?"

"I don't think I've seen my sister look so pleased in a long time," he confirmed.

"Good."

"You're staying the night?"

"I don't think that would be appropriate."

In a few hours, it would be the end of my contract. At midnight, technically, I'd have no more reason to be inside this cabin I'd poured so much energy and work into the past few weeks.

"You're staying tonight," Aaron rephrased, more finality in his tone as he turned me around to face him.

I nodded, not second-guessing. Because, really, I didn't want to leave.

"I'll stay," I said. "Go back out with your family. I'm going to finish cleaning up in here."

"I can help."

"No, go ahead," I encouraged. "I'll only be a second."

After some hesitation, he headed back into the dark living room, where the movie was still playing, so that I set up brunch plates and hot chocolate mugs for easy access tomorrow. However, Aaron didn't get far, stopped by the door, where I could overhear him and Sarah.

I paused my work as I listened.

"Thank you," Sarah said to her brother softly.

Aaron responded with one of his small scoffs, as if dismissing the conversation before it even began. "I didn't do anything."

His sister didn't relent. "You did. You know, it wouldn't be awful if you stuck around. It wouldn't be the worst thing to let yourself be happy where you are for once."

He sighed. "I'm … happy."

"I can see that. I think you're telling me the truth too," she said.

"I am."

"I just—I don't want you to lose it."

He didn't reply.

"I don't want to lose you either," she continued.

"What are you talking about?"

"It's obvious," she insisted. "Anyone who's walked through this place, let alone spent more than an hour with you two, could see that she isn't just doing her job anymore."

"That isn't any of your business."

"You're right; it isn't. But I know you, and I know that unless I say something, you're going to ruin whatever it is that you're creating here because you're stubborn."

"There's nothing to ruin, Sarah," said Aaron. "She has things to do. Jobs to accomplish."

"I've never thought of you as someone who'd stop a woman from enjoying work," his sister replied with just enough snark.

"I'm not," he mumbled.

"So, what's the problem? What's making you want to leave still?"

I couldn't help but listen in closer because I too, was curious about what the answer was.

"Nothing. I've decided. After this is all over, I'm selling this place now that it's fixed up. So, enjoy it. I'm moving on. Starting fresh. I think we all deserve that. Don't you?"

"I think my kids would like to get to know their Uncle Aaron more than they've been able to. I think I'd like to spend more time with my baby brother."

Aaron stuttered as he tried to come up with something to say next, but he was interrupted.

"Mom!" Liana called out. "Can we please open one present tonight?"

"Just one!" yelled Gavin.

"Who said that we did that?"

"Please?" both the kids begged, cupping their hands together.

"Just one," Sarah sighed, glancing at Aaron's gifts under the tree. "Do you mind?"

He shook his head. "Go ahead."

Cheers rang out through the living room, startling their father awake.

I giggled, causing Aaron to return to stand next to me.

"You okay?" he asked.

"Uh-huh." I forced a small smile, hiding that I'd heard what was discussed between him and his sister.

For the rest of the night, I watched as a spectator among the gratified family. After the kids ripped open a single present, Sarah led them to bed and tucked them in good night. I watched as she and Nathan came back out for one more glass of wine, sitting together in front of the fireplace and talking softly, just the two of them.

It was perfect. This home. This day. All of it. I couldn't have designed it better.

This cabin, at some point, had become so much more than I'd ever realized.

I changed houses and cabins into homes where memories were made.

A home.

Only I had to realize it now.

I had to realize, even if I got to pretended for a little while …

This home? It was never going to be mine.

twenty-seven

. . .

Aaron

"WE KEEP FINDING OURSELVES LIKE THIS," I whispered.

My nose trailed up the side of Poppy's neck toward her cheek in a way that made goose bumps spread over her skin.

"It's becoming a habit," she agreed, her voice turning small. "Not sure we should break it."

No. We shouldn't.

I should tie her to my bed. Right here. Then, I could keep her where I wanted her. With me.

"Your parents are expecting you tomorrow," I said.

"Plan on keeping me longer?" Poppy tried to joke.

"Wouldn't dream of it," I said, albeit a bit clumsily, as the conversation turned.

I pulled my head back away so I could see her face better in the darkness. The small light in the bathroom remained on for Oz. It gently cast a gentle glow across the bed.

"The other night, when I ran into them picking you up at the party, I could tell they really love you."

"I hope so," Poppy replied. "Though I gave my mom a rough time after I graduated from high school."

"I can't imagine that. From what I do remember, you were always a hard worker. Confident in who you were."

"You must still be thinking of some other girl from high school who had an obnoxious crush on you." She shook her head. "And that was before you left. After high school, I was … a bit lost. I started college at a great placement, but it was hard to move forward when I ended up having to drop out because I was in so much pain, which no one wanted to explain or take seriously. Eventually, I felt like everyone thought I was faking it, even my mother, who tried to be positive about the whole thing, which only hurt me more. I felt like a burden," I said.

"Do you still think that?" I asked.

"Sometimes."

"You shouldn't."

"Wow." She smirked. "Cured me."

"Not that easy?"

She shook her head, but the two of us were both smiling.

"Happy with how everything turned out?" she asked me.

I took a deep breath, seeing the way her eyes flared as if she already knew what I was going to say.

Let me be happy with you, I wanted to say.

But I didn't. I didn't deserve to. I couldn't ask that of her when I knew that she'd even said she chose work over relationships—and this wasn't even a relationship. This was just …

As if sensing my thoughts, Poppy whispered with a shake in her voice, "Is this really it?"

I took a deep breath, clearing my throat as my fingers trailed along her cheek. "That was always the plan, wasn't it?"

And if there was anything Poppy did, it was sticking to her plans.

"Professional, right?"

She shook her head. "Threw that out the window long ago."

"We did," I said, voice dipping.

For a house so full of people, it was so quiet. There were only the soft breaths that passed between us since night had fully fallen.

In my bed, as we lay next to each other, it was as if we were the only people in the cabin. In the woods. In the town. In the state. It was just me and Poppy. I liked it. I liked it more than I ever should have.

It looked like Poppy was thinking the same thing, forehead furrowed.

"Stop thinking," I whispered against her cheek. I pressed another gentle kiss there.

She shook her head. "You don't even know what I'm thinking about this time."

"Yes, I do," I ventured. "But I'm going to tell you what you should think about now."

"Okay," she said, staring directly at me. Waiting.

"Good," I replied, buying myself some time as I thought. "Because what I'm going to tell you is that after today, everything is going to work out. I'm going to …"

I didn't know what the hell I was going to do.

I continued anyway, lying through my teeth with the truth of a good lie. "I'm going to get my leg sorted and see if my body's still worth something." Somewhere, even if it wasn't here anymore because I wasn't sure if there was anything for me here after all this.

I didn't know if I wanted to stay to find out if there was anything left here for me either. This house held too much. The memories of how I'd first arrived here. The moment I left. The moment I came back, more broken than I ever had been before, only for a woman to walk in and startle us both back to some kind of life.

"You're worth something."

I shook my head. "We're not talking about me right now," I insisted. "We're talking about you."

"Me?"

"Yes. We're going to talk about you and how you're going to

get back into the city and never have to drive these terrible roads back into the mountains every day—or ever again if you're lucky."

She chuckled.

"You're going to go work your job that you love. You're going to see how much you wowed them by transforming this shack of a place. Shock them all. You're going to have the promotion and the job you earned."

Poppy tried to be discreet, but I noticed the tears begin to build in the corners of her eyes, no matter how many times she attempted to swallow down the thick emotion.

I cupped her face in my hand. "Don't cry."

"I'm not," she argued.

She was lying. One tear escaped, dripping out from the corner of her eye and over her lashes before slipping down over her cheek.

Why would I ever make her cry? I could stop it. I could tell her the truth. Because, the truth was, I didn't want this to end. Screw her contract saying it was over. Screw her ever having to drive the commute to work every day. We'd make this work.

We could. Somehow.

I just didn't know the answer as to how.

The best I could do, unable to say the words, was press my lips against her temple, taking her wet salt with me. Turning her head, she forced me to look her in the eye when she kissed me. She gripped me tightly before her hands slid, tracing me as if she was afraid to forget the way my nose bridged or how there was a scar along my jaw or what it felt like when my breath hitched in my throat, all because of her.

I did the same, slipping her shirt over her head and making sure that I took note of every dip and freckle she had. I reached out and pulled her against me until her nose pressed against the space at the base of my throat, breathing in and out. I was certain she could hear the way my heart raced in my chest, and my head screamed at me.

What the hell was I doing, thinking I could let this girl go?

It was for the best. I kept hearing myself say that, and yet there was also another voice, screaming in the back of my head.

Stop. Don't go.

I feel better when you're here. I don't want this to end. Do you?

But when morning came around and I felt her slip out from under my arms ... I didn't reach out to pull her back.

twenty-eight

· · ·

Poppy

I KNEW ALL MY AFFIRMATIONS. I knew how to say I was doing my best and pray to whatever great heavens I wanted to believe in that day to make it so. Because I wasn't sure what else to do, and if it wasn't sure what to do, I was positive I'd fall apart altogether if I didn't have at least one truth in my life.

I knew what I had to do to keep moving. I'd learned the steps well to keep my heart beating and my lungs breathing and the rest of me from completely giving up once and for all.

But I'd never had to do it when it felt like someone had carved an entire hole out of my chest. Even though it was me who had done it.

I knew that I had basically done this to myself. I gave in. I thought that it would be okay and that I could handle a short holiday fling even though I should've known better. Now, I was forced to deal with the consequences.

I needed to keep going. I needed to keep doing what I knew I was meant to do.

When I walked into the office on Friday and saw the bright smile on Alison's face, I knew exactly what was going to happen before my ears heard it.

I sat in Michelle's small yet sophisticated office, which always used to set me at ease when I was on edge.

"I hope you all had a wonderful holiday, if you celebrated. I called you in here before the end of the year to give you some positive news," Michelle said from where she sat across from us at her desk.

I took a deep breath. I thought there would be more lead-up about how both projects were a success and that she was proud of specific things within our work.

But Michelle didn't sugarcoat things. I used to admire that about her.

"I am happy to congratulate Alison on receiving the promotion," Michelle announced quietly as we sat in front of her in the same seats that we had sat in when she first put down the gauntlet over a month ago.

It'd felt like it was so much longer.

I schooled my face into a look of unhurt, though my aching heart sank deeper into my stomach. I turned toward Alison and plastered one of my best smiles on my face.

She didn't see through it.

Neither did the formidable Michelle Maven.

No one ever did.

"Congratulations, Alison. I saw the work you did on your home. It was remarkable," I said.

It wasn't a lie. Alison's project *was* amazing. It was classy and modern and had a hint of antique to work well with the original architecture of the building. It was exactly the kind of home that Home Haven readers would ooh and aah over.

Alison's wide smile faded before she dipped her head in a small nod. "Thank you, Poppy."

"Thank you for coming in to see me today," Michelle said. "I won't keep you longer than necessary, so please get out and enjoy the rest of your day. Your calendars should list upcoming projects. I hope you both are as excited as I am about what Home Haven has in store."

Alison pushed back her seat and rose, thanking Michelle before heading toward the door leading back into the main office space. I did the same.

"Poppy, could you please remain for a second?" Michelle asked.

Alison caught my eye, holding the door open. She gave me another small smile before shutting the office door behind her.

Michelle cocked her head at me as I slowly lowered myself back into the chair I'd sat in a moment ago.

Smoothing out my pants, I took a deep breath. I was wearing the stretchy dress pants with the bows on them again. I'd worn them the first day that I started on the cabin. I remembered the way that Aaron's eyes had caught on them in what looked like disgust, but I'd noticed that when we were in bed, it was almost like he was still remembering them on my legs, tracing his fingers over my skin in small twists and loops.

That moment that had brought us together.

Back together.

But that wasn't meant to be. A lot of things weren't right now.

Maybe it wasn't the right time, or the universe had other things in store for me soon. Or maybe that was all bullshit. Because when it came down to it, all the affirmations were just words. What mattered was what you did with them afterward.

How do you make each positive phrase true?

"Poppy," Michelle started, catching my attention, "I wanted to check in with you."

"Of course."

"I know the promotion was previously discussed with you before all this mess. In this case, Alison simply had what I was looking for, for the magazine, as a lot of our smaller projects and minor home DIYs were already included. We needed a big piece to fill the spread," explained Michelle.

I nodded.

"It had nothing to do with the quality of your work," she went on, making sure that I understood how she had come to the decision.

I did.

What I didn't—what I held inside myself, knowing that it wasn't polite or professional—however, finally broke free as I met her gaze, still held tightly on mine.

"Did I have a chance?" I asked.

"Excuse me?"

"Did I ever really have a chance?" I repeated.

But I felt like the answer was sitting right in front of me. For so long, I was always the woman who was walked all over and told to try better next time, and I believed it because I thought this was the way of the world. It was what it was. *C'est la vie.*

As long as it pleased everyone else and they liked me enough, I let it go.

But for some reason, I couldn't right now. It was all too much, even as I bit the inside of my cheek.

"I've worked hard here," I explained, standing up for myself. I'd never thought I could, but I did against Aaron. At least until the end. I was able to speak my mind, even if my voice shook and my eyes filled with water. "I put in extra hours. I take on the extra training. I devote myself to the work and the mission here. I'm not saying that Alison hasn't. I'm not saying that seniority is the correct way to hand out promotions, but I have worked so hard, and I love what I do, and I wanted it so badly, and right now, I feel like I ... what have I gotten for it?"

Michelle watched me carefully as I went on, not interrupting.

"Half of the senior design team don't even know my name beyond the girl who color codes their calendars." I whispered. "I'm not asking for a *thank you* or a *job well done*. I want proof that all the work I do without being asked, that's praised, is worth it. I mean, did you know that I built those custom bookshelves in that cabin?"

"I didn't know that."

"I did. Not only that, but when we were behind schedule, I

spent days and nights staining the original hardwood floors. I doubt half the other designers even know how to use a nail gun if push came to shove and they needed to make the vision happen themselves. But I did. I do. I don't *deserve* this promotion. I earned it."

But was my constant need for perfection and doing whatever I had to do, throwing health and family and love to the wayside if that's what it took, worth it in the end?

My job, my work was what I always chose. It was why I still lived with my family, so close to the office, especially after Lincoln left me, because what else did I need to move for? It was why I'd made sure to keep myself under lockdown for so long, so I would be at full alertness at Home Haven while everyone else did whatever they wanted. Yet somehow, they still managed to be so many steps ahead of me.

I cut myself off, trying to catch my breath.

"Sometimes, in this job, you're the only one who can fully know you did your absolute best," said Michelle. "And that should be worth something."

"What if it's not enough?" I pressed my lips together.

"It will be," Michelle said, sadness filling her tone. "For so many of us, even when we're struggling, it has to be."

I should've nodded. I should've been the one to thank her for the opportunity, like I always did before asking if there was anything else she or the other designers needed from me, which I would fulfill, no questions asked.

But I didn't. And now, I was stuck here, under her studying gaze.

"I'm sorry," I apologized. "I'm tired, as I mentioned, from the late nights and making sure that the cabin and the holiday were put together for the Hayes-Preston family."

"You've had a very productive year. I hope we can move forward from here and continue this trend," Michelle said. "This isn't the end of something. It's just the beginning."

It was easy for her to say. No matter if Michelle had gone

through trials or struggled to make Home Haven what it became after years, she didn't understand where I was coming from.

She has no idea.

I could nearly hear Aaron's stiff arrogance leaking through my thoughts, the same words he'd spit at me during the first two weeks of my time at the cabin.

"You have no idea what I'm going through, and to be honest, I don't need you to pretend to care."

Tears started to stream down my face.

Michelle reached across the desk, and I couldn't even pull my hands away before she had them in her grasp. She held my hands tight, not caring that they were in fists.

"You're going to do great things, Poppy. You can be afraid right now. But don't let yourself stay like this—one foot out and one in. Take the energy you need. Dig yourself out and start again."

"You said I had potential."

"And you know when I say that, I mean it," said Michelle, her tone switching from soft to serious. "Dive into this feeling. Dive in until you have no choice but to try and swim."

I stared at her, wondering what she would do if someone spoke to her like this. If she would suddenly jump up and shout for joy after failing?

Again.

"Can you make it out of here this evening safely? Would you like me to call you a car?"

I shook my head.

"Go home, Poppy. You've done a lot of good work. Get some rest and come back ready to jump in one hundred percent like I know you want to. Good things come out of it. That I can promise. Because you do have talent. Right now, however, I think it's your job to take some time for yourself and have a wonderful new year. Have a good rest of your day, and thank you for taking this time to talk so vulnerably with me."

I swallowed, standing up. "Thank you."

I made my way back to my desk, and the cubicle I shared with Hannah felt tinier than I remembered. I sat down before I could turn off the monitor and pull my tablet into my bag like I should've, doing what was expected of me. But I knew what would happen if I did. I would pack up and sling my heavy bag over my shoulder and turn off my desk light on the way out. I'd try to call Hannah, though I knew she was going through her own stuff, and I shouldn't bother her. I'd walk home or catch the bus at the nearest stop. When I went inside, my mother would ask me a million questions, knowing I'd heard back about the promotion that she always assumed I'd receive.

How couldn't I after all?

I'd given so much time. So much effort. It almost felt like I'd given everything I had left of myself.

I wasn't ready for any of it.

So, I did what I always did.

I got back to work, opening my email and checking through upcoming appointments for the next project I'd be on as an assistant to another senior designer.

twenty-nine

· · ·

Aaron

"HERE WE HAVE THE KITCHEN. The entire place was recently renovated and refinished by the wonderful Home Haven, right in the city. Design choices were made to create an authentic yet timelessly elegant cabin experience." The realtor prattled on as she walked through the house, casually letting her hand slide against the countertops or wave toward the new appliances like she was on a game show, displaying the prizes.

The woman had had a constant purse to her lips, like a duck, since she'd walked in the door. She had yet to let go of her husband's elbow. It didn't surprise me, considering the first thing she'd asked when she arrived was the likelihood of gray wolves.

Gray. Specifically.

If Poppy were here, she would've jabbed her elbow into my ribs for how hard I rolled my eyes.

But she wasn't here.

She'd probably never be here again. I'd let her leave.

"Hmm," the potential buyer hummed. "The cabinets are a little different in color than what I was expecting."

"We've worked with Home Haven clients before." The realtor persisted with the couple. "The designers are often willing to make a few alterations to make sure that the interior is to your liking as well, if you'd like me to make a few calls."

The whole kitchen hadn't even been done for a few weeks. The cabinets were barely used, and they were already going to change the color of them.

"It's a little *woodsy*." The woman giggled, suddenly happier now that the realtor seemed to be speaking her language. "And if we're making changes—that's all right, isn't it, honey?"

"If we decide on this retreat from the city," her husband agreed.

"Then it's a bit dark in the living room with the—what is it? Dark green paint?"

"Another simple alteration. Not to worry."

"Wonderful. I want something bright and airy. Our home is a crisp white in many of the rooms. Makes the other colors pop."

Just like that? Without pausing to consider the rest of the place and what had been put together in such a short time, they were going to change it all.

They were going to change everything Snow Angel had done to this place.

I stepped out into the mudroom, where Oz sat, patiently waiting for me. Taking a deep breath, I tried to calm my nerves and push away the feeling of wanting to run back inside and kick out the realtor and the couple still exploring every inch of my house.

This is what I wanted, I reminded myself.

It was.

A new start, where I would finally be able to put everything behind me once and for all, was days away. It just wasn't helping that everywhere I looked in the house, I thought of her. And apparently I wasn't the only one. Oz, who at some point became my dog, started to look for her, likely because of her constant pampering. He probably liked her better, especially when she showered him with gifts including a lifted dog bowl set and collar. *Oz—K9* was burned into the leather.

Vassar probably would've gassed the boy up with how handsome he looked in it. I could also imagine how long Poppy must've spent deciding on the color and font before purchasing it.

I had to believe it was all for the project. To get the perfect report from my sister. To get her promotion and move on. Just like I wanted to get back and move on. As best as I could anyway …

But was that all our short yet significant relationship boiled down to? A house renovation she'd completed with determination before going back to her own life as if nothing had changed? As if I was no one to her but the boy she had a crush on in high school.

Doubt lingered. Everything would work according to plan though. That was what she always said.

Or maybe, that was her affirmation app.

But it wasn't that simple.

Oz ran back up to me, twirling around once with his tongue hanging out of his mouth. I breathed a short chuckle at the sight of him against the snowy backdrop.

"Yeah, Vassar would be pretty happy, knowing you're here, finally getting to be a dog, huh?"

Oz didn't answer, but like always, he looked pleased with himself, running back into the yard.

I glanced up at the gray sky. "What do you think, Vass? Any tips about what the hell I'm supposed to do? Come on? Anything to offer your hopeless friend you left here to take care of your dog?"

Again, there was nothing.

I shook my head. Oddly enough, I felt the tiniest curve to my lips.

I cupped my hands in front of me, letting my elbows rest on my knees. "Figured I'd give it a shot. Thanks anyway."

Behind me, the sound of crunching slush rolled up the driveway, though I didn't think there was another house showing tonight after the last. I narrowed my eyes at a familiar black SUV pulling up, lights passing over me before my sister jumped out the driver's side.

She was about to head towards the front door when I whistled. She did a double take before noticing me.

"Aren't you freezing?" My sister walked to meet me.

I raised my eyebrows, not answering her. I had an appropriate coat on unlike her thin peacoat clearly made for impressing clients rather than warmth. "What are you doing here?"

"Liana lost one of her sweaters. She's upset, so I thought I'd take a drive and see if she left it here."

I waved towards the side door. "You can go on in. Realtor is here with a couple looking at the place."

With a nod, she took a step toward the door. Then, paused. Sighing, she brushed some snow and sat down next to me. "You're really going through with this?"

"I said I was." Multiple times.

"Well, you look thrilled."

"Aren't you supposed to be going to get a sweater or something inside right now?" I asked.

"How are the home walk-throughs going?" she asked.

Oz was still wandering around the yard. When he spotted Sarah, his head snapped back, and he rushed toward us through the snow.

I huffed. "They're going fine."

"So, terrible?" she clarified for me even though I didn't reply. "You don't need to run away."

"I'm not running away," I grumbled.

"Yes, you are." She could contradict me all she wanted; I wasn't having this conversation with her. "I mean, you don't see Poppy running away just because she finished one of her largest projects and, apparently, it still wasn't enough. In my opinion, that company's becoming too big for themselves. Who do they think they are, HGTV?"

Wait.

"She didn't get the job?" I asked.

Sarah narrowed her eyes. "You didn't know?"'

"Sarah," I warned.

"No, not that I know of unless something changed. I wrote a high-praise letter to the company on her behalf. I got a response, letting me know my thoughts were considered, however, the other candidate was promoted. From what I heard, it seemed unfair, considering they had a bigger leg up to begin with but—"

"Poppy didn't get the promotion."

"Are you really going to make me repeat myself?" Sarah raised her brows.

Why didn't Poppy call? Why didn't she tell me?

Probably because I told her that it was over and I'd be fine for her to go.

"I'm glad I came over and got to tell you," said Sarah. "Though I did have ulterior motives."

"I would've never guessed your impromptu visit wasn't about picking up a child-sized sweater," I replied sarcastically.

"I also came to see if you would reconsider coming home with me to celebrate the new year with us."

"Don't you have some fancy corporate party to go out to?"

"Not this year." My sister shook her head. "Staying in with the family. I wondered if maybe you wanted to see them a little more too. Since, didn't you have another doctor's appointment yesterday?"

I had.

"How did it go? Get your sign-off, like you wanted?" Sarah asked.

Oz pressed up against me, grumbling at me until I petted his hips.

I'd arrived at the doctor's office, a sleek, modern building in the heart of the city. After I checked in at the front desk, a nurse led me to an exam room, where I waited for a few minutes. Finally, my doctor breezed in, glancing through my file as he asked me a few quick questions.

He barely looked up from his notes before giving me the all-clear and slapping my back with a casual, "Take care out there, serving your country, son."

And just like that, my appointment had been over in less than fifteen minutes.

The other doctor who had looked me over first the other week was right—I'd have no problem finding a doctor to sign off on me if that was what I wanted. And I had.

I looked down at Oz. He didn't move away from leaning against me, panting from his exertion in the snow. He adjusted his leg to find a better position, trying to find his own comfort and balance in a way that didn't strain him. His bent, torn-up ear flopped to one side when he peered around to look at me.

I raised my eyebrows. I shit you not, I was sure he raised his right back.

When would I start to feel relieved? My whole goal since I'd gotten home was to leave it. My entire purpose was to be back in the military. There I belonged. I was doing something meaningful —worthwhile even.

But then Poppy came into my life, making me feel valuable from the day she'd laid eyes on me. And I cherished every moment—from her first bickering at me to finally yelling back whenever I got in the way of her rebuilding the cabin into a home just like my ancestors had almost a hundred years ago. For the first time, I didn't mind being stuck here.

I might've even enjoyed it.

I was supposed to go back to the military. I was supposed to leave the past behind and start fresh somehow even if I wasn't sure how. But what if there was no such thing as leaving things behind or starting fresh? That wasn't life. It wasn't possible.

Who was I to make that decision for both of us, even if Poppy hadn't gotten her promotion?

None of it made a difference.

I only wanted it to. Could that be enough. A sign, maybe?

I glanced back up at the gray sky.

"Stay here." I jumped away from Oz and Sarah, casting her in a spray of snow.

"Hey!" She brushed herself off, a crease forming between her brows in confusion.

"Stay. Just for a minute. I'll be right back. I'm going to need a ride."

I paced away from her and back into the house, where the realtor was pointing up at the painted bookshelves. Poppy's bookshelves were still filled with my and my grandmother's books.

"Excuse me."

They acted like I wasn't even there.

"Excuse me," I snapped a little louder.

Then, people wondered why I felt the need to be rude.

The couple and realtor turned toward me.

"Oh, Mr. Hayes—"

"I need you to reschedule," I told the realtor.

She blinked at me. "Pardon—"

"I need to go, and I'm not leaving you all here with your terrible interior design choices," I said, yet no one moved. "Did you not hear me? I need you to get out of my house. *Now.*"

thirty

. . .

Poppy

MICHELLE TOLD me to dig deep? I was going to dig myself into the biggest pile of work I could and block everything else out. This was what I loved, right? Home design for Home Haven, even if I wasn't going to be promoted.

Yet.

Ever.

Who knew really at this rate?

"Do I need to drag you out of here, or can I trust you to leave at a reasonable hour?" Hannah packed up her things for the evening after finishing her last call, which was a doozy—the caller had needed a last-minute gift but did not appreciate any of Hannah's usual suggestions.

Wrapping up her headset, she gently set it alongside her computer. She looked tired with her hair twisted up in a bun and circles under her eyes from the long hours.

"Or are you still moping?" she asked.

"I'm not moping. I'm working."

"Sure you are. Those emails look like they are taking care of themselves at the speediest of rates," teased Hannah.

Unfortunately, after practically living here since getting the promotion notice, I didn't have much to do. I needed to make the work stretch.

"You know your house looked amazing. Stunning. And you know that I don't like the outdoors," Hannah praised me. "Even I would stay there for, like, a night or two. As long as you were there and promised me there weren't any axe murderers lurking in the trees outside."

"Thanks, Hannah."

"Want me to say it again?"

"I'm pretty sure I believed you the first time. And the twentieth today."

"Just making sure those pretty ears of yours are listening," she said. "And we are only getting more calls and projects coming up, which means more opportunities for you to overwork yourself into a creative masterpiece."

"I'm fine. I'm … what's the step beyond grieving?"

"Denial?" Hannah ventured. "For your job or the GI Joe you left behind in the forest upstate?"

I rolled my eyes. "Can we not talk about it?"

"Fine. Fine. I have to get going anyway before I'm late. Again."

"You headed somewhere more special than your couch to eat popcorn with your roommates?" I asked.

"I have a date." Hannah's mouth twisted as she weighed the final word. "Sort of."

My eyes widened with sudden shock. "No, you don't."

Hannah cocked her head.

How was I just hearing about this? And on New Year's Eve, no less?

"That's not what I meant. I knew something was going on. I can't believe that you didn't tell me. What's his name?"

"Grant."

"Grant," I repeated. I didn't know any Grants, though I didn't know many people. "How long have you known Grant?"

"Remember that guy I was telling you about at the bar? The one who called the hotline before the holiday?"

"The ham guy?" I gasped.

She rolled her eyes. "He'd be delighted to hear that's his nickname. He sort of tracked me down and ..."

"Tracked you down?" I needed more details.

"It's no big deal. He's just someone I've been seeing—not even seeing. It's not like that exactly."

"Tell me more about how it is since you've been hiding this information. You've been trying to get my mind off the promotion and you've been holding out?"

"I didn't want to distract you," she said, glancing away, as if embarrassed. I'd never seen this side of Hannah before. "Work has been busy, as you saw today. Other things have been going on, like family stuff, so it's been hectic."

"Family stuff?" I asked.

I reached out a hand, which Hannah took. As far as I knew, Hannah didn't speak much with her family, if at all. It was one of the topics neither of us broached, covered in barbed wires.

"You know I'm here for you if you need anything, right?"

"I do. But tonight is going to be a good night."

"It is," I agreed. "Take a picture of your outfit for me."

"I will. I have to go home now though and fix all of *this*." She waved her hand over her face and hair situation she had to deal with. "Promise you'll get out of here before midnight?"

I nodded, though I didn't say anything.

She huffed. "I'll message you if I don't hear anything from you."

"I'll be fine."

"Uh-huh." Leaning down, she pressed a glossy kiss against my cheek before tugging her coat over her shoulder. "Love you, Pops."

"Have fun. It'll be great."

She chuckled, turning down the aisle toward the door leading out of the office. "It'll definitely be something."

With that foreboding thought, I turned back to my computer again, trying to remember where I had left off. One email at a time, I worked through my list, adding things to the senior interior designers' calendars and making sure everything was perfect for when everyone returned to the office.

Why shouldn't I after all? By doing this, I was still doing the thing I enjoyed even if I was the last one in the office. There was no point for me to leave. I had no parties to go to. Even my parents had plans with friends to watch the ball drop and cheer with cheap champagne to bring in the new year, moving us one step forward into the rest of life.

I sighed.

Everyone seemed to be moving on with their lives, except for me.

Rubbing my eyes, I tried to focus on finishing the next contract and invoice that would need to be sent out for … someone.

Reaching for my stack of papers, I sorted through different folders of last names. Larson, McLucas, Hayes—

I paused, picking at the edge of the Hayes-Preston folder, detailing all the first images I'd had for the cabin's design before I even saw it the first time. There were swatches of tans and greens and more plaid than I thought Aaron would've ever stood for. The original design plans had held the same feeling I wanted in the end, but also so much had changed before it became the final product that I was proud of. I had no idea how I'd managed it all in such a short amount of time with all the hiccups. I certainly wouldn't have without Aaron helping me.

Aaron inundated my mind. Was he celebrating New Year's with his sister? How had the showing for his house gone? The people looking at it would be crazy if they didn't buy it. It would surely go quickly. And when it did sell, was he going to reenlist?

I forced myself to push those thoughts aside and concentrate on work. I couldn't dwell on Aaron Hayes or the cabin right now. It was over. I needed to move forward.

But how?

Tears pricked and threatened to spill from my eyes as I thought about how pathetic I must look, sitting alone in the office after hours while everyone else was out, enjoying their lives. Why couldn't I?

I missed Aaron with his infectious laugh and love for his dog that he tried to hide. Underneath his facade of strength, I could see the cracks of grief that he tried to disguise, and it felt like a gift meant just for me.

Maybe I was pathetic, but I couldn't let myself sit here, blinking at a screen any longer. Reaching to turn off the monitor, I pressed back all the emotions that threatened to surface even though it didn't matter. Who was here to judge me? My stapler? The little flower sticky notes Hannah had somehow stocked in bulk?

"Super pathetic," I muttered as I got up from my chair and slung my bag over my shoulder.

That was it; I was heading home and then driving to the cabin.

Was it crazy? Yes. Did it border on desperate? Also yes. But if he wasn't there, then maybe that would be a sign. And if he was? Well, I didn't know what would happen then, but—

"I disagree," a voice said.

Aaron stood in front of me, halfway up the aisle to my tiny cubicle in the corner of the office.

I wiped away the tears that finally slipped down my cheeks as I cleared my throat. "What are you doing here? It's New Year's. You should be—"

"Where should I be, Snow Angel?"

How was he here? He shouldn't be …

I couldn't find the words.

"I finally understand why you hate driving the back roads into the city now more than ever," he said.

"What?" I asked.

"It took way too long for me to get to you." He took a step towards me, then another until he was directly in front of me.

"Then, I stopped by your parents' house, thinking that you would be home—"

"You went to my house?"

"And then I figured if you weren't there, you had to be here," he said, looking around and taking a deep breath as if it were the first one he'd managed all day. I stared, watching him take it. "Why are you here, Poppy?"

"I'm … I'm working."

He paused. "I heard you didn't get the job."

"Oh. Right. I mean, that's true. I didn't get the job, but that doesn't mean you had to feel sorry for me and come down here."

"I wanted to see you."

I swallowed hard, self-conscious under his intense scrutiny. "There's no need to check up on me. I'm fine," I replied a little too quickly, my voice coming out sharper than intended.

"Fine?" Aaron raised an eyebrow, unconvinced by my feeble attempt at reassurance. "You don't seem fine," he observed, taking a hesitant step closer to where I sat, frozen at my desk.

I felt the tension crackling in the air, uncertain of how to respond to his unexpected presence. Aaron's gaze was unwavering, as if he could see through my facade. With a sigh, I finally relented, dropping the pretense I had been desperately clinging to.

"What do you want me to say?" I shifted uncomfortably in my chair, the weight of his gaze making it hard to breathe. "I said I'm fine," I repeated, trying to sound more assertive this time. But the words sounded hollow, even to my ears.

He didn't contradict me. He knew better by now.

I swallowed, feeling a renewed wave of emotion swell behind my eyes. I swung my hand to the side. I couldn't hold it together anymore. Again. "Goodness. Why are you here, Aaron? Why did you have to show up here now? I was going to come to you so you didn't have to see me this way. At my lowest. If only you'd stayed home for another two hours or something."

"You were coming to see me?"

"Yes!" That was why I was pathetic.

Aaron pressed his lips together, as if he couldn't help the smile that I once couldn't believe I was seeing. Even if his eyes were still sad, calculating.

"Why were you coming to see me, Snow Angel?" he asked. "Coming to yell at me again?"

"No."

"Visit Oz maybe? I kind of figured that you would miss him."

I snorted and shook my head.

"Then, why, homemaker?" he asked again. "Tell me."

I rolled my eyes. "You're the one who showed up here."

"Oh, I get it. You want me to say it."

Say what? I couldn't even begin to assume.

"I think I'm in love with you, Poppy Owens."

My eyes widened.

There was no way he'd just said that. I was imagining things.

"No. You didn't—you can't just say that, Aaron."

"What if I said it? I did say it. And you know what? There's no *thinking* about it. I love you."

His words echoed the feelings swirling inside me, unspoken but palpable.

And as I looked into his eyes, I saw my reflection—my mirrored desires and fear. Aaron had been on my mind constantly, his absence leaving a void that I couldn't seem to fill, no matter how hard I tried. Yet here he was, putting words to it.

"I can't stop thinking about you," said Aaron. "You're all I think about every second I walk through the cabin. I see you everywhere—in those bookshelves and in the paint color on the cabinets that some snooty couple touring the place want to redo in some ugly beige."

"You told them that it was a terrible idea, right?"

"I held myself back," he admitted with a small chuckle. "Not that it matters. I don't think I'm going to be leaving the place."

"You aren't?"

"I think I'll have something to keep me here. Or at least, I hope I will," he said.

I stared at him, sniffing as I held myself together. "Really?"

"Since losing my parents, I never realized how much I wanted to have a place that felt like I was meant to be there. A place with good meals, even if they're burned. I don't care. A place with laughter bouncing off the walls and way too many knickknacks that I don't get the purpose of. And you helped to make that. You created this place for me that I love more than I thought I could, and after you were gone, I realized that it wasn't the cabin that was home for me. It was you, Poppy. You're home."

Aaron stood there, vulnerable yet resolute. His words hung heavily in the air. My heart pounded in my chest, a whirlwind of emotions crashing over me as I processed his confession.

"I know we agreed on not being together because of your job and my desperate need to escape this place. That would have been the easy solution for us. The neat, tidy, predictable version of us. But then I figured, since when have we ever followed a plan?" He chuckled, as if it was some sort of inside joke. "I should've never let you leave the other morning. I woke up, and all I could think about was how I could drag you back into bed, and I didn't. I thought I would regret what happened in the Army or not going back, but that morning—I don't think I'll ever regret anything more than not stopping you then."

I swallowed, staring at him.

"I guess what I'm saying in all of this is that I hope you feel even a little of the same way here." Aaron chuckled with his arms open before letting them fall to his sides. "Because I'm done pretending or preparing to run away. I want to stay here in the cabin that you made a home. With you."

I searched his eyes for any sign of insincerity, but all I found was raw honesty and a flicker of something more. Hope maybe. It was a fragile thing, this unspoken connection that silently grew, but it was there, undeniable and potent.

For a moment, neither of us spoke. The silence stretched taut with all the truths laid bare. And then, without conscious thought, I found myself stepping away from my desk until we were mere inches apart.

The weight of his gaze was both comforting and terrifying. It pulled me in like a magnet.

I couldn't help but feel torn apart by conflicting emotions. My body ached for him despite all the pain he had caused me before.

Could I let this happen again?

He *wanted* me. Despite everything that had happened in the past, Aaron Hayes wanted me now.

And you know what?

"I love you too." My voice was barely a whisper.

Aaron closed the gap between us until our breaths mingled in the small space that separated our lips. "We can figure it out together," he said softly, his hand reaching out tentatively to brush against my cheek. "Everything. I won't hold you back, and I'm going to figure out my mess to make *us* work."

"We can work with a mess," I said. "I'd work with a complete disaster for you."

He kissed me, not pausing for another word. Our mouths spoke the rest, tasting sharp and sweet.

Our kiss deepened, a blend of longing, passion, and unspoken promises. It felt like the rest of the world screaming for the new year to come had fallen away, leaving the two of us in our bubble of existence in the middle of the Home Haven office.

I laughed against his mouth, still in slight disbelief over what was happening, letting the tears slip down my cheeks.

He pushed them away with his thumbs, checking to make sure I was all right before kissing me again.

Breathless and flushed, I ran my fingers through his hair, feeling the tension in his body slowly melt away as he wrapped his arms around my waist, pulling me impossibly closer.

Our noses brushed against each other again before Aaron leaned back. Still holding me against his chest, he glanced around the empty office for the first time since he'd arrived, and he laughed too.

I loved that sound.

And how he wasn't letting go of me.

"Where do you want to go, Snow Angel?" Aaron asked me. "You say the word and I'll take you."

There was only one answer as I held on to him tight.

"Home."

epilogue

. . .

Poppy

I **LOVED** the sounds that came with a home. There were so many of them. The distant sound of laughter filling up a room. Music drifting from the kitchen, where a couple might find themselves dancing over the tiles.

Today, there was the sound of champagne glasses clinking together like the most beautiful chimes.

"Congratulations." Alison approached me, tapping her tall glass against mine one more time. "You earned it."

I basked in Alison's words, feeling a surge of gratitude for the friends that surrounded me on this warm evening that stuck to my skin like honey.

The soft rustle of the trees in the gentle breeze provided a soothing backdrop to the joyful chatter. As the sky darkened into shades of deep indigo, the stars twinkled above us like little diamonds scattered across velvet.

I took a sip of champagne, savoring the effervescent bubbles that danced on my tongue. The cabin seemed to come alive with light, casting a renewed and cozy radiance over our little gathering. I caught snippets of conversations and laughter around me, feeling a sense of contentment settle in my chest as I celebrated myself for the first time in my life.

At Aaron's insistence.

A month ago, following a variety of design projects, both in the city with senior interior designers as well as small-budget productions on my own no one else wanted to take outside of the city, I'd gained recognition for my work on the cabin. Maybe it was with that newfound confidence that I'd scheduled a meeting with Michelle.

"One of the things I realized the most when working on the house was how much I missed doing the renovation and seeing everything come together. I love designing—of course I do, as I've been here for nearly three years now," I told Michelle, sitting across from her in her office, much calmer and at peace than I had been the previous year. "But I like to see my project through from the moment I get the vision of how everything should look to extensive remodel rather than just choosing the color scheme and shaping."

Michelle listened intently as I spoke, appearing thoughtful and calculating behind her glasses. She nodded slowly, considering my words.

"I see where you're coming from," she finally said, tapping her pen against the notebook in front of her. "You have a real passion for the hands-on aspect of design, don't you?"

I nodded eagerly, excitement building within me just from talking about it. It was amazing, considering how many times I'd already gone over everything with Aaron at home in our little cabin in the woods.

This was my chance to finally step into a role that resonated with my creative spirit.

"Exactly," I replied. "I want to be more involved in the entire process—from the initial design concept to the finishing touches. I believe there's a niche in the market for clients who want a more personalized and hands-on approach to their home transformations. I want to bring my visions to life in a way only I can."

At the end of my presentation, a smile tugged at the corners of Michelle's lips as she leaned back in her chair, regarding me with a newfound respect. "What kind of title do you think that position would have?"

My business card still read *Poppy Owens*, but instead of *junior interior designer*, my title was *Home Haven renovation specialist*.

I still did the design and some event work when appropriate, but now, I had the job I'd always dreamed of—hands-on as I brought my visions to life.

I looked around the outside of the cabin, scattered with friends and family. My parents were talking loudly with Aaron's sister by the firepit, where Liana and Gavin argued over whose marshmallow had come out better. Barrett was leaning against a wall, talking with one of our newest hires from Home Haven, who wanted to know more about the upcoming project of redesigning his homestead rescue later this summer, headed by me, which was a huge honor. And responsibility.

Hannah was surely around here somewhere, partaking in a glass of champagne, or set to arrive at any minute.

I glanced around one more time as arms snaked around my waist.

"What's going on inside that head?" Aaron hummed in my ear.

Oz slipped by my legs, rushing into the yard before turning back to look at us.

It was as if he was asking, *Are you coming?*

"All good things," I said.

"Dangerous. What's next? Flower beds next spring? Redoing the entryway how you wanted with the glazed front window was last month. What's going to happen in the fall? A garden so you can stop complaining about how far away the grocery store is?"

"How did you know about that?" I shook my head as I looked at him accusingly.

The corners of Aaron's lips quirked as he leaned in closer, his breath warm against my ear. "I have my ways," he murmured, his voice sending a shiver down my spine. His arms tightened around me, pulling me closer against his solid frame.

"I know you, Poppy Owens," Aaron said, his tone playful yet tinged with something more intimate. "And I know that your creativity knows no bounds. You've already worked wonders with this home of ours. Who knows what magic you'll conjure up next?"

His words stirred something within me, a fire of determination and excitement that blazed brightly in my chest.

With him by my side, I felt invincible, ready to take on any challenge that came our way.

He ran a thumb over my cheek before threading his hand through my hair. When he leaned in close, my eyes closed, and I felt the way his breath touched my lips before he did.

His mouth was warm against mine, a soft and gentle pressure that sent sparks dancing across my skin.

Surrounded by laughter and music, bathed in the soft yellow glow of the fairy lights strung up around the cabin, illuminating his features, casting shadows and highlights that made him look almost ethereal, it was as if everything had aligned perfectly at last.

All the pieces of my life falling into place with us at the center.

"So, is this it? When are you going to be mine, Poppy Owens?"

I grinned. The answer was so clear, so obvious.

The dog started barking, rushing to Barrett, nearly sending him straight over the stone wall and into the yard. The crowd we'd asked to join us for a beautiful summer night chattered with love and joy. The fire crackled as it put out heat.

And Aaron looked at me like I was the person he'd been looking for, for years. But I'd make sure to tell him, I had known it first.

I was his.

I was home.

"I already am."

acknowledgments

As I write this, I know that soon, *When in December* will be going out to its first readers. Knowing that, it feels like I've crossed some kind of finish line. Only, when I cross it, I'm gasping for air and trying to figure out why no one is cheering other than my heartbeat, rapidly pounding against my chest. When writing, however, that's simply how it is. It's an anticlimactic process most of the time. It's solitary. The only person usually there when you hit The End is yourself, and your computer you've been begging like a friend not to give up on you before you finish edits or hit publish. I definitely felt this truth while writing *When in December*.

In my acknowledgements, I often take the time to thank the few people who helped me put all this story together along the way. I also like to shed a bit of light on how I got to this page myself as a self-publishing author who often wears all the hats besides that of cover artist—Thank you to Echo Grayce for creating my romantic winter-themed "people cover" as I like to call them—and editor, the wonderful Jovana. Jovana, you will never cease to amaze me with how you make even the most messy sentence sound exactly how I heard it in my head. You are truly the grammar (and my readers') MVP.

After *Call You Mine*, I was left with an overwhelming sense of unease as writer. *Call You Mine* was my first book I put out there where I went, *"This is it. This is going to be the book that changes things for me."*

Only, it wasn't.

There's a phrase often used in the publishing world as much

as it is used in the author world when you ask how someone managed to go from part-time writing to full-time, or hit the best-seller's list. It goes something like, *"It was all luck."*

And oh, how I hate that.

But, in the end, sadly, I'll admit it's true. Beyond all the hours of writing, editing, marketing, and never-ending work, often, whether a story does well comes down to that single word. *Luck.* And as an author or creative in general, from that point there is only one way forward.

You have to try again. You have to write another book. You have to build yourself back up again.

It took me a little while longer than I'd like to bring myself back to the page after *Call You Mine.* I debated on whether I should go back and keep writing more of the Barnett Witches, but then came along When in December.

Here we are.

But, again, no matter how much hard work and dedication goes into a book, it's truly the readers and the people along for the ride who make a book worthwhile. So, I want to take the time to thank all the wonderful people in my life who support and love me while I write love stories.

My parents, who rise up and cheer me on both loudly and quietly to be confident and enjoy the things I do—and who also love a good Christmas romance.

To Collin, through sticking it out through the many moments where I felt too overwhelmed to write or wasn't sure if I could ever write another book again and achieve my goals. Your confidence in me to write something beautiful and to take risks to make the dream happen means more than perhaps I will ever be able to express.

To the wonderful fellow romance authors who support and help me learn something new every time I publish a new story, you're the absolute best. You all make me proud to be an indie romance author.

And thank you, my readers, for sticking along for the ride. Thank you. Thank you. Thank you.

There are still many stories to be told.

about the author

Kendra Mase is the author of emotional, romantic, sometimes magical love stories including *Call You Mine* and *Bewitched by You.* You can visit her online at kendramase.com.

also by kendra mase

ASHTON

The Strings That Hold Us Together

Everything You Never Had

Words That Burn Like Ash

The Way We're Meant To Be

BARNETT WITCHES

Bewitched By You

Put a Spell on You

HOME HAVEN

When in December

STANDALONE

Call You Mine